STAY DOWNWIND

RICK COOPER

Stay Downwind

Published by Rendini • PO Box 722, Mount Dora, FL 32756

Paperback: ISBN 979-8-9939214-0-2

for Mrs. Hemphill
my teacher, my mentor, my friend

Marion Hemphill-Palmer
1926 - 2019

Confess yourself to heaven;
Repent what's past; avoid what is to come.
  —William Shakespeare

Victoria LaRue was about to enter another world, to step from light into darkness, a darkness that had nothing to do with the late hour.

It wouldn't be the weirdest place she turned a trick. That trophy went to the walk-in cooler and the guy who claimed he could only get it up when he was freezing his ass off. But a *cemetery?* What kind of pervert would want to do it in a cemetery?

Their paths crossed that afternoon on a Lower Broadway sidewalk in a part of Nashville known as The District. She was on her way to meet a friend when she noticed a man walking step for step beside her. In his early thirties, good-looking and trim, he sported an athlete's body. She thought he was just flirting, but casual conversation soon turned to business.

He told her his name was John, but names didn't matter—they were all johns to her. It did bother her that he knew she was a prostitute. She long ago quit the risky street hustle to work for somewhat safer escort services. She wasn't dressed like a hooker, she wasn't walking like one, she wasn't sending out any of the usual signals. And yet, he knew.

He said he would give her two hundred in advance and eighteen hundred more if she would meet him at Mount Olivet Cemetery at midnight. He flashed a wad of cash to show he was serious. She agreed to his request and the details were set. He pressed a couple of hundred-dollar bills in her hand and walked away.

Victoria feigned interest in the john's pitch but she had no intention of going to the cemetery—she would take the sucker for the easy two bills and forget about it. Several hours later, while shooting up for the second time that day, she knew she would soon need the extra eighteen hundred.

It was more than just the money or a fix, even if she was reluctant to admit it to herself. She recalled a time when her body would turn any man's head, but that was years ago and the drugs had also taken their toll. She couldn't remember when she last made two grand in a week, yet this guy was going to pay her that much for one night. He could have found a younger, more attractive woman, but he wanted her. She just hoped he wouldn't ask her to do anything too weird, like screw on his mother's grave.

She went to the granite boulder where the entrance road forked left and right, and the first wave of wariness arose when he was not there to meet her. She spotted something at the base of the stone. There she found a folded piece of paper, a small flashlight, and a single red rose. She inhaled the fragrance of the delicate flower and allowed herself a moment of fantasy, before the reality of what he wanted from her again set in.

She unfolded the paper and switched on the flashlight. The note said she would find directions that would lead her to the part of the cemetery where he would be waiting. She was to follow all instructions exactly as they were stated, or he would not pay her another dollar. At the bottom of the note:

Walk in a straight line from the back of the boulder up the hill, until you find Mr. Nickel and Mr. Gardner.

Victoria stood still in the darkness, listening but hearing only traffic in the distance. The August night was muggy, suffocating, and she weighed turning back against pressing on. To survive in her line of work she needed to be spot-on about first impressions. She serviced many scary men over the years, but this john, despite his cemetery fetish, was polite and cordial. Harmless. Besides, money was money.

She climbed a short slope and crossed the right branch of the road that wound its way up the hill. She came upon two small crypts built into the hillside a few feet apart, the one on the left belonging to A. Nickel and the one on the right to E S Gardner. There she found another rose between the crypts and a second note.

Walk a straight line for 75 paces to Mr. Carter and look for Medora.

She surveyed the sea of geometric shapes that rose from the soft ground. An imaginary hand brushed its bony fingers across the back of her neck. She shuddered and glanced over her left shoulder and then her right. Was the sound she heard the rustling of tree branches, or something else?

She stepped off her paces and counted to herself. At seventy-five steps she did not see the name "Carter" on any nearby stones. While her steps were short and tentative, his were likely long and certain. It took another fifteen paces before she found the Carter marker.

It was at least thirty feet tall and looked like a miniature Washington Monument. She moved closer and played the light upon the inscription. John J. Carter perished in the Baldwin Hotel Fire in San Francisco on November 23, 1898. *"TRUE IN PURPOSE, COOL IN JUDGMENT, OF UNFLINCHING COURAGE AND STAINLESS INTEGRITY, HE NEVER COMPROMISED PRINCIPLE, NOR SACRIFICED HONOR HE WAS DISTINGUISHED FOR KNIGHTLY BEARING, AND ABOUNDING CHARITY, WHICH WAS FREE FROM CALCULATION, AND WITHOUT OSTENTATION."* Her first thought was that the stone carver had omitted a period; her second thought was *Why couldn't I have met someone like John J. Carter?*

Several feet to the right of John J. Carter's grave she found Medora. The monument was weathered and worn, its right angles rounded over the decades by the elements. *"MEDORA, DAUGHTER OF ... "* she couldn't read the rest of the faded inscription in the dim light nor did she care to. She bent down and picked up another red rose laid across another note.

Walk 75 paces straight ahead until you find Mr. Hill.

Eighty-six steps later she found John M. Hill, his wife, Phebe, a rose, and a note. Was there a reason the john chose certain grave markers to guide her through the cemetery? She looked again at the monument in front of her. *"THE RIGHTEOUS HATH HOPE IN HIS DEATH,"* and several lines below, *"THE AGED PILGRIMS WHO LIFE'S PATHWAYS TROD, ARE NOW IN HEAVEN AND WALK WITH GOD. "*

She cut to the left ten paces—thirteen for her—and walked along a narrow road, the crunch of gravel beneath her shoes. She would use the flashlight sparingly in case security patrolled the grounds.

A few steps beyond a sign that read "Section 2" she stopped. To her left was a small crypt set back a few feet from the road. *Someone is standing on top of the crypt!*

"Hello ... is that ... you, John? Hello?"

She switched on the flashlight and raised the beam up the side of the crypt, past the name "Thomas" above the doorway. The light reached the figure and her body sagged with relief. Still, she was too scared to laugh. On top of the crypt and partially hidden by the branches of a tree was a life-sized statue of a man. She didn't know what the statue was—she was happy enough to know what it was not.

She came to an intersection with a grass triangle in the center. She again referred to the john's latest note.

Go straight ahead on the same path, until you see the cross.

There were graves all around her now, in every direction, and she felt like a farmer in a field of stone. In death, as in life, the difference between the haves and the have-nots was clear: next to ornate obelisks she would find small rectangles of cement embedded in the ground like stepping stones in a garden, with only the last names, or even just the initials, to remind visitors that someone had once lived. And died.

Victoria questioned why she wanted to deny that the corpses buried beneath the gently rolling hills were once living, breathing, human beings. It was as though her mind set aside a separate dimension for the dead, an area not meant for the living, because once the line was crossed it was too easy for the memories and the pain to wash over her.

She came upon a monument to John L. Nolen that wasn't mentioned in the trick's note. A statue of a man stood over the grave, the figure's right hand on its chest. The inscription read *"ERECTED BY THE ODDFELLOWS OF TENNESSEE."* She had erected a few odd fellows in Tennessee herself.

The road curled to the right. She came upon a short cross and again switched on the flashlight. She found another red rose at its base, along with a new note.

Walk in the direction pointed by the rose for 115 paces. There you will find Mr. Burk sawing logs.

She was tiring of the john's game. She wanted the cash, but this was getting ridiculous. She turned off the flashlight.

The grass was spongy and damp beneath her feet, and the thought of rolling around on wet ground was not at all appealing. She should have packed a blanket.

Victoria was counting her steps when she felt the small, coiled snake brush against her right ankle. She let out a shriek and kicked wildly, sending the snake through the air. She fumbled for the switch on the flashlight. What she saw was not a snake, it was a piece of line from a string trimmer.

She had to backtrack to the cross and start over.

She counted one hundred fifteen steps and saw no marker that bore the name "Burk." *What does he mean by sawing logs?*

It took nearly ten minutes of searching in the darkness to find the marker belonging to Captain R. C. Burk, who lived from September 7, 1853, until September 12, 1903. It was shaped like a tree trunk with its limbs cut off. The trunk was about six feet high and rested on four shorter logs. It was so life-like in the darkness she had to touch it to confirm it was actually stone. The marker had been donated by *"THE WOODMEN OF THE WORLD."* A rose and a note were nestled between the trunk and one of the shortened limbs.

Victoria had to read the note two times. "You're a sick little puppy," she muttered to herself. She unbuttoned her blouse and took it off. With her blouse and purse in one hand and the roses, notes, and flashlight in the other, she cut over to the road on her left and headed deeper into the cemetery.

She felt someone's eyes watching her. *His eyes.* She had neither seen him nor heard him, but he was there, moving with her in the shadows. She stopped and thought about turning back. This was not her first bizarre trick, she reassured herself, nor would it be her last.

She came to a tree that sheltered the deceased members of the Schott family. She turned ninety-degrees to the left and kept going until she reached another gravel road, where she was to take the left fork. She had lost all sense of direction—maybe that was part of the john's plan.

She stopped in an area of grass rimmed by a circular drive, in the center a towering granite monument. Three smaller bases were layered above a massive square base, and on top of all four stood a statue of a soldier, ten feet high or more. It was the Confederate Circle. She looked around until she found a rose and another note.

As directed, she unzipped and removed her skirt.

She was to take the south walk heading from the Confederate Circle. *How am I supposed to tell directions without the damn sun?* She searched and spotted a rose and a note behind the monument. The rose aimed toward a cathedral-shaped crypt.

Halfway to the crypt she heard a noise and spun around. Her flashlight splayed a wide path, but she saw no movement. If it was the john he was staying out of sight.

Maybe it was because the Acklen crypt looked like a small cathedral, or maybe her nerves were rubbed raw at that point, but it struck Victoria that she was on sacred ground, invading the slumber of the long-deceased residents of Mount Olivet Cemetery. She could imagine thousands of lifeless eyes staring with disgust as she took the john inside of her and moaned in false ecstasy. She felt ashamed, disappointed with herself for what she was about to do.

Despite her disdain for organized religion—several local preachers were among her best customers—she would sometimes reach out to God. She mouthed a prayer of forgiveness, and she vowed she would return to the cemetery one day soon to make her peace with the dead.

At the Acklen crypt she turned ninety degrees and walked for sixty steps to the marker of Henry Edward Lauman: November 5, 1844 - July 20, 1881. *"HE SAVED OTHERS HIMSELF HE CANNOT SAVE."* She picked up a rose and a note.

From Lauman she turned left for thirty-four steps and found the Wood family, identified by four simple rectangular slabs in the ground. She went right for sixty-three steps to McCormack. Fifteen steps at an angle to the right from McCormack she found the small angel standing guard above Joe S. Aylor, who died on July 29, 1909, before his third birthday.

As she looked down at the child's grave she thought of a prayer buried deep in her memory:

Now I lay me down to sleep; I pray the Lord my soul to keep. If I should die before I wake, I pray the Lord my soul to take.

She read the note she found there. She crumpled it and tossed it to the ground along with the roses and the other notes she had carried through the cemetery. She turned off the flashlight and placed it with her purse on top of her skirt and blouse. Under the faint pale glow of the crescent moon she unfastened her bra, took off her shoes, and slipped off her panties.

She sensed movement behind her and turned to a blinding light.

"Hey! What the hell are you doing?" She crossed her arms over her breasts and squeezed her legs together.

"Take it easy. It's just a camera, to shoot video of our date. To remember you by."

Squinting against the glare, Victoria couldn't see his face but she recognized the voice. It was only a small comfort to know it was the john.

"No video. You never said a word about video. I thought this was just supposed to be sex."

He turned off the light on the camera and stepped closer. "When did I say anything about sex?"

"Shit, are you a cop?"

"That's really funny. Just relax, okay?"

Still clutching her arms against her chest, Victoria shivered despite the hot breath of the summer night. "Look, John, or whatever your name is. Let's just get this over with. What do you want from me?"

He reached out and brushed her cheek with his hand. "I want nothing more from you than what you want from me."

She inched backward and bumped into a marker that scraped her bare skin. "I want the money you promised."

"You will get your money, Victoria. And in return I want your time, that's all. It's your time and my money. A fair exchange."

"How do you know my name?" She was sure she hadn't told him.

"I know everything about you, Victoria."

Damn, this is getting real.

"Look, why don't we forget this whole thing, okay? I'll even give you your money back. Somehow."

His hand gently closed around her arm before she had a chance to pick up her panties.

"I've upset you. It's just that I had to meet you here because I have what you might call ... special needs." He turned her arm over and ran his thumb across the needle scars above her veins. "You know about special needs, don't you, Victoria?" His other hand pulled hundred-dollar bills from his pocket and held them in front of her face. "I can help you with your needs. Are you still willing to help me with mine?"

Her gaze moved from the money to his eyes, then back to the money. He released her arm and didn't protest when she picked up her blouse and wrapped it around her. She tried to swallow the tightness in her throat.

"What do you want me to do?" she asked.

"Follow me."

He led her a short distance to the mounded dirt of a fresh grave. A few feet away she saw a tripod, a duffel bag, and a rolled-up mat.

"This will do," he said.

He untied the mat and spread it over the grave. She watched as he moved to the tripod and attached the camera. The recording indicator blinked red just before he turned on the bright light again.

He hummed softly and took the blouse that Victoria had put around herself. He folded it and placed it on the ground with her skirt and purse. She again was naked, but this time she did not cover her breasts.

"Lie down." He pointed to the grave.

"What? I don't think so. Not there."

"I'll say it one more time. Lie down." His tone was now stern, commanding.

"Hey, you can screw yourself. I've had enough of your crazy games."

"It's your choice, Victoria. I can walk out of here with my money, but I'll also walk out of here with your clothes. That would be rather awkward for you, wouldn't it?"

"You son of a bitch." She considered her choices. He was bigger and stronger than she was, so she couldn't overpower him. He looked menacing dressed entirely in black, but maybe that was because he had something on and she didn't. And if he was not bluffing about keeping her clothes it *would* be awkward. Awkward as hell, and she would end up getting busted before the night was over.

"All right, but I want the money first. It'll cost you three hundred more to video it. And no posting online, promise?"

"It seems the lady doesn't trust me." He counted aloud as he peeled off twenty-one crisp hundred-dollar bills and tucked them into her purse. "Satisfied?"

Her gaze never left his face. She eased herself onto the mat, on her hands and knees, with her buttocks upraised. The mat felt waxy and smelled like balsam. She swiveled to him.

"No, no, that won't do. You have to lie supine. On your back."

"I know what supine means." Victoria sighed and turned over. The guy in the walk-in cooler had serious competition.

The john opened his duffel bag and reached inside.

Lipstick and a blonde wig, she thought. She couldn't count the times a john had painted a god-awful shade of red lipstick on her lips and made her wear a cheap blonde wig. Maybe this guy's girlfriend was dead—that would explain the freakin' cemetery. Was this her grave?

"You need a skin?" she asked. "I have one if you don't."

"I have a condom, but there's no need to rush things." His voice sounded friendly again. When he pulled his hand from the duffel bag he was holding two syringes. "I have a little bonus for you first."

She felt her eyes narrow. "What is it?"

"Just a little H. I thought it might make this easier for both of us."

She sat up and considered his offer. He didn't seem the type to do heroin and that worried her. But he also didn't seem the type to meet a working girl in a cemetery at midnight.

"Good stuff?" she asked.

"The best."

"Which one is mine?"

"Your choice." He extended his hand.

She picked up a syringe and tried to see what was inside but it was too dark. There was nothing she could do now but trust him, for she was far beyond any point of return. And she wanted the smack.

He handed her a scarf from his bag. She tied off and pushed the needle through her skin. The john dropped his unused needle to the ground.

She eased onto the mat.

"Close your eyes," he said. "You have to keep your eyes closed or you don't get your money."

She closed her eyes tightly. She didn't *want* to see.

She heard a zipper being worked, but the sound seemed to be getting farther away. Her head was spinning, her stomach turning over. She almost opened her eyes when the stream of liquid splashed first her feet, then her shins, but her eyelids were too heavy. *What is he doing?* It finally registered.

"You bastard. A golden shower's gonna cost you a lot more."

The stream went up her thighs, across her pubic area, and saturated her stomach as the strength drained from her body.

When it reached her chest and spattered her face, she sniffed something different, something ...

God, no!

For the tiniest slice into which conscious time can be divided, the stillness of the night amplified tenfold, as everything around her was being sucked into a vacuum of sound, an auditory black hole from which nothing, not even a scream, could escape.

She opened her eyes to the strike of a match.

Luke O'Connor took a long look in the mirror and decided he wasn't happy with the soft, pudgy figure staring back at him. He swore off desserts, cut back on the Heinekens, and bought an extra-large jogging suit and a pair of New Balance running shoes. That was a year ago. Now thirty pounds lighter and the veteran of eight 5K races and his first marathon, he turned into Mount Olivet Cemetery from Lebanon Pike in the middle of his twelve-mile training run.

The morning air was light and easy to breathe. He left his home in Donelson at six-fifteen to finish by eight-thirty, before the sun blistered the pavement and made outdoor exercise unbearable.

It was Sunday, and later in the day the cemetery would be a gathering place for families bringing flowers to their departed loved ones, but for now O'Connor was alone.

The small, crushed stones beneath his running shoes were a welcome relief from the unyielding asphalt of the highway. He ran in the cemetery to enjoy the sights and sounds of nature greeting another day—the ground squirrels scampering among the gravestones, the cheery yodeling of a Carolina wren, butterflies fluttering about, the elaborate spider webs still glistening with dew, and the random raccoon or possum foraging for food. That he found so much life in a setting reserved for the dead was a paradox not lost on him.

O'Connor was running at a comfortable pace, his feet pounding out a steady rhythm on the stones, when he noticed a faint odor that grew stronger with each stride. It became a nauseating stench. He looked to his left and slowed to a stop, horrified by the scene before him.

He took a few cautious steps closer.

The badly burned body was lying on its back, its arms contracted in a defensive posture. Flies circled mottled skin that was cracked in places and seeping body fluids. Clenched hands, more like claws, held several long-stemmed red roses, unharmed by smoke or flame.

The heat had drawn the skin taut, leaving eyes, cheeks, nose, and lips as no longer recognizable features on what was once a human face. Patches of scalp had split and peeled away, exposing a skull the color of slate. A white wooden cross tilted upside-down between the corpse's legs.

His mind snapped into action and he retreated to the gravel road to call 911.

-3-

To Alita King, every sunrise was unique in its beauty and its promise.

She dug her toes into the sand and gazed eastward at the sliver of light on the distant, endless line that separated sea from sky, the warm ocean breeze caressing her face. There wasn't another place on the planet she would rather be. Less than fifteen miles south of Daytona Beach, New Smyrna Beach also welcomed thousands of vacationers and visitors every year, yet it retained a quaint, small-town vibe. More than anything else, it was home.

Alita was the younger, by nine years, of the two daughters born to Carl and Marjo King, and she had always been her mother's favorite. From her earliest memory, Alita dreamed of becoming a fashion model when she grew up. But it took the accident—or, more accurately, *the scar*—for her to realize that she was merely a lump of clay in Marjo's hands, to be molded and shaped to fill some unknown void in her mother's life.

As a freshman at New Smyrna Beach High School, Alita had been a member of the Florida Class 4A District Champion diving team. Her mother disliked Alita's diving—Marjo was against anything that distracted her from her promising modeling career—but Alita convinced her that it was an excellent way to maintain muscle tone and avoid her mother's greatest fear: weight gain.

It was Alita's last dive of the day, an inward two-and-a-half somersault in the tuck position. In the dozens of times she replayed the dive in her mind she never could pinpoint exactly what went wrong.

Her press and takeoff from the 3-meter springboard was normal, but as she threw her arms down and began to spin in her forward rotation she knew she was in trouble. She tried to duck away from the board but she struck it just above her left eye. Though it happened in an instant, the split-second fall to the water seemed to take an eternity. There was no pain, and it wasn't until she surfaced and saw the red cloud encircling her neck that she was overcome with a sickening fear. Not of the injury, but of her mother.

Marjo burst through the emergency room entrance and shrieked at a volume that could jump-start a heart when she saw the angry purple bump and two-inch nylon suture line above Alita's left eyebrow. Dr. White, the emergency room physician, had closed the wound with a 6-0 atraumatic plastic surgery needle so that it wouldn't leave a scar. At least that was what he assured both Alita and her mother.

"You stupid, foolish girl! Your future is over, do you hear me? You stupid, foolish girl!" Those were the words Marjo said to Alita when they were leaving the hospital, right after she threatened a malpractice suit against everyone from the insurance clerk and Dr. White to a passing maintenance worker with a cart full of fluorescent light tubes.

From Alita's birth, Marjo planned for her to become a model. Even though Alita won the Dade County Baby Beautiful Contest at five months of age, Marjo had no way of knowing that genes would eventually bless her daughter with the height—five feet, ten inches— and weight—one hundred fifteen pounds, perfectly distributed—that many women would kill to have. Add Alita's sky-blue eyes, high cheekbones, Greek nose and shoulder length, full-bodied blonde hair, and you had ... well, you had a fashion model, which was exactly what Alita was raised to be, what she thought she wanted to be. Until the scar.

You stupid, foolish girl.

Alita developed an interest in art at an early age, especially painting with acrylics. She favored seascapes, which she painted at every opportunity, but not as often as she wished because her mother was so discouraging. She loved the antics of sandpipers playing tag with the tide, the grace of pelicans cruising parallel to a breaking wave with their wingtips almost skimming the wall of water. She captured those scenes on canvas with a delicate brush and an eye for detail. Her paintings won several awards in local competitions, but Marjo always found a reason to ground Alita and take away her art supplies for a week or two, just long enough to get her focused on her modeling career again.

You stupid, foolish girl.

For someone paraded in front of crowds of people from an early age, Alita never felt comfortable in the spotlight. She was the center of attention not for any achievement on her part, but for a superficial quality beyond her control: her "beauty," as judged by others who knew nothing else about her.

She didn't remember the town or the name of the shopping mall where she was featured in a style show, modeling back-to-school clothes for pre-teens. But she would never forget walking down the runway of the temporary stage in the center of the mall and seeing the girl with the cleft palate whose stare bored right through her. The girl was about Alita's age—ten or eleven at the time. Alita knew the other girl played video games, just like she did; the other girl rode a bicycle, helped bake cookies, and did many other things just like Alita did. But Alita was on the runway modeling clothes and the other girl was standing on the sidelines simply because adults found Alita to be beautiful and the other girl to be not so beautiful. For reasons she did not fully understand at the time, Alita felt a deep sadness. Maybe that was her first scar, an inner scar, but a scar nonetheless, and an awareness that maybe she didn't want to be a model after all.

You stupid, foolish girl.

The skin above Alita's eye was still a reddish purple when the stitches were removed a week after her diving accident. "It looks a lot worse than it is," she said to her mother. Marjo didn't speak. Her glare was enough.

Several months later it was obvious that Dr. White overestimated his stitching abilities because a scar did form, a small but permanent reminder of her encounter with the diving board in high school. If she truly wanted to pursue her modeling career it would not have been a big deal—a touch of makeup, several passes with an eyebrow liner, and it was almost completely hidden. But the accident, and the scar, served two useful purposes. For the first time in her life Alita began to think for herself, and she knew she would not be happy as a model. In temporarily closing one eye, the diving accident opened both of her eyes and led her to pursue the path in life she wanted, instead of the one her mother wanted for her. More importantly, the accident shattered Marjo's fanatical focus on perfection for her daughter. Alita knew that her mother could never again look at her and not see it: the scar, the blemish, the slight imperfection that in Marjo's mind negated Alita's chances of ever attaining superstardom as a model.

You stupid, foolish girl.

The sun was twenty degrees above the horizon when Alita walked the two blocks from the beach to her house on Condict Drive. In the beauty of the sunrise she forgot that she was to go to work early to tag new inventory with Meg Zorn, her business partner. She checked the time. Meg would have finished her breakfast at The Beacon and already be at the shop. She rushed a shower and dressed for the day. On her way out the door she grabbed two folders crammed with sketches and tucked them under her arm.

The Sunriz Boutique was less than a half mile from home, but as she backed her red Miata convertible from the garage Alita wished that an hour's drive and a hundred curves were ahead of her. She had long wanted a small sports car that was both fun and affordable. When she was behind the wheel the car became an extension of herself. She liked that feeling.

Alita knew she would be lost without Meg to keep their shop running smoothly. She had opened the Sunriz Boutique five years earlier with a dream but little business savvy. She just wanted a shop to sell beachwear and souvenirs. She decorated it using pieces of her original art, with the hope that she might also sell a few of her paintings.

Alita didn't even have a business plan when Meg, a former marketing manager for Walt Disney World, stopped by her boutique the week it opened. In her mid-fifties and already bored following her recent retirement, Meg was looking for something to do after moving to New Smyrna Beach. She was impressed with Alita's artistic talents and amused by her raw inexperience. She offered to work part-time in the shop and mentor Alita, an offer that was quickly accepted.

Meg soon turned Alita's paintings of sunrises and beach scenes into eye-catching designs they printed on T-shirts, hats, handbags, beach towels, and other accessories. She educated Alita on every aspect of running a successful small business and nurtured her flair for fashion. As sales and profits steadily rose, Alita gave Meg a full partnership in appreciation for all she had done. In their third year together they started their "Sunriz" line of casual women's clothing. Several beach stores from St. Augustine to Fort Lauderdale stocked their apparel. They planned to one day expand distribution and set up an online store, but for now their focus was on their small shop on Flagler Avenue.

Alita pulled into her parking spot behind the building and saw that Meg's car was already there. A glance at the cloudless blue sky told her there was no need to raise the convertible top. She picked up her folders and headed for the back entrance.

She caught the aroma of fresh coffee as she walked through the storage space and office area at the rear of the shop. She dropped the folders on her desk and headed straight to the coffeemaker.

"Is that you?" Meg called out.

"Sorry I'm late." Steam rolled from the mug of coffee Alita poured for herself. She was tired from working past midnight on a painting and climbing out of bed to catch the sunrise. A little caffeine would help.

Meg walked into the office area, box cutter in hand.

"Watch broken?" she asked.

"You should have seen the sunrise. It was spectacular."

"I saw it. But I was also here on time." Meg was smiling. "There's one more box out front and then we're finished. It was a light shipment."

"I swear, Meg, there are times that if we weren't partners, I think you'd have to let me go."

The phone rang before Meg could respond. "I'll get it," she said. "I guess we're open for the day."

"Sunriz Boutique … I'm sorry, from where? Okay. Uh-huh … uh-huh … no, I'm not, but she's right here." Meg looked at Alita and motioned her closer. "Yes, yes, she does." Alita saw the concern on Meg's face. "And what is your name again? Okay, I'll put her on."

Meg held out the phone to Alita. "It's a Detective Blate, from Nashville. He asked me if you have a sister named Victoria."

W arm tears trickled down Alita's cheeks. Meg handed her another tissue and put an arm on her shoulder.

"When did it happen?" Meg asked softly.

"Two weeks ago. Detective Blate talked to a Lyft driver who took her to a cemetery just before midnight on Saturday. A jogger found her," Alita's eyes closed, "found her body the next morning."

"Why did it take so long for them to notify you?"

Alita dabbed her eyes with the tissue. "He said she was burned so bad that ...."

Her chest rose and fell with heavy, painful sobs.

"I'll be all right," Alita said, her voice cracking. "I'll be all right." She closed her eyes and again saw her sister, her face a mask always hiding something. The pain, the lies ... the truth.

Alita slammed her hand down on the desk with such force that Meg jumped back.

"Dammit! How could she be so careless? I told her that something like this could happen, but would she listen? Would she ever listen to me?" Alita rose from her chair and shoved it back against her desk. She turned and took a few steps toward the front of the shop, then whirled to face Meg. Before she could speak she felt the strength drain from her, and new tears tracked down her cheeks. "Why, Meg? Why did it have to be Victoria?" She dropped to her knees and began sobbing again. "It's all my fault."

Meg rushed over and held her close. "Don't talk like that. You did everything a sister could possibly do." She consoled Alita until her tears finally dried.

"I need to go to Nashville," Alita said. "This afternoon. I'll go see that detective when I get there. To get some answers. " She dropped into her chair and leaned back until it squeaked in protest. "Why would she go to a cemetery that late at night?"

"What if the Lyft guy is lying?" Meg asked. "Maybe she got into his car to go somewhere else, but that is where he took her."

"Anything's possible, I guess. But I would think they've already checked into that."

Alita pulled open the middle desk drawer and took out a bottle of Tylenol. The slight throbbing over her temples was now railroad spikes being driven into the sides of her head with a sledgehammer. She shook out two caplets.

"Let me get you some water," Meg said.

"No, I'm good." Alita tilted her head back and forced down the caplets. "I have to run home to throw a few things together, so would you see if you can get me a flight? And a rental car and hotel room?"

"I'll take care of everything and text you with all the details. And plan on me driving you to the airport."

"Thanks, Meg. I don't know what I'd do without you."

Alita was almost to the door when she stopped and turned around. "Meg ... buy two tickets. All the info you need is in my Contacts on the computer."

Meg looked puzzled before nodding. "Did they already notify her?"

"No, I'm going there now. I want to tell her in person."

F airgreen Estates was less than five miles from the Sunriz Boutique, via the North Causeway over the Indian River. The last
time Alita went to her mother's house was three years ago, at Thanksgiving. The two of them decided to put aside the past and attempt the
ritual of being together on a holiday. After an hour of pleasantries, the
argument began when Alita pointed out that a family gathering would
never be complete without Victoria. It ended a short time later when
Alita walked out her mother's front door and heard it slam behind her.

Alita and Marjo occasionally crossed paths—New Smyrna Beach
was small enough to make it inevitable. Each time Alita would return
her mother's icy stare. They didn't exchange words. She could always
see in her mother's piercing, judgmental eyes that familiar look of
disappointment: *You stupid, foolish girl.*

Tidy, single-family homes lined both sides of the street. Marjo
made a lot of money through the years selling houses there, and she
listed and sold a few of the properties multiple times.

Alita turned onto Lake Fairgreen Circle and within a minute pulled
into her mother's driveway. She switched off the ignition and took a
deep breath. Tylenol relieved the penetrating headache that earlier tore
her skull apart, but no known remedy could stave off the black veil of
dread that was closing around her heart.

Alita tilted the rearview mirror and leaned forward. She moistened
two fingers with her tongue and rubbed them across the makeup that
covered the skin just above her left eyebrow. A scar was exposed, so
slight there was likely only one other person in the entire world who

would notice it immediately.

She went up the walk toward the screened front entrance. A curtain moved in the living room window. She pressed the doorbell button and looked down at the "Welcome" mat. *Yeah, right.*

On her third press of the button the door opened, just as she was about to turn away.

"Well, well. Isn't this a treat. Hello, Alita."

"Hello, Marjo."

A brief silence followed. Marjo's eyes settled on the upper left part of her face.

"May I come in?"

"Oh, certainly." Marjo opened the door wider. "But you'll have to excuse the place. It's a mess."

Alita stepped inside and noted the polished marble entryway. "Nice." She tapped the toe of her sandal on the shiny surface. "When did you do this?"

"It's been a couple of years. Patrick Jeffrey put it in for me. He does such great work."

Alita followed her mother into the living room. A grandfather clock she had not seen before was dividing infinity into measurable units of time. The white contemporary sofa and matching recliner were new additions since her last visit, as was the teal carpeting.

They made their way to the kitchen. Like the living room, it was spotless.

"Coffee?"

"No, thanks."

Alita was not sure how to begin. She took a moment to focus on her mother. Her auburn hair was pulled up in the back and pinned, just as it always was. Although Marjo had spent her entire life in Florida's sunshine, Alita used to marvel how her face remained unlined and youthful. Now, at fifty-two, age had announced its presence with creases and bags where skin used to be smooth and tight. Marjo was an inch shorter than Alita and had never varied more than a pound or two from the one hundred and ten pounds she weighed during her college days at Stetson. She was even thinner now.

"So, what brings you here?" Marjo paused just long enough to arch an eyebrow. "Money?"

Alita felt a slow burn creep up the back of her neck. "Of course not."

"Don't tell me. You're getting married to that fellow, what's his name? Kevin Stone?"

"It's Gavin, not Kevin. But we're not getting married. We broke up, a couple of years ago."

Marjo folded her hands in front of her and offered a saccharine smile. "Then this is just a social call. How nice."

"No, it isn't." Alita swallowed hard. "I'm sorry to have to tell you this ... Victoria is dead."

Marjo's face went blank. Alita could hear the ticking of the grand-father clock in the living room.

"How?" she finally asked.

"She was murdered. In Nashville. I just found out an hour ago. I'm flying up later today and I was hoping that ... that you'd go with me, to bring her home. Meg is getting tickets for both of us."

Marjo looked away and drew an audible breath. Her head nodded several times like she was confirming something to herself. She looked back at Alita.

"That's a shame. And I'm sorry you wasted your money on my ticket. Maybe you can get a refund."

Alita glared at Marjo. "You'll never change, will you? It was crazy to think that for once you might actually care about someone other than yourself. But no. I tell you that your daughter—my sister—is dead, and that's how you respond?"

"I'm sorry about your sister." Marjo's voice stayed empty of emotion. "But my daughter was dead to me years ago."

Alita felt herself trembling. She was ready to turn and head for her car, but there was something she couldn't leave unspoken.

"And now you are dead to me."

A lita leaned back in her seat and closed her eyes. Five miles above the ground, somewhere between Daytona Beach and Nashville, she thought of her first airplane rides, with her sister long ago. Alita was four or five. Victoria would lie on her back, upraised hands on Alita's sides, and "fly" her through the air until her arms grew tired and they crashed in a heap of sisterly hugs and giggles.

Her eyes were still smarting from all the tears she cried that morning. She was bone tired from the most devastating day of her life. When sleep finally came, it was a welcome respite.

In a dream she and Victoria were kids again. They held hands as they hurtled through a tunnel of brilliant light. An unseen force propelled them, almost a living entity unto itself. A man in the distance, dressed in white and floating on a cottony cloud, beckoned them. Alita felt a great deceleration and a sound like a needle on a turntable spinning to a stop. The man before them was their father. He cradled Victoria in his arms, pressing her against his chest and stroking her hair. He took no notice of Alita. His lips moved and he began to speak.

A flight attendant tapped Alita on the shoulder and asked her to put her seat in the upright position to prepare for landing. She adjusted her seat and closed her eyes to rejoin the dream, but it was gone. Just like Victoria.

The wheels bounced several times before the plane settled on the runway. She turned off Airplane Mode on her watch and saw it reset an hour, to Central time.

She stopped at a newsstand in the terminal to buy a copy of *The*

Tennessean, Nashville's daily newspaper. She tucked the paper under her arm and didn't open it until she had ordered a cup of coffee in the North Lounge.

Victoria's murder wouldn't be in the headlines or even on the front page—over two weeks had passed since her sister's body was discovered—but Alita did hope to find something about the investigation. She turned every page, scanning each column from top to bottom. *Nothing.*

"Coming or going?" The server dropped a napkin in front of Alita and set her cup of coffee on it.

"Excuse me?"

"Did you just get in or are you getting ready to fly out?"

Alita wondered why it mattered. "Just getting in, from Daytona Beach."

"Really? I've been to Daytona for the 500. Remember Darrell Waltrip? He was one of the best drivers of all time. From Franklin, you know. A local hero 'round here."

"That's nice." The name wasn't familiar nor did Alita feel like making small talk. But a thought did cross her mind. "May I ask you a question?"

"Sure."

"Have you heard any details about a murder a couple of weeks ago? The woman they found in a cemetery."

The server's brow wrinkled. "You're talking here? In Nashville?"

"Yes."

The server shook her head. "Sorry. I haven't heard anything about a murder in a cemetery. And I stay up on all the local news, plus I hear about everything working in this place. What happened to her? And what cemetery was it?"

Alita focused for a few seconds on a circular coffee stain on the table. *How could Victoria's murder not be major news?* She raised her head to meet the other woman's eyes. "Never mind. But thank you for your time."

"Sure thing." With a tight, unsure smile, the server turned and walked away.

A soft rain was massaging the world outside. Alita opened her eyes to the early morning darkness in her room at the Sheraton Music City Hotel. Her fingers found her phone on the nightstand. It was four-fifteen. Strange thoughts crept into her mind, thoughts of a graveyard, her sister, and a stranger. Could it have happened at four-fifteen a.m.? Was that why she awoke at that moment?

She resisted an urge to throw on her clothes and drive to Mount Olivet Cemetery. She had no idea where the cemetery was, but a feeling told her that she would find it, that she would be led to it. Victoria would guide her. *But what would I do then?*

She thought about Victoria's killer. Where was he? Did he flee the city, or was he still in Nashville? Maybe he was the man who stood too close behind her at the Alamo counter when she picked up the rental car, the man with the olive complexion and the shiny black hair and the hot breath reeking of garlic. Maybe he was the creepy guy in the hotel who leered at her when she was inserting bills into a vending machine full of empty calories, giving in to the gnawing demands of a stomach that had gone without food since dinner the night before. Or maybe he was in a bedroom on the other side of the city, sleeping next to a wife who was unaware of where he went and what he did after midnight just over two weeks ago. He could be any of them. Or anyone else.

In less than twenty-four hours since learning of Victoria's murder Alita was already struggling with many questions that, once hypothetical, were now a part of her reality. She had always been against the death penalty. She believed that no one was beyond rehabilitation, no soul was beyond salvation. Now she wasn't so sure. What type of man could do that to another human being? A type that maybe didn't deserve to live? She was ashamed to think that she might even be willing to administer the lethal injection herself.

Alita looked at her cell phone. She wished she could talk to Victoria just one more time. She scolded herself yet again for not calling her sister the last few weeks. Being busy at work was not an excuse. She considered calling Victoria's number to hear her voice on the recording, but thought better of it because of the murder investigation. Was her phone being held as evidence and monitored for incoming calls? Had they even found her phone? A chill trickled up her spine. What if her killer still had it? And she called. And he answered ….

She couldn't go back to sleep, so she turned on the TV and watched a few minutes of one channel and then another.

She startled when her phone buzzed.

"Hey, Meg." Alita sat up and switched on the lamp.

"I'm sorry if I woke you, but I wanted to be sure I caught you this morning before you headed out."

"What's up?"

"Well, I hope you don't mind, but I called Phil Krynak just to get some information. You haven't contacted a funeral home up there yet, have you?"

"No, why?"

"I know you're not thinking about the money, but I found out it's a lot less expensive to have a funeral home down here make all the arrangements. Phil walked me through how everything works. He handles a lot of out-of-state transfers."

"What do I need to do?"

"Just tell anyone who asks that Wilkins-Mader Funeral Home in New Smyrna Beach is handling everything. Phil said that once you claim the body, the medical examiner's office will help you arrange to have it released to a local funeral home in Nashville. Let me or Phil know what funeral home it is and he will take it from there. He'll arrange to get a shipping casket, and if you call me as soon as you know when you're flying back, he'll see to it that the casket is on the plane with you."

"Okay, I think I have all that straight."

"Don't you worry about anything. And Alita ... please be careful up there."

A warm shower didn't relax her and she barely touched a muffin. She dressed in the outfit that was on top of the short stack of clothes in her suitcase and opened Maps on her phone. The Metro Police Department Hermitage Precinct was located at 3701 James Kay Lane, six miles and eleven minutes from her hotel.

The light rain stopped and the sun had broken through the puffy gray clouds that framed a skyline much different from the one that inspired a Bob Dylan album. Alita joined the flow of traffic heading east on Lebanon Pike.

Victoria had been renting a unit in the Hunting Creek Apartments complex off I-24 near Harding Place. Alita knew that was another stop she would soon have to make.

She turned on the radio in her rental car and heard an unfamiliar country singer with too much twang in his voice. She turned it off again. She loved music, but today she preferred the drone of road noise.

Alita parked in a space for visitors and took a moment to study the modern precinct building with its concrete and steel portico. Was Detective Blate inside, or on the streets working a case? Maybe Victoria's case? She would soon find out.

She scribbled her name on the sign-in sheet and clipped on a visitor badge. A few minutes later a balding, forty-ish man in a brown suit stepped around a partition and walked stiffly toward the counter. His carriage reflected formality but not friendliness. Alita saw him look at the man behind the counter, who nodded in her direction.

"Miss King, I'm Detective Harold Blate." He didn't offer a handshake. "Again, my condolences. I didn't know you would be coming to Nashville this quickly. It would have been better if you had called first. I only have a few minutes. Please, come with me."

Alita followed him as he led her down a corridor to a closed door, which he opened and held for her.

"I need to get a couple of things, then we'll go where there is a little more privacy," he said.

The desks in the room were covered with stacks of files and paperwork. Alita saw four men in suits gathered in a corner of the room. She resented that they had time to chat, drink coffee, and stuff their faces with Egg McMuffins. Why weren't they out trying to catch a killer?

She watched Blate sift through a pile of papers and slip several pages into a folder. He picked up a pen and notepad and walked back to her.

"First trip to Nashville?" he asked.

"No, I was here once before. Several years ago."

He nodded absently as he held up the folder. "This is all I need, so let's get out of here. This place can be a zoo."

They went down the same corridor to another room, much smaller than the first. Blate closed the door behind them.

The furnishings were spartan—a rectangular conference table, four straight-backed chairs, and a black telephone with a chunk of plastic missing from its side. He took out a toothpick and put it between his teeth. She sat down across from him.

"So, what can I do for you?" he asked.

Alita took rapid stock of Detective Harold Blate. His voice was gravelly, maybe a product of years of smoking, but free of any accent.

He had a birthmark on his forehead like Mikhail Gorbachev's map of Italy, but his was smaller and looked more like New Jersey. He was broad-shouldered and muscular, a cop who could handle himself if an arrest turned into an altercation. There was a distance about him that she could not further define or label. She normally wasn't so attentive, but this man was in charge of finding her sister's killer. She wanted to satisfy herself that he was up to the task.

"Miss King?"

"Oh, sorry. I'm here to get information, and to tell you anything I can about Victoria that might help your investigation."

"I appreciate that. What questions do you have?"

"Okay, I would like to know ..." The dryness in her mouth made it hard to talk. "Do you, do you have a suspect yet?"

"No suspects, no leads on anyone at this point."

"How about a motive?"

"Motive could be anything. Look, I'm sorry to be so blunt, but your sister was a prostitute and a drug addict. That's a tough life that often doesn't end well. Our working theory is that it was a drug buy that went bad." Blate chewed on the toothpick and scribbled on his notepad. "Do you know how long she was using? And could she have been dealing, too?"

Alita looked away. She recalled snippets of conversations she'd had with Victoria about her sister's drug abuse. *Promises to change, promises broken.* She looked back at the detective. "She's been on and off drugs forever, but mostly on. Eighteen, nineteen years, I don't know. That always worried me. You know, where she bought them. She swore she had good sources, people she could trust who wouldn't sell her bad stuff or rip her off. But I know she wasn't dealing. She would never do that."

"Addicts keep secrets, even from those closest to them. We can't ever be sure of anything."

As much as Alita wanted to disagree with him, there were many things about her sister's life that she would never know.

"How did you find out it was Victoria?"

"It took a while. We couldn't get fingerprints because ..." She saw him bite down on the toothpick when his voice trailed off. "Then we got lucky. We received a call from a woman who said her friend was missing. She gave us your sister's name, and when she described the tattoo that's on her ankle we were pretty sure of the ID."

Alita recalled the small monarch butterfly tattoo on the inside of Victoria's left leg, just above the ankle. Victoria always loved butterflies. Because they were beautiful, because they were delicate, but mostly because they seemed to be so free as they fluttered about. Now beautiful, delicate Victoria was free at last, too.

"Wait, what do you mean by pretty sure? You don't know for certain?"

"We couldn't know for certain just on the basis of a tattoo. A lot of women have butterfly tattoos on their ankle."

Alita felt a flicker of hope. "Then how do you know it really is Victoria?"

"Once we had her name it gave us a place to start looking, but it still wasn't easy. Your sister's been busted a few times so we knew her line of work, but all the booking information was dated. Her driver's license had expired and she had moved from that address anyway, plus she didn't have any vehicles registered in her name. We were finally able to track down the escort service where she was working, and we obtained her current address from them. I talked with neighbors and the apartment manager but that didn't yield anything helpful. When we checked her apartment we found a calendar on the wall where she wrote down her medical appointments, including one with her dentist. We had a forensic odontologist review her dental records." Blate paused. "It was a match."

He must have seen something in Alita's eyes. "I'm sorry," he added.

Alita barely nodded.

"How did you find out about me?" she asked.

"I found letters in her apartment that you sent to her, so I called the New Smyrna Beach Police Department. I love small town cops. They knew you and gave me your shop's phone number."

Alita tried to remember everything she had written in letters that were meant only for her sister to read, but it was too much for her to think about.

"I have a question for you," Blate said. "You're a King, she was a LaRue. Was that her married name, maiden name, were you stepsisters, or what? I came up blank on that."

"She never married. She was Victoria King until her early twenties, then she changed her name to LaRue."

"Where did that come from?"

"I was a kid when she did it. I never asked her. But you said a woman called you, a friend of Victoria's. Who is she?"

Blate leaned back in his chair. "She wouldn't give us her name."

"You found out where Victoria worked. What's the name of the place?"

"It's not a place, it's just a cell phone number that johns call. The service sends a girl to wherever they are. Right now it's Satin Dolls, but names and numbers change often to try to stay ahead of the Gambling and Prostitution Unit. A buddy of mine in that unit crossed paths with your sister a time or two, and that eventually led us to Satin Dolls. Like I said, they gave us your sister's address but that was about it. They're not exactly in the record-keeping business and they avoid talking to cops. They did say that your sister wasn't working for them that night. But take that with a grain of salt."

"What do you mean?"

"We weren't able to talk with anyone in person, just on the phone and not for long."

Alita closed her eyes and shook her head. It was a world she couldn't imagine. She remembered one of Meg's concerns. "Did you check into the Lyft driver?"

"Of course. He's in the clear. Everything checked out."

"Her cell phone. Did you find it? Do you have it?"

"No. It last pinged the night she died. It's been turned off, destroyed, who knows. It wasn't at the crime scene or her apartment. Or her purse, wallet, anything like that."

Alita let out a small, defeated sigh. None of the answers were helping at all.

"You told me yesterday that a jogger found my sister in the cemetery. What's his name?"

"I can't tell you that."

"Why? I should at least know who found her, so I can thank him."

Blate pulled the toothpick from his mouth and rolled it between his fingers, perhaps weighing her request in his mind. After a pause, "His name's Luke O'Connor. And trust me, there's no way he was involved in your sister's death. No way."

Alita filed the jogger's name in her memory. "So if you still don't have any idea who killed my sister or why she was killed, what do you have?"

A light on the telephone blinked on.

"The fire eliminated any evidence. There were no witnesses, at least not any who have come forward. About all we know for sure is that she was killed where we found her, she wasn't dump—uh, she wasn't brought there from another location. So again, we're thinking a drug deal."

"Was it the fire that killed her, or was she shot, stabbed, something else?"

Blate seemed uneasy as he again shifted position in his chair. "I can't say anything more right now. It's an open investigation. That's the best I can do."

Alita folded her arms and sat back in her chair. "You don't have a suspect, you don't know the motive. You won't tell me how she died. Why should I even believe that it's my sister? Just because you tell me that it is? What if that forensic dentist is wrong?" She looked into the detective's eyes. "I want to see the body myself. I want to be sure it's Victoria."

"I told you we're sure it's her. The dental records are an exact match, there is no doubt." Blate reached across the table to pat Alita's arm but she pulled it back. "I know this is hard on you, but don't make it any worse. I was there, I saw her. It's not something you want to see."

"That's not your decision to make, Detective."

8

Alita turned down Detective Blate's offer to meet her at the Medical Examiner's office to view Victoria's body. She didn't know if he made the offer as a courtesy, or for a reason that would benefit him.

It was a short drive to the Metro Forensic Services facility. The modern brick building with a two-story atrium looked nothing like the aging edifice she had pictured in her mind.

On the walk from her car to the entrance, she thought about the inevitability of the moment. Victoria was on a path to self-destruction for years, and that path finally ended in a Nashville cemetery. Although she died by the hands of a stranger, in the end, as it was sure to be from the beginning, she was the victim of the guilt that seized her after the death of their father and sent her in a downward spiral. In that sense, their mother was right—Victoria had died a long time ago.

Alita went inside.

"May I help you?" The receptionist's tone was friendly.

"My name is Alita King. I came here to see my sister. Victoria LaRue."

"Of course. If you'll take a seat, I'll call Dr. Carringer for you."

Alita sat in one of the steel and fabric chairs along the wall. She inhaled through her nostrils, not finding a smell of formaldehyde or disinfectant. The only sound was the clack of the receptionist's keyboard.

The double doors opened and a Black man walked toward her. He was medium in height and weight, about thirty-five, and dressed in blue scrubs.

"Miss King, I'm Dr. Carringer, Assistant Medical Examiner. Detective Blate called to let us know you'd be coming. But there's really no need for you to do this. There's no doubt about the identification and—"

"I've been told that, Doctor. But I need to see her for myself."

Dr. Carringer nodded. "That's what I thought you'd say, so I went ahead and prepared everything. I can take you back now."

"Please."

Alita followed him through the double doors and down a hallway. They walked in silence to the rear section of the building. He opened another door for her.

The room was designed with ease of cleaning in mind. It would be a simple task to wash blood or anything else from the tile walls and floors.

Alita saw stainless-steel tables on wheels, and a type of heavy lift or hoist. A large scale sat in a back corner of the room.

Dr. Carringer stopped at a steel door with a one-foot by one-foot glass window. Alita squinted but could see only darkness. She moved closer to the window.

"Can you describe any of her tattoos for me?" he asked.

He said "tattoos"—plural—and that gave Alita another faint hope there could have been a mistake. "I know of only one tattoo she had. It was a butterfly, above her left ankle. A monarch."

"Would you recognize it?"

"Yes."

Dr. Carringer raised his hand to a light switch. "Your sister's body suffered severe damage, especially anteriorly, but her lower legs were not burned quite as badly. Her tattoo is still visible." He paused. "Are you ready?"

Alita nodded.

Dr. Carringer flipped the light switch.

What she saw was not at all what she expected. The dim light on the other side of the steel door illuminated the outline of a body covered with white sheets. The body was on a cart with a curtain pulled close around it, blocking her view of whatever else might be behind the door. The sheets were arranged to expose an ankle, and above that ankle Alita saw Victoria's tattoo. There had been no mistake.

"Miss King, you can't go in there."

Alita hadn't realized she was pulling on the door handle. It was locked.

"I'm sorry. But I need to see the rest of her body. That's why I came here. I have to see her."

"I can't let you. And believe me, it would serve no purpose anyway."

Alita wanted to lash out at him, but she couldn't when she saw the pain on his face. "Please, it's very important to me. Don't I have the right to see her?"

"No, not here." Dr. Carringer flipped off the light switch. "But there is a way if you insist. Once we release the body to a funeral home, the decision to view it there would be up to you."

Alita didn't respond. She just stared at the darkness behind the window.

9

Alita signed the paperwork to release Victoria's body to the Graham-Slivka Funeral Home. She added a note that stated Phil Krynak would be in touch to handle the transfer to Florida.

Dr. Carringer called the funeral home to arrange pick up, and a staff member told him the body would be ready for viewing at three o'clock.

"Here's the address." He handed a piece of paper to Alita. "Do you have a GPS?"

"On my phone."

Dr. Carringer looked at his watch. "You have several hours. I can suggest places you could go for lunch."

"I'm not hungry. I'll just drive around."

"Of course." He paused. "If you just want time to clear your mind, you might want to stop by Centennial Park. It's on your route, you can't miss it. There's even a replica of the Parthenon. You'll find it peaceful there."

"You've been kind. Thank you."

Alita followed Dr. Carringer's suggestion and drove to Centennial Park, mostly because she had nowhere else to go. She didn't care about the Parthenon or anything else in the sprawling park, she just wanted to walk in isolation and think about Victoria. It was a peaceful setting, as Dr. Carringer said, but she did not find peace of mind.

She pulled into the parking lot of the Graham-Slivka Funeral Home on 25th Avenue North just before three o'clock. She looked at the white, one-story building that Dr. Carringer said was built in the

1860s. She also saw the structure at the rear that was once a carriage house. That's where Victoria would be.

She walked under an awning and up the steps to the front porch. There was one thought she could not block from her mind—she hoped they had been gentle with her sister's body. Not just the people at the funeral home, but everyone who had come in contact with her body to that point. Victoria's last moments were filled with terror, violence, and pain. It would be comforting to think she had been handled gently and with dignity. Were they careful when they placed her on the gurney? Did they wash her and clean her and dress her in something pretty? Was her head now resting on a pillow?

A reserved but cordial man asked Alita a few questions about Victoria. He handed her a form and told her to read it carefully before signing it in several places. With only a glance, she scrawled her name in the proper blanks and gave it back to him.

"Are you sure this is what you want to do?" he asked.

"Please, I just want to see my sister."

"Okay, then. Follow me." He led her out back, to the converted carriage house.

Inside, Alita did not look around the small building. She was drawn to the sheet-covered body on the table.

"I'm sorry to have to do this." The man's tone was somber.

Alita closed her eyes. Her fingernails dug into the palms of her hands.

At the sound of the sheet being pulled back, she opened her eyes.

They had not been gentle with Victoria. Nor had her killer. The sight before her was a thousand times worse than anything she had seen in her life, and it was multiplied a thousand times more because she was looking at her own sister.

Alita fought through the shock and horror to find the resolve to touch the body. She delicately turned the left ankle just enough to see the monarch butterfly tattoo that had escaped the devastation done to much of the rest of the flesh.

Her overloaded senses shut down. If there was an odor, she didn't smell it. She heard nothing. She felt no pain from where she had bitten her lower lip, and the drops of blood left no coppery taste in her mouth. The man pulled the sheet back into place.

Several minutes later she was sitting in her rental car. She couldn't remember if she thanked the man, or if she said anything more to him at all. She couldn't even remember walking out of the building. But there were two things she would never forget. One was the sight of her sister. The other was the vow she made that she would find the monster who did that to her.

10

If there was two birds sitting on a fence,
he would bet you which one would fly first.
    —Mark Twain

E d Potter told his friends that he lived life for the next day's
    mail. But Potter was always at least two days away from
success. And the gap never seemed to narrow.

Fate gave him one good break in his life, when he was a young literary agent with the prestigious Harrod Rawlins Agency in New York
City. That was the day he found the first novel by Artemus Logan, a
high school English teacher from Duluth, Minnesota, in the stack of
manuscripts on his desk.

Potter read *The Devil's Finest Hour* and found it to be a brilliant
work of fiction. He was sure he could sell it for a sizable advance and
was already calculating his commission when he gave Artemus Logan
a call. Before Potter could identify himself, the distraught woman who
answered said that her husband had been killed two days earlier in a
car accident. The idea was already forming in Potter's mind when he
hung up the phone without another word.

His good break was that he could have sold the book, cashed nice
commission checks, and climbed a rung or two on the agency ladder
at Rawlins. But Potter had other plans.

From Artemus Logan's letter that accompanied his manuscript,
Potter knew that he was the first and only literary agent to look at the
work. Logan also mentioned that no one other than his wife had read

his novel or even known he had written a book. It was easy enough for Potter to create a substitute title for *The Devil's Finest Hour*. He made up a pseudonym and rented a post office box using that name. He even took the step of mailing a copy of the manuscript to himself, just so he would have the envelope with the pseudonym's name and return address.

Potter invented a story hinting of the anonymous author's high-ranking position within the Catholic Church and the need for secrecy and a pseudonym, which meant no bio, no photo on the book jacket, and no media interviews or book signings. He dangled juicy bait in front of publishers—a thinly-veiled tale of altar boys, priests, and cover-ups that went all the way to the Vatican. One publishing house took the bait, offering a two-hundred-thousand-dollar advance that stunned him—it was a huge sum for an unknown author at the time.

It seemed so easy to Potter. He doubted that Logan's widow would ever follow up on her dead husband's manuscript, but if she did, Potter would respond with a standard rejection letter and a comment that the work was hopelessly flawed. She would put her husband's papers in a trunk in the attic and that would be the end of it. And once the book was published under a new title and with a different author's name, what were the chances she would ever pick up a copy? There were thousands of new books published each year and she wouldn't even be looking for that particular title, the new one Potter created. He was willing to live with the odds. He would get a commission from the advance and a check for the balance would be sent to the pseudonym's post office box. The same for future royalties. The checks would be relatively simple to deposit in the account he set up, and since he was working both ends he could manipulate his employer's paper trail. And if a publisher offered an even bigger advance for a second book by the anonymous author, well, Potter had always wanted to write a novel. Even if it turned out to be garbage he would still have the advance. Potter congratulated himself for being so clever. But there was one possibility he failed to consider.

The book was a smash. Not just a bestseller, but the number one, *must read* book of the year. So popular, so publicized, that even a still grieving widow in Duluth, Minnesota, bought a copy. A week later she met with her attorney.

Ed Potter carried an attitude with him when he walked into his second-floor office in the two-story white brick building on Beverly Boulevard in Los Angeles. Short, thick, and blotchy faced, with buggy eyes and a bulging abdomen, he was well aware of the effects of time not only upon the body, but also upon the mind. Almost fifty, he was convinced that he was destined to wither and die in L.A. He hated the thought as much as it haunted him. New York seemed like a faraway dream, stored in a box in the deepest recesses of his memory, a small blip on the radar screen of his life.

"Warm enough, Sam?" Potter loosened his tie and felt as rumpled as the cheap sport coat that clung to his chunky body. The air inside the office was as stifling as that from which he had just escaped.

Sam Brocklesby—*not* Samantha, she allows a person to make that mistake but once—offered Potter a glare along with the bundle of mail in her hands. Small tributaries of sweat trickled down her forehead. She was in her early forties, and while not what most men would label attractive, she was not unpleasant to look at. She had piercing eyes and a venomous mouth that was always ready to strike.

"Get something done about the damn air conditioning or I'm not coming back until you do," Sam said. "And I had to eat lunch at my desk because you're just now showing up."

"Yeah, yeah," Potter mumbled. He grabbed the mail from her hands. "I'll take care of it."

Potter trudged to the rear of the office suite. He dropped the mail on his desk. Between his first and second shots of Johnnie Walker Black, he called the building's management company and was promised the air conditioner would be fixed within the hour. The same promise he'd been given the last three times he called. The blue-tinged smoke from his Marlboro cigarette hung in a stubborn cloud over his head. Potter felt as gray and as battered as the metal filing cabinet that sat in the corner.

He settled into his faux leather chair. It had a gash in the seat and a frozen wheel that turned him sideways whenever he pushed himself from his desk. He picked up the mail and slipped off the rubber band. Three nine-by-twelve padded envelopes were among the junk ads and bills.

His business card and the plate on the door told the world he was a literary agent, but only he and Sam knew that Potter Literary Associates had sold just two books in the last three years, and neither made a ripple in the publishing world. It was no longer fallout from *The Devil's Finest Hour* and the mess he left behind years ago in New York. After a seven-figure settlement with Artemus Logan's widow—paid by insurance companies for both the book's publisher and Potter's former employer—and a long period of being shunned by all reputable publishing houses, Potter was able to wiggle his way back into the business. None of the editors Potter now worked with had any idea of what he had done in the past. No, the problem today was competition. There were too many literary agents and too few good books. Add ebooks to the mix and the fact that any no-talent could self-publish, and it was all that Potter could do to keep his nose above water.

To survive he charged writers a fee to read and critique their manuscripts. He encouraged writers with little or no talent, writers whose manuscripts had no chance for publication. He played on their egos and aspirations—*"You did a good job on this rewrite, but it still needs work. Send me another five hundred dollars and I'll show you how to fix it."* He could milk several thousand dollars that way before the writer suspected a scam or ran out of money. Either way, the next day's mail always brought more lambs to the slaughter.

Potter was old school and preferred printed submissions instead of electronic files. He also found it was easier to dupe writers who weren't tech-savvy, and there were plenty of them. One of his current clients still used a typewriter to compose her stories.

He picked up a padded envelope and opened it. The manuscript was a rewrite from a housewife in Pennsylvania who wanted desperately to be a mystery writer. Potter turned a few pages, enough to see that her writing style was as desperate as her dreams. Another rewrite would be in order. He slid the woman's check from under the paper clip attached to the first page of the manuscript.

The next envelope contained the third rewrite of *Me 'n Boomer*, a novel about a boy and his dog. The author was a highway worker for the State of Oklahoma and his story was based on a dog he had as a child. The enclosed letter, addressed to Sam, stated the author could not afford to pay for additional critiques and that he hoped Mr. Potter could now sell his revised work "as is." Potter glanced at a few pages. *The guy's not a terrible writer—at least he's better than the Gillian Flynn wanna-be from Pennsylvania—but who wants to read about a boy and his stupid dog?* Potter wrote a note to Sam telling her to call the guy and use her charming, sexy voice to say how close he was to getting it right. And mention that if he'd pay for just one more critique ….

The last padded envelope was postmarked "Old Town, Florida," but the return address was Potter's office address. Puzzled, Potter ripped open the envelope and pulled out six chapters and a query letter.

"*Stay Downwind,*" Potter said to himself as he noted the title. "Not bad." He skimmed the query letter and settled on the author's name at the bottom: W. Dawdy.

Potter almost never read anything for free, but this writer piqued his interest. He read the first page of *Stay Downwind*. And then the second. And third. When he finished the fourth page he hit a button on his phone.

"Yeah, what do you want?" Sam asked. "I'm melting here."

"I've taken care of that. Look, I don't want to be disturbed for a while. Hold my calls, will you?"

"Your calls? That's a laugh."

Potter ignored the sarcasm and turned back to the pages in front of him.

The first six chapters of *Stay Downwind* consisted of thirty-nine pages of double-spaced print. Potter was halfway through the sample chapters when the vent above his desk rattled several times and spat out a blast of air. He barely noticed.

Potter finished the last page and picked up the query letter to read it a second time. His office was cooler now but he was still sweating. He buzzed Sam's extension.

"Yeah?"

"Can I see you a minute?"

"Thanks for getting the air back on." Sam's tone was almost pleasant. She sat in a chair in front of his desk as he nudged the cover letter and sample chapters of *Stay Downwind* toward her.

"What's this?" Her bored tone annoyed him.

He nodded at the stacked pages. "Go on, Sam, look at it."

She shrugged and picked up a couple of pages. "Okay. What am I looking at?"

"A million bucks, if the rest of it is as good as this is." Potter took a final sip of whisky and reached for another cigarette.

Sam sat up in her chair, taking more interest in what she held in her hands. She pointed at the author's name. "W. Dawdy. He hasn't sent us anything before. I'd remember that name."

"I don't know if it's his real name or not. He didn't include an address or phone number or any contact information. He's on the road all the time and said it would be easier if he does the getting in touch." Potter took a long drag on his cigarette. "I don't think you understand what we may have here. This guy can write, and I'm hooked. If the rest of his book is as good as these chapters, we could be sitting on a gold mine. This stuff is what's hot now, what's selling the big numbers."

"Tell me about it."

"Well, it begins with a prostitute in Nashville. She doesn't know it, but a serial killer's been shadowing her."

"Like stalking?"

"Yeah, whatever. But this serial killer learns everything about the hooker. I mean, everything. He's a real computer wizard, knows how to use the Dark Web, and even hacks her phone remotely. He can track her every move, listen to her calls, read her texts. It's amazing. When he's finally ready, he propositions her on the street and promises to give her two thousand bucks if she'll meet him in a cemetery at midnight. She goes expecting kinky sex and instead the guy dopes her up and sets her on fire. And he films the whole thing! Great, right?"

Sam shrugged. "Doesn't sound all that great to me."

"Like hell it isn't." Potter leaned forward in his chair. "It's real creepy, this hooker wandering around the tombstones at night. Dawdy wrote in his query that he went to Nashville to do the research and found a cemetery that was a perfect setting. He walked through it at midnight so he could get a feel for what it would be like. He said the tombstones he describes and the names on them are freakin' real. This guy is special. You don't get that kind of research effort from new writers."

"But don't you think serial killers have been overdone?"

"Are you kidding me? It's a sick world out there, and people just eat this stuff up. Besides, he claims to have come up with a unique angle for a serial killer novel. Maybe we can make a few bucks from him in reading fees and then actually sell his work. Sell his work! What a concept! God, I love this country."

"So what do we do now?"

"The only thing we can do. Hope we hear from him again."

11

A lita parted the thick hotel drapes and looked eastward at a palette of yellow and orange hues. In another setting, under other circumstances, she would have watched the sunrise, a ritual she had enjoyed countless times before. Today, she released the drape and turned away. She needed to hear a friendly voice.

"Hey, I was getting ready to head to the shop," Meg answered. "Are you okay?"

"I just wanted to tell you I'm going to fly home tomorrow. I'll come back here after the funeral but right now I want to get my head together and take care of Victoria. Would you book me a late afternoon flight, and do whatever's necessary to make sure she is on the plane with me? I don't care what it costs. Just put it on my Amex and I'll worry about it later."

"Consider it done. What about the funeral? Phil was asking."

"I don't know. Maybe next Thursday. A week should be enough time to get everything arranged, don't you think?"

"Do you still want to go with just the graveside service?"

"There's no reason to do anything else. I'm sure it's just going to be you and me." Alita looked at her watch. "I have to get going. But thanks, Meg. For everything."

Mount Olivet Cemetery was only four miles from the hotel. Alita hadn't found the time or mustered the resolve to research the cemetery online, but soon she would see it in person.

When she turned into the entrance she saw the large building that housed the cemetery office and funeral home. She drove on, not ready for the questions she would soon need to ask.

In front of a large boulder the road divided into opposite directions. She took the road to the right. Halfway up the winding grade she saw two weathered crypts built into the side of the hill. Her eyes briefly settled on the names carved in stone: *A. Nickel and E S Gardner.*

Not until her car crested the hill did she realize that the cemetery was much bigger than what could be seen from the road. The panorama in front of her looked like a giant green chessboard with an endless variety of pieces scattered across its surface.

The road split again and she took the path that went to the right. Several turns later she was well into the cemetery. She drove up and down the narrow roads, some gravel, others paved, uncertain of the emotion she was feeling. She was surrounded by the dead—and this was where her sister was murdered—but she felt no fear. The anger had calmed. The grief behind so many tears was gone. She was numb.

Several more turns later, Alita reached the edge of the cemetery. She was so lost at this point she didn't know if it was the back of the cemetery or one of the sides. She kept driving, unsure of where she was going or what she would find.

She lowered her window and took in the scents. Flowers, trees, and freshly cut grass. Over the crunch of the stones beneath her tires she heard the happy call of a songbird perched in the leafy canopy overhead.

She thought of another, smaller cemetery from her past. It was outside Miami and she had not been there in years. She pictured a gravestone, a spire so tall that to an eight-year-old it looked like a small rocket made of granite. The first time she saw the monument the ground was still raw and uneven. Marjo took her hand and forced her to touch the stone. She told her it was Victoria's fault that her daddy was dead. That Victoria had killed him. Marjo was grieving for her husband—or maybe for herself—but she had no right to manipulate the mind and the feelings of a little girl who just lost her father.

Alita threw herself upon his grave, scratching and clawing and digging to get to him. An older man rushed over to lift her off the ground, and an older woman took out a handkerchief to dry her tears and wipe the soil from her face and hands. Alita told them her sister had killed their daddy, and that he was now in Heaven and they took her sister away. Marjo just stood there, silent.

A straight stretch of road was in front of her and Alita could once again see Lebanon Pike in the distance, and the cemetery office and funeral home. This time she would pull into the parking lot.

A pleasant-faced woman, plump but well-groomed and nicely dressed, greeted Alita when she went inside.

"G'mornin.' I'm June Wickliff and I'm happy to help you." The woman had a Southern accent. "Here, let me give you a brochure." She handed Alita a tri-fold pamphlet with the words "Confederate Circle at Mount Olivet" on the front panel, above a tall monument topped by the figure of a soldier.

"It tells about a lot of our war heroes," June said. "Fourteen hundred and ninety-two of them are laid to rest in the Confederate Circle. Fourteen hundred and ninety-two, same as the year Christopher Columbus discovered America."

"But I came here to—"

"Let me show you the map." June unfolded the pamphlet in Alita's hands. "Now here's where we are, see the 'B' right there?" Her index finger pointed at a small, darkened symbol on the map of the cemetery. "And there's the Confederate Circle, see where it says 'D' there?" She ran her finger upward about two inches. She was so close that Alita caught the nicotine and morning coffee on her breath.

"But what I—"

"This here tells you about Major General William Brimage Bate."

June's active index finger was pointing at pictures of men long dead. "He was wounded three times and had six horses shot out from under him. And my favorite is Colonel McGavock. McGavock Pike was named after the McGavocks, you know. He's in Section 1, with the rest of his family. Let me show you on the map."

Alita gripped the pamphlet firmly in her hands, not allowing her to turn it over. "Look, I'm not here about the Civil War. I'm here to find out where my sister died."

June's rosy cheeks reddened a shade brighter. "Oh my. I thought you were the lady who called earlier. She said she was on her way over to do research about the Confederate heroes buried in our cemetery. My mistake, I get carried away by the history of this place. Tell me your sister's name. I'll check the records to see where she is located."

"No, you still don't understand. My sister was Victoria LaRue. She was murdered here two weeks ago."

June's mouth fell open. "Oh, that was such an embarrassment for us, you know. We're not used to things like that happening around here."

"Excuse me? My sister's murder was nothing more than an embarrassment to you?"

June lowered her head and her chin disappeared in the roll of slack flesh beneath her jaw. "You're right," she said. "I am so sorry about your sister. Please forgive me."

"Look, can you just show me where she died? Then you can be done with me."

"Of course. Of course I can do that. It's a ways back in the cemetery but let me take you there."

June retrieved her keys and asked another staff member to cover the front desk. She led Alita outside to her car, and babbled on about the cemetery until they came upon the Confederate Circle. She stopped talking until it was behind them. At the next intersection they turned to the right.

"It's just ahead, over there." June eased the car to a stop at the side of the gravel road. "Is this close enough, or—"

"I'd like to see exactly where it happened."

They got out of the car and walked between the rows of gravestones. She watched as June stopped to replace a bunch of petunias in a planter that had fallen over.

"Were you and your sister close?" June asked.

"Yes."

"I got four brothers and three sisters but we all fight like cats and dogs." With each step June's breath became more labored and audible.

They stopped in front of a gravestone and a low mound of dirt.

"This is it," June said. "This is where it happened."

Alita looked at the brown soil and the gray marble marker, the surrounding gravestones, and trees. The flowers and grass.

The gravestone wasn't Victoria's. She wasn't lying beneath the dirt at Alita's feet. There was nothing to suggest that Victoria had ever been there, nothing to suggest that her killer had ever been there. No blackened patches of grass, no signs of a struggle. No blood. Just someone else's grave. Again, thoughts swirled in Alita's head, crashing into images and feelings of long ago.

"June, were you here the day they found her?"

"I wasn't working that day, but I came to the cemetery as soon as I heard about it. A coworker called me. But the police wouldn't let anyone get close. We weren't allowed all the way back here until several days later."

"What did it look like when they finally let you come here?"

"Same as it does now. Why?"

"But the fire …"

"Fire?" June looked puzzled. "What do you mean?"

Alita paused, baffled by what she saw, by what June had said.

"Do you know how my sister was killed?" she asked.

June shook her head. "They didn't tell us that. They just said a woman had been murdered in the back of the cemetery."

"I was told that a jogger named Luke O'Connor found my sister's body."

"Luke O'Connor?" June put a hand on her chest. "Oh, my."

"You know him?"

"Not personally, but I know he's a big wig in the music industry. My son talks about him all the time. Wow, Luke O'Connor was the one who found her. Mercy."

"Do you know how I could get in touch with him?"

"Sure. He has an office over on Music Row. I don't know the address but I can tell you right where it is. I'll write down the directions. My son wants to be a country music singer and I was with him once when he was driving up and down the Row. He pointed out Mr. O'Connor's office and I told him he should—"

"Directions would be great. I'll pick them up before I leave, but I want to spend a little time here by myself. I can walk back to the office."

Alita looked down again at the patch of ground, more confused than ever.

12

The directions that June Wickliff gave Alita were easy to follow, but traffic on I-40 West was heavy, testing her patience. On 17th Avenue South she had no trouble finding the two-story brick building with a covered front porch that June described. She circled the block and parked in back next to a Ram pickup with a Texas tag. A sidewalk led to the front of the building.

There were bars over the windows in the lower level and all the blinds were drawn. She didn't see a doorbell so she turned the door-knob. Unlocked. She opened the door and took a tentative step inside.

She stood in the foyer, not sure what to do. She could hear the click of computer keys coming from down the hallway. The sound didn't stop when she shut the door audibly behind her.

Before her was a polished hardwood staircase with a finely crafted oak banister. Plush carpeting ran from the base of the staircase throughout the interior. She could see the doorways of three rooms down the hallway on the right, with light from the middle room casting a parallelogram on the carpet. At the far end was a closed door.

"Hello? Anyone here?" No response. Alita headed toward the room with the light.

When she reached the middle doorway she saw a young Asian woman sitting at a computer. The woman took off her AirPods.

"I'm sorry, I didn't hear you come in," she said to Alita. "May I help you?"

"I'm not even sure I have the right place. Is this Luke O'Connor's office?"

"Yes, but we're not accepting any material right now. I'm sorry."

"I'm not in the music business. I need to talk with him about a personal matter."

"Oh. Is he expecting you?"

"No. He doesn't even know who I am. But it's extremely important. Please."

Luke O'Connor's receptionist was trained to be efficient at screening the many singers and songwriters who walked through the door, but the look on her face said this situation was different.

"I can check and see for you. What is your name?"

"Alita King."

"And this is about?"

"I'd rather tell Mr. O'Connor myself."

The young woman picked up the desk phone and punched a button. She spoke in Japanese. About thirty seconds passed before she paused and looked up.

"Mr. O'Connor is busy right now. He needs to know why you wish to see him."

"Tell him it's about the woman in the cemetery. He'll know what I mean."

The receptionist again spoke in Japanese as she twisted the phone cord around her index finger.

She cupped her hand over the receiver. "Mr. O'Connor does not wish to talk with the media. He will not be making any statements."

"I'm not the media. Tell Mr. O'Connor that I—"

Alita grabbed the phone from the startled receptionist. "Mr. O'Connor, the woman whose body you found in the cemetery was my sister. I need to talk with you. Please."

A pause. "Okay. I'll be out in a minute."

Alita handed the phone back to the young woman who looked wide-eyed at her. "I'm sorry, but I just have to talk with him."

The door at the end of the hallway opened and a man walked toward her. The man who found Victoria.

"I'm Luke O'Connor," he said.

Alita detected wariness in his voice. She expected someone dressed in cowboy boots and faded jeans, but O'Connor wore casual slacks, a pullover shirt, and tennis shoes. He was an inch or two over six feet and on the thin side. He had short blond hair, a chiseled jaw-line, and a stubble beard.

"My name is Alita King. May I ask you some questions?"

"You're truly not a reporter or any type of media person?"

"She was my sister, like I said. I'm just here to get more information. But first, I want to thank you ... for finding her."

"I'm not sure I have any answers for you, but I'll try. Let's go on back to my office." O'Connor turned to his receptionist. "Marika, don't worry, you did just fine."

The young woman offered an embarrassed smile that she covered with her hand.

He led Alita to the end of the hallway. In addition to a massive desk, the office was comfortably furnished with high-backed chairs, an overstuffed couch, a heavy glass coffee table resting on a chunk of granite, teakwood paneling, and a small wet bar. Four acoustic guitars on stands were clustered in one corner, and gold records, plaques, and autographed pictures covered the walls.

O'Connor sat behind his desk and gestured at one of the high-backed chairs. "Please, sit down. I am truly sorry about your sister. What was her name? They didn't tell me."

"Victoria LaRue."

"Victoria. I'm glad to finally know her name. When Marika told me you wanted to see me, I thought you were a reporter who somehow learned I was the one who found her."

"That's not common knowledge?" Alita regretted telling June

Wickliff at the cemetery.

"No. I haven't talked about it with anyone. How did you find out?"

"Detective Blate. He's handling the case. I told him I wanted to thank the person who found Victoria. And I hope you'll tell me what you saw that morning."

"What have the police told you so far?" The wariness that had left his voice returned.

"Hardly anything, that's why I'm here. My sister was an adult escort, she battled drug addiction for years … she had a rough life. She was in the cemetery late at night, so Detective Blate thinks she met someone there for a drug deal. Something went wrong, she was murdered, and they set a fire to destroy any evidence. That's all he said. So please, tell me what you saw when you found her."

"You're her sister, you have a right to know. I'm just not sure how much of it you really want to hear."

"Mr. O'Connor—"

"Luke. Please call me Luke."

"I saw her body at the funeral home, Luke. Nothing you tell me could be any worse than that."

"Then you know."

Alita nodded.

"Okay." Luke sat forward in his chair. "I'm a runner, and I go through the cemetery on my Sunday morning long runs. It's a big place, but by chance I happened to take a path that led me right by your sister. When I found her she was lying on top of a grave. On her back, on a kind of blanket or bedspread. It had burned, almost completely gone, so it was hard to tell what it was." Luke paused. "You saw her, so I don't need to describe what the fire did to her."

"No."

"Do you know about the roses?" he asked.

"What roses?"

"Victoria … she had four or five red roses in each of her hands. Long-stemmed roses, and they had to have been placed in her hands after the fire was out because they weren't even singed."

"That's … that's bizarre."

"The grass around the grave was burned, too. And something else. There was a white cross. Upside-down, between her legs."

Alita was angry that Detective Blate had not told her any of this.

"Why would someone do that?" Her question was more for herself than Luke.

"I don't know. When I called 911 they told me to stay there if I wasn't in any danger. The first squad car arrived in less than five minutes and then more officers kept coming. They needed me to give a statement, but for a few minutes they forgot about me as they secured the scene. You know, taping it off. I could hear them talking. They said the body was posed—because of the cross and the roses—which suggested a serial killer to them."

"Serial killer? Oh, my god."

"I shouldn't have told you."

"I asked, I needed to hear it." She dabbed her eyes with the tissue he handed her. It took a few seconds to compose herself. "Have you been back to the cemetery?"

"No. I haven't been able to make myself run since that day."

"I just came from there. A woman in the office took me to the spot where you found Victoria. I'm not sure what I expected, but it just looked … normal. No signs that anything had happened there. And the woman didn't even know about the fire."

"That's strange. The burned patches of grass wouldn't have grown back already. And I remember the marker on the grave was streaked black with soot. You couldn't have missed that."

"Maybe she took me to the wrong spot." A tear trickled down her cheek.

"If you have time, we can go there now. I just need to tell Marika."

On the short drive to the cemetery Alita tried to assemble a puzzle in her mind but no two pieces fit together. An unsettling thought crept in when she remembered Detective Blate's words when he told her that Luke O'Connor was the man who found Victoria's body: *"there's no way he was involved in your sister's death."* But what if Blate was wrong, and she was not only riding in a car with the man who killed Victoria, but they were driving back to the scene of the crime?

The thought was absurd and she dismissed it.

Alita heard the tick of the turn signal as they came to the entrance to the cemetery. She was about to direct him before she remembered he knew exactly where he was going.

"This is the route I took that morning. I run here every Sunday, and it seemed like just another day until …"

She gazed at the grave markers that surrounded them.

"Did you see anyone else here?" she asked.

"No. I rarely do because I run so early to avoid the heat."

"I forgot to ask the police or the medical examiner what her time of death was," Alita said. "I know what time she was dropped off by the Lyft driver and what time you found her, but I don't know when she died. That's about a seven-hour window."

"Maybe you could get the death certificate."

"Right." Alita added one more mental note to the list.

Luke made two more turns and parked on the grass.

"It's over there," he said.

Alita nodded. "That's where the woman from the office took me."

They walked up to a recent grave topped by mounded dirt.

"The grass along this side of the grave was burned, but they've replaced it." Luke bent down and brushed his hand through blades of grass. "That's odd. This hasn't been here long, but it's not new sod. See that line?"

He pointed to an irregular seam separating patches of grass.

Alita frowned. "I don't understand."

"Putting down new sod would have been the easiest thing to do. It's like they took grass from somewhere else and tried to match it, like it's always been here. That's a ton of extra work, but why?" Luke put a hand on the gravestone. "And this was black from the fire when I saw it, but it's already been sandblasted or scrubbed off."

Alita read the engraved names. "Merle and Helen Tanner." She shook her head and tried to process everything. "They were born the same year. The husband died eight years ago, and his wife must have passed recently because they haven't added that date yet." Alita turned to Luke. "Do you think there was a reason he chose this spot to … to do it? Maybe the killer was connected to this couple."

"We could search the web, see what we can find out about them."

"I'm going to take a few photos." Alita pulled out her iPhone to get close-ups of the names and dates, and capture the scene from different angles.

"You heard the officers mention the possibility of a serial killer because of the way Victoria was posed," she said. "There was virtually nothing about the murder in the news. And Detective Blate was so evasive with me. Maybe they don't want people to know there could be a serial killer in Nashville who just burned a woman to death."

"You might be on to something." Beads of sweat dotted Luke's forehead. "A serial killing would have been all over local TV and in the paper. And being Nashville, it'd be national news. Tourists are the lifeblood of this town and a serial killer would be bad for business. But if they made it seem like just another drug deal gone wrong, no one would really notice or care."

"That could be it. Or it could be something totally different. I know there are answers out there, I just have to find them."

"I want to help if I can, Alita. I mean that."

She stopped taking photos. "You've already helped so much, Luke. Just by not judging my sister."

13

A lita called Metro Police but Detective Blate was not available. She left a message for a call-back she doubted she'd receive. Blate knew what happened to the crime scene after it was processed, but would he tell her?

Traffic was busy on I-40 and only a bit lighter when she merged onto I-24. Alita didn't know what reception she'd get at her next stop, but her experiences thus far in Nashville prepared her for almost anything.

She took the Harding Place exit and saw the street sign for Linbar Drive.

Alita remembered the phone conversation from four months earlier, when Victoria was excited about her new apartment. She moved in during one of the many brief periods when she tried to stay clean. There was pride in Victoria's voice when she talked about not using for six weeks. She told Alita she wanted to quit the escort business for good and find work as a receptionist or sales clerk. She even mentioned going back to school.

Alita sent her a volume of inspirational poetry as a housewarming present, along with a crystal glass sculpture of a butterfly in flight, a piece she found at Dian's Galleria de Arte just across the street from her own shop. Victoria begged her to come to Nashville to see the apartment and spend some sisterly time together. Alita promised to visit right after the Labor Day weekend, when business slowed a bit. Another log on her pile of regrets.

She turned off Linbar Drive and parked in front of the Hunting

Creek Apartments office. Inside, she saw an attractive woman sitting behind a desk. She wore a colorful geo print top and styled her hair in locs.

"Hi, may I help you?" The greeting was friendly.

"My name is Alita King. My sister, Victoria LaRue, rented an apartment here and—"

"Oh, Alita. I'm so sorry about Victoria." The woman rushed around the desk to give her a hug. "She had her problems, but she was such a sweet soul." She patted the top of the chair in front of her desk. "Please, sit down. I'm Jamila Crockett, the manager here."

"Jamila. What a lovely name."

"Thank you. It's Swahili, says my mother. She named me after her grandmother. Alita … your name is lovely, too. And not very common."

"I have no clue how my mother came up with it." Alita sat down. "Jamila, I would like to see my sister's apartment if that's not a problem."

"Of course it's not."

"Do you need my ID or anything?"

"Girl, all you had to do was say your name and I knew who you were. Victoria bragged about her little sister Alita all the time."

Alita felt the tension leave her body, relieved she had one less battle to fight.

"I flew up from Florida so I can't clear out her apartment this trip, but I can come back soon to take care of it, if that's okay. I just wanted to see it today."

"Sure. She paid August rent, and when a tenant moves in we ask for the last month's rent in advance, so you have until the end of September to come back and get her things. Let me grab a key and I'll walk down there with you."

Alita surveyed the older cars and pickup trucks in the parking lot, several with dented doors or fenders and paint that didn't match the rest of the body. One car missing tires rested on cement blocks.

"We have mostly low-income tenants here," Jamila said. "Many are on government assistance of one type or another. Just collecting rent is a full-time job for me. But not with Victoria. She didn't get any government help, and she paid on time."

"She was homeless for a while a few years ago," Alita said. "She told me she would never let that happen again."

They followed the sidewalk to the second building on the left, then up two short flights of interior stairs. Jamila opened the fire door and stopped at the first apartment on the right, B202. She put a key in the lock and jiggled it several times before the knob turned.

"There we go." Jamila gave the door a slight push. It creaked open on worn hinges and a warm, musty smell hit them. "Whew. I better turn on the air conditioning. I'm not sure why it's off." She went inside and disappeared around a corner.

Alita stood in the doorway and peered into the small apartment. On her left was a tiny eating space. A dinette table with a laminated wood grain top and a missing leg had only a single chair pushed under it. The chair had suffered a jagged rip in its vinyl seat that exposed a foam cushion. A few feet beyond she could see the back of an ancient easy chair, its brown fabric soiled and worn. The right armrest was broken and hung off the side. In the compact living room was a green and blue couch in worse shape than either of the chairs.

Alita took a couple of steps into the apartment. When Victoria first moved in she bought new furniture and proudly sent pictures of it to Alita. What happened to the lovely southwestern-style couch? The overstuffed recliner the color of desert sand? The glass-topped dining table with the cute white wrought iron and yellow canvas chairs? *Drugs.* When Victoria could no longer stay clean, she sold everything to buy more drugs.

Alita heard Jamila say something about dirty-looking water, followed by the sound of a toilet flushing and a faucet running. She walked into the living room.

Against the wall was a wooden console table with gnarled legs, but it was not the table that drew Alita's attention. It was the items on it that caught her eye.

A Voice of Hope, the book of inspirational poetry she sent to Victoria, sat on top of the table next to her other gift, the glass butterfly in flight. The book's value was only sentimental, but she could have sold the butterfly sculpture. Knowing that Victoria kept those two gifts left Alita feeling sad and empty.

For the first time she noticed the photo on the wall above the console table. She last saw it a few years earlier when she stayed with Victoria in a different apartment after her sister's appendectomy. She was amazed at how youthful the face in the photo seemed to grow with the passage of time. Her father had always looked old, but most adults seem old to a young girl of eight. Now, as Alita studied the photo, her father didn't look old at all.

"Someone you know?"

Alita was so lost in thought that she hadn't noticed Jamila standing next to her.

"From a long time ago." Alita picked up the glass butterfly and cradled it gently in her hands. "Did you ever see my sister's new furniture?"

"I did. Very nice. But … you know."

Just as I thought. "So where did this stuff come from?"

"It's sad. I remember the couch and chair by the dumpster. Somebody pitched them when they moved out. Victoria asked a couple of the guys who live here to carry them in for her. I imagine that's where the rest of this came from, too."

Alita shook her head. "I don't know what I'll do with all this. I don't think even Goodwill would want it."

"I'm sure they wouldn't. But don't worry about it. I can have it carried back down to the dumpster. And who knows, my renters might take some of it."

Jamila went to the sliding glass door and pulled back the curtain. She gave the door handle a tug. "Just checking to make sure it's locked. I should get back to the office, but feel free to stay as long as you like. Here's the key, just lock up and drop it off when you're finished."

"Thank you again, Jamila. You've been so kind."

Alita explored the rest of Victoria's apartment. It consisted of a single bedroom, a bathroom with a shower bath, and a small closet. The bedroom had several cardboard boxes stacked in a corner and a mattress on the floor, but no bed frame or box springs. A beat-up three-drawer dresser sat against the wall by the mattress. Both the mattress and the dresser looked like rescues from the trash dumpster.

She opened the drawers and found items that were out of place in a cheap, particle board dresser. She pulled out a snowy white teddy with black scalloped lace trim, a pale pink camisole and tap pant set, and an aqua chemise and robe, made of silk. She found lacy bra, bikini, and garter belt sets, and a champagne bustier with matching panty.

Alita sighed as she closed the dresser drawers. She knew the fine boudoir items were not luxuries that Victoria allowed herself. They were tools of her trade, paid for with her body and a piece of her soul.

She went to the kitchen and opened the fridge. She quickly closed it, not wanting to know the source of the smell that assaulted her. In a drawer she found personal letters she wrote to Victoria, bound by a rubber band. There were dozens of business cards and scraps of paper with names and phone numbers. She wondered if one of the names belonged to the man who killed Victoria. *Why did the police leave all of this behind? Did they even look at it?* More questions she needed to ask Detective Blate in the morning.

She decided to take the business cards and scraps of paper with her, along with her letters, the book of poetry, and the crystal glass butterfly. As for the rest of Victoria's possessions, Alita didn't have the time or energy to go through them before her flight home. She'd return to Nashville soon, and what didn't go to the dumpster could be packed and shipped to Florida.

She didn't know what she would do with her father's photo.

14

E d Potter stubbed out another cigarette and looked at his watch. Sam was already an hour late coming back from lunch. Covering the phone was not much of a chore as Potter didn't take any calls while his secretary was out of the office.

He was trimming his fingernails over the open pages of an old issue of *Publisher's Weekly* when the phone rang.

"Potter Literary Associates."

"Yes, I'd like to speak with Mr. Potter."

"I'll see if he's in. And your name is?"

"Winston Dawdy. I sent him sample chapters of my book. I just wanted to know what he thought."

"Mr. Dawdy! I'm glad you called. I'm Ed Potter. So, the W is short for Winston. Like the cigarette?"

"Churchill. Mr. Potter, have you read my chapters?"

"I have them on my desk right now, and yes, I've read them. Several times."

"And?"

"They're not bad. They could use a little work, of course." Potter couldn't think of anything that needed to be changed, but he always played all the angles.

"What do you mean, a little work?"

Potter noted the edge in Dawdy's voice. "Oh, nothing major at all. Light editing, just a few cosmetic things, nothing we need to talk about now." It had been a long time since Potter actually wanted a writer's work, not just his or her money, and he didn't want this one to get away. "You know, Mr. Dawdy, I might be interested in representing you. I've only seen part of your manuscript, of course, but your plot is intriguing so far. And you can certainly write."

"The plot is just beginning, Mr. Potter."

"Wait a minute, you mean all you have are the six chapters you sent? I thought you had a complete book. I can't sell six chapters."

"I'm well aware of that, Mr. Potter. No worries. The chapters I sent you are the most recent ones I've written. I sent them as a sample. My book is almost finished, and it is practically writing itself. I'm just getting a head start in my search for an agent who believes in me. An agent I know I can trust."

Potter took a drag off the fresh cigarette he had just lit. "Well, Mr. Dawdy, I want to be that agent. But I need you to send me everything you have so far, and the remaining chapters as soon as you finish them."

"You're rushing things, Mr. Potter. I haven't decided yet if it's you I want to represent me. That's why I gave you only six chapters. But I think you can tell from what I've already sent that I'm not like other writers who contact you."

"No, Mr. Dawdy, you're certainly not."

"Nor will my book be like anything you've ever read, which is why I'm not going to send more of it to you or any other agent until I am sure I've found the right match for my work."

"You've submitted chapters to another agent?"

"No. Just you."

"Well, I hope you keep it that way. This isn't how it usually works, I'm sure you know. Agents want to see the entire manuscript. But I have a good feeling about you, Winston—may I call you Winston?"

"Of course."

"By the way, is Winston Dawdy your real name or a pseudonym?"

"It's my name, Mr. Potter."

"Well, it definitely sounds like an author's name. It would look good on the cover of a book, the book I want to represent." Potter picked up a pen. "Winston, give me your phone number so I'll have it if I need to get in touch."

"I prefer to call you, Mr. Potter. I travel a lot, and when I'm writing or doing research I cannot have any interruptions or distractions."

"Okay, fine, but at least give me your e-mail address so I can—"

"Goodbye, Mr. Potter."

***

Winston Dawdy turned off his burner phone and opened his laptop. Potter jumped through the hoop, just like Dawdy knew he would. Hacking Potter's office computers to install keyloggers and other remote access spyware had been just as easy. Now that Potter had his full name, Dawdy knew what would happen next.

He entered a series of keystrokes and a window opened that displayed Ed Potter's computer desktop. Less than a minute after their conversation was over he watched Potter do a web search on "Winston Dawdy."

Potter would not find what he was seeking. Dawdy did not lie to Potter when he said his name was Winston Dawdy, because that was his name. For now. But he had other names in the past, just as he would have other names in the future, and no amount of searching the web would reveal anything about any of them.

15

Alita's anger rose. "You can't give me a precise time of death because she was burned so badly. You say there's no connection to the Tanners' gravesite where she was found. You don't have any suspects, you don't have a clue why she was murdered. Look, I have a flight back to Florida in a few hours, but I don't care if I miss it." She stared into Detective Blate's eyes. "I'll sit here all day if I have to, until you finally give me straight answers."

"Miss King, I don't know how to say it any other way. All we're doing at this point is speculating. Maybe it could have been one of her johns with a weird fetish, but if you want my honest opinion, I think your sister was killed over drugs. Again, that is pure speculation. We have nothing, believe me."

Blate's left eye twitched.

"I was in Victoria's apartment yesterday," Alita said. She took out a sealed Ziploc storage bag from her purse. "I found these business cards and slips of paper, with names and phone numbers. I'm sure these are men who have used her services. One of them could be her killer, so isn't all of this evidence? Why did you just leave it in a drawer? Why aren't you investigating them if there's a possibility it could have been a customer? It's because you don't give a damn about Victoria, do you?"

"Come on, you know I do. And what you found there is not really evidence, but we did log all of that and—"

"You're lying."

Blate sighed. He opened a folder on his desk and leafed through its contents. He took out a dozen or more paper-clipped pages and pushed them toward Alita. She looked through them and saw multiple business cards and notes arranged and photocopied on each page, front and back.

"Okay, so you've done that," she said. "But are you checking these guys out?"

"Miss King, you have to be honest with yourself and face the facts. You know your sister's profession, and she was in that line of work for a long, long time. She has come in contact with many men over the years. The vast majority of them wouldn't be stupid enough to give her their contact information. I have no idea why these guys would do that. Drunk, most likely. But we simply don't have the time or the resources to track all of them down, especially when there is nothing that points to a specific person. We copied what we found so we'd have it to cross-check if we get a lead on a suspect. That's the best we can do. But I think we'd be barking up the wrong tree if we went that route, and the same with drugs."

Alita was playing chess with the white pieces and caught the slip that Blate just admitted. "You really don't think it was a customer or a drug deal, do you?"

Alita saw redness creep up the detective's neck, and even the New Jersey birthmark on his forehead seemed to darken a bit. Alita enjoyed his discomfort.

"Look," he began, "we don't know what we're dealing with. It doesn't make sense that it was a john because a cemetery would be an odd place for that kind of encounter. Plus, as I told you when you were here on Wednesday, your sister's escort agency said she wasn't working that night. Same line of thinking applies to a drug buy. Why there? Your sister had a supplier, and if he wasn't available, drugs are easy to find in this town. You don't have to go to a cemetery late at night to get them."

Alita felt a tiny breakthrough.

"Then why did you tell me on Wednesday and again just a few minutes ago that you thought it was connected to drugs, when now you say it likely wasn't?"

"Your sister was an addict. You have to admit, a drug buy gone bad would be on the list. I wanted to at least give you a theory, something that would assure you that we are truly working on your sister's murder. Which we are. But there are things in any homicide investigation that can't be released to the public, even to the family. We can't put information out there that only the killer knows."

Alita knew it was time to play her trump card, to end whatever game Blate had been playing since the minute they met. "Like the roses and the upside-down cross between her legs?" she asked.

Blate closed his eyes for a few seconds and shook his head.

"Luke O'Connor. I knew that might come back to bite me in the ass when I told you his name. He shouldn't have said anything to you, but I doubt you gave him a choice." The slightest of smiles creased his lips. "I do admire your tenacity and what you're trying to do for your sister. I really do."

"You keep saying 'my sister' every single time, like she doesn't have a name. Her name is Victoria."

"Of course. Victoria. I'm sorry."

Alita wasn't going to stop until he admitted what she needed to hear. "If you really don't think it was a drug deal or one of her customers, what was it? Why would she go there? Why the roses and the cross?"

Blate shrugged. "That brings us full circle. We don't have anything to go on. We didn't find any footprints, fingerprints, DNA evidence. We just don't know."

Alita leaned forward in the chair and glared. "You're not going to consider the possibility that Victoria was the victim of a serial killer?"

If Blate was taking her measure, the look on his face showed he didn't like the results.

"Okay. What was done to your sister—I mean, Victoria—was cruel and deliberate. Her body was placed in an unnatural position. We call it posing a victim. That is a common trait of serial killers. The roses in her hand and the upside-down cross, that's bizarre stuff. We don't know what those things mean, but they meant something to her killer."

"What about the gravesite where she was found? Why were all traces of what happened completely erased? And if you don't tell me, my next stop is to go back to the cemetery and demand an answer from them."

Alita had Blate in a corner and he clearly knew it. He would either become defensive and send her on her way, or give her the information she wanted to keep her from seeking it elsewhere on her own. When his body relaxed in his chair she had her answer.

"Everything I've said and am about to say stays between us. If you talk about any of this to anyone and it gets out, it could seriously jeopardize our investigation and we may never find who killed Victoria. I know you don't want that."

"I understand."

"It was a joint decision between us and the cemetery. As I explained, in a homicide investigation we don't want details getting out to the public. The cemetery's management felt the same, but from a business standpoint. We kept the area off limits for a few days to process the scene and restore everything to how it was. Before the fire and all. They brought in an out-of-town company so even the cemetery's own staff wouldn't know what happened there."

Alita knew that Blate was still holding a few cards back, but at least he was giving her something.

"Thank you for finally being honest with me. And you know …

even your own officers said it looked like a serial killing to them."

Blate groaned. "Luke O'Connor again. He and I need to have a little talk."

"Don't blame Luke. You should have told me all this from the beginning."

Blate lightly drummed his fingers on his desk.

"Miss King, there are varying definitions out there, but the FBI defines serial murder as the unlawful killing of two or more victims by the same offender, in separate events at different times. We don't know who killed Victoria, so we don't know if she was the killer's first victim, tenth victim, whatever. We did a search on ViCAP—that's an FBI database—to see if there were other homicides that matched any of what we found in the cemetery. We didn't get any hits. Had we found similar cases, that definitely could have suggested a serial killer. So we can't label this a serial killing based on what we have at this point, which is one victim."

"But your gut feeling, Detective. Unofficial, off the record. Please."

Blate's fingers stopped drumming and his jaw tightened. "I think we're dealing with someone who has killed before and will kill again. Someone who's so cunning he could persuade a street-smart woman to go to a cemetery alone at midnight. Someone who doesn't make mistakes. And someone we'll be damn lucky to catch."

-16-

A lita had a window seat on her flight to Daytona Beach. She gazed at the layers of marshmallow clouds far below and looked back on the three days since she landed in Nashville on Tuesday.

If she hadn't met Luke O'Connor she might never have learned the details about Victoria's murder that Detective Blate tried to keep from her. Luke was sympathetic and kind. Although he was one of the top record producers in country music, he took time to drive her back to the cemetery to the spot where he found Victoria. His business card was a reminder of his offer to help in the future.

Jamila Crockett, the manager of Hunting Creek Apartments, said there was no rush to clean out Victoria's apartment. Most of her furniture came from the trash dumpster in the parking lot and would be returned there. Alita wished she could load everything on a truck and deliver it to Marjo's house, to be stacked on her front lawn so her mother could see for herself how much of a struggle life had been for the daughter she abandoned.

Her thoughts turned to Detective Blate and his words that had seared her mind … *someone we'll be damn lucky to catch.* She remembered a true crime show on TV that said nearly forty percent of all homicides go unsolved. The fact that almost three weeks had passed since Victoria's murder, without any suspects, witnesses, or leads, gave her little reason to hope that an arrest would be coming soon. In her anger she had crossed a line with Blate, and she needed to take a step back and let him do his job. But how much time should she give him? And if she didn't keep the pressure on him, who would?

Alita closed her eyes and leaned her head against the coolness of the window. The drone of the jet engines and the gentle vibrations of a cylindrical tube cutting through smooth air soon lulled her into much needed slumber.

On final approach to Daytona Beach International Airport Alita found she could no longer keep a certain thought from her mind. Deep within the belly of the plane was cargo much different from the luggage around it. She knew Victoria's journey home was almost complete.

Meg was waiting in the terminal just beyond the security gate. They rushed together in a warm hug.

"You poor thing, you must be exhausted," Meg said. "Let me carry your bag."

"I got it, it's not heavy. But … do we need to make sure that—"

"It's all taken care of. There's no way we'd be allowed to be there anyway. I asked Phil to let me know he was here and he texted me an hour ago. He'll take her right to the funeral home, and he'll send another text once he's there."

On the thirty-minute drive from the airport to Alita's house in New Smyrna Beach she told Meg almost everything that she had seen, heard, and done while in Nashville. Almost everything.

Alita pulled into her driveway and parked.

"You have been through so much," Meg said. "Take all next week off, too. Whatever you need."

"What I need is a glass of wine, and I don't want to drink alone. Are you in a hurry?"

"Aren't you tired?"

"I think I'll be tired the rest of my life. Come on in."

Alita poured two glasses of red wine and they sat side by side in wicker rockers on the screened lanai. She kicked off her shoes and stretched. "It feels good to be home."

"I'll bet. But there's something else we need to talk about, isn't there?"

"You know me better than anyone, don't you?" Alita took a full swallow of wine. She set the glass back on the table and rotated the stem several times. "You set up my meeting with Phil Krynak tomorrow morning at the funeral home."

"Right, and I'll go with you. I should have already thought to have offered."

"No, Meg, that's not it. I can go by myself."

"Then what is it?"

"It's … it's Victoria. You know that I went to see her at the funeral home, but I didn't tell you what I saw there."

"I can't imagine."

"It was horrible." Alita closed her eyes for several seconds to block the image that formed in her head. "But I need to make a choice when I talk with Phil."

"About?"

"Even though I'm all Victoria had, we never really talked about, you know, what to do if something happened."

"You mean, like a will?"

"I don't think she even had one. She had nothing to leave to anyone, anyway. I'm talking about what to do with her … body."

"Oh. Whether to bury her or cremate her?"

Alita nodded. "Yeah."

They sat in silence, each taking sips of wine. Meg, who had given sage advice to Alita many times before, was coming up empty this time. She broke the silence with a gently spoken question, "What are you thinking you want to do?"

"I don't know. You should have seen what was left of her, Meg. It was like she was half-cremated already. If I tell Phil I want to go with cremation, it's like I'm finishing the job her killer started. But I can't bring myself to have her buried the way she is, either. I don't think she would have wanted that."

"Hon, what happened to Victoria in Nashville and whatever you decide to do here are two different things. What you're doing is out of love, no matter what you choose. Just remember that."

"I will, Meg," Alita said, still no closer to a decision. "I will."

A lita opened the front door and stepped inside the Wilkins-Mader Funeral Home, a three-tone chime marking her arrival. Phil Krynak, a short, bearded, middle-aged man in a black suit and white shirt, came down the hallway, an iPad tucked under one arm.

"Hi, Phil," she said.

"Good morning, Alita." He gave her a light hug with his free arm. "I'm so sorry about Victoria."

"Thank you. She was a wonderful sister, I wish you could have met her. And thanks so much for all you did last night."

"It was my honor and privilege. Please, come on back."

Alita followed him to a large room with dark brown walls, two couches, four leather chairs, heavy window coverings, and electric candles that framed the solemn setting.

"Can I get you coffee or a bottle of water?"

"No, I'm good. I just want to get this over."

"Of course. I understand." They sat in chairs that faced each other. "I can give you any number of options, and work with whatever budget you have."

"It's not about the money, Phil. I don't care about that at all. And I think Meg told you I want to go with just the graveside service. She and I will be the only ones there, so there's no need to have calling hours, either."

"But Alita, if I may, visitation is as much for you as it is for Victoria. You have a lot of friends in town who I'm sure would want to pay their respects. And you haven't mentioned your mother. I haven't seen Marjo around town recently."

Alita took solace in knowing her issues with her mother had stayed mostly within the family. Unless Marjo told someone, which was unlikely, Meg was the only person in New Smyrna Beach who knew of the deep bitterness between mother and daughter.

"No visitation. I just want the graveside service."

"That's fine. No problem." His many years in the funeral business had clearly taught Phil that some questions should go unanswered. "Are you still looking at this coming Thursday?"

"If that works for you."

"I already had it down." He tapped his iPad screen and swiped his finger across it several times. "Let's see, there it is, Victoria LaRue. Time TBA."

"Maybe ten o'clock?"

"Ten it is." Phil typed an entry on his iPad. "Would you like to take a look at caskets now?"

"I'm not sure. Do I need a casket if Victoria is going to be cremated?"

"No. A casket is not required for a cremation in Florida, but that might change the timetable. To have her cremains back in time for a service on Thursday the process would have to be expedited. I would need to call first thing Monday to see if they could even do it in time. But before I do that, are you sure that's what you want to do? We can talk about options."

Alita fought to control the now familiar sadness that again washed over her. "Have you seen Victoria's body?"

"Yes," Phil said softly.

"I decided to have her cremated. I've thought about scattering her ashes, but it would also be nice to get a spot in the cemetery where I could visit her. Buy her a nice granite stone, plant flowers."

"You could do both, you know. You could scatter part of her cre-mains in a place that would be meaningful to her memory, and get an urn to bury the remainder in the cemetery. That way you could still get her a monument and visit whenever you wanted."

Alita thought about the options.

"Yes," she said. "I like that idea. That's exactly what I want to do."

"But I think you're putting too much pressure on yourself. We can take care of Victoria in the normal time frame, which would give you a few more days to find a nice place in a cemetery for her. Then you can have the graveside service, and scatter her cremains later whenever you're ready."

"No, I want to get this behind me and get back to work." Phil probably thought she meant the Sunriz Boutique, but her main focus now was to stay on top of the investigation into Victoria's murder. "I'll get a plot on Monday, in Edgewater-New Smyrna Cemetery. If you can expedite the cremation, I want to go with a graveside service on Thursday and bury some of her ashes like you suggested. I'll scatter the rest later."

"I will do my best to make it happen, Alita. For you, and for Vic-toria."

***

"You're not supposed to be here," Meg said. "How was your weekend?"

Alita arched an eyebrow and tilted her head toward two women who were looking at beach towels near the front of the shop.

"They're just browsing," Meg whispered.

Alita moved closer so the women wouldn't overhear, but they waved a "thank you" and headed out the door.

"Phil's been wonderful," Alita said. "After I met with him on

Saturday, he called the cemetery's general manager and asked her to meet me there this morning. I bought a nice plot that gets shade from a live oak. Then I got a text from Phil about an hour ago. He made sure the cremation will be done on time. The service is all set for Thursday at ten."

"Did you go with Edgewater?" Meg asked.

"Yeah. It's close enough, and I think it's the prettiest."

"Can I help with anything?"

"It's just going to be you and me. And Phil, of course. I asked him if he'd say a few words. Victoria wouldn't have wanted a preacher."

Alita stayed at the shop long enough for Meg to run a few errands. She came back with vegetarian fajitas from Mi Mexico. An early afternoon downpour gave them a break from customers and a chance to eat their lunch.

"I'll be going back and forth to Nashville," Alita said between bites, "and I don't want to feel guilty about leaving you alone. Maybe we should think about hiring some help."

"You go whenever you need to," Meg said. "I'll be fine."

"But—"

"No buts!"

Alita knew it was hopeless to press the point. Meg was a workaholic who loved every minute she spent in the shop.

"Okay," Alita said. "As long as you let me make it up to you."

"You get out of here. I'll see you on Thursday."

-18-

In the time it took for Alita to silence the alarm that rustled her from sleep, she felt the soul-crushing awareness of what would soon take place in a cemetery just a few miles away.

She ran a toothbrush across her teeth several times before slipping into a T-shirt and shorts. She dressed without turning on a light, taking refuge in the darkness. Even the muted glow of an LED bulb would bring reality a little closer. A reality she wanted to put off for as long as possible.

She could have asked a friend to walk with her on the beach, but today she needed to leave a solitary set of footprints in the sand.

The sun was hidden in pink-hued clouds before it edged above them. Alita stopped to let its rays wash over her. This stretch of beach was hers alone now, as were the gulls, the pelicans, the sandpipers, and the scurrying sand crabs near her feet.

She walked down the beach until she came to The Breakers, a popular bar/restaurant at the end of Flagler Avenue with a panoramic view of the ocean. The large pink building was quiet and empty at that hour, but before the day was through it would be packed with a mix of locals and vacationers, all seeking and usually finding a good time. One summer not many years before, Victoria had talked about moving to New Smyrna Beach and staying with Alita until she could find a place of her own. A friend of Alita's who managed The Breakers even promised Victoria a job, but drugs once again dragged her down and she never made the move. Alita turned around and headed toward home. If only Victoria had moved to New Smyrna Beach to live with her, had taken the job at The Breakers, and had overcome her addiction. Her life would have been so different.

After a walk on the beach Alita liked to enjoy coffee on her lanai, but she held no desire for a cup this morning. She could not go about her normal routine on a day that would be anything but normal.

She showered and put on clothes for a second time, a peach-colored dress with a matching belt and white sandals. Victoria would not have wanted her to wear black.

A few minutes in front of the mirror and her hair still looked flat and lifeless. She set her brush on the counter. She could have fussed with it all day and it still wouldn't be right.

Meg called a second time to offer her a ride to the cemetery, but Alita again turned her down. She wanted to drive there by herself. Maybe later, after the service, she would drop the top on her Miata and head up A1A, to St. Augustine or beyond. Just the wind in her face, the sun on her shoulders, and the ocean to her right. For as far as she could see.

Phil Krynak would bring Victoria's cremains to the cemetery, a portion in a stainless-steel silver urn for burial and the remainder in a temporary plastic container for Alita to take with her. She had ordered a custom ceramic urn topped with a beautiful multicolored butterfly that she found online. It was handmade by a pottery artist in California and could take up to eight weeks for delivery. She had elected a third option. Some of Victoria's ashes would be buried. Some would later be scattered. The rest, she would always keep with her in the butterfly urn.

A check of her watch, a bit of panic. The service was at ten o'clock and she couldn't be late. She took a last look in the mirror, grabbed her purse, and headed out the door.

Alita was stopped at a light when her cell phone rang again. The caller's ID was blocked so she didn't answer. No message was left.

She turned into Edgewater-New Smyrna Beach Cemetery and was dismayed to see that a large funeral was about to take place. Several dozen cars were parked along the interior drives, and people were standing in small groups. *How inconsiderate*, she thought. Why would they hold two services at the same time in nearly the same area of the cemetery, even if only she, Meg, and Phil Krynak would be there for Victoria?

She pulled to the side of the entry drive just inside the cemetery and turned off the engine. She sat there, thinking of what she should do, when a woman broke from one of the groups and walked briskly in her direction. *Meg.*

Alita climbed out of her car, even more confused now.

"What's going on, Meg? Whose funeral is that?"

"Everything's okay. Just come with me." Meg took Alita's hand and they walked along the gravel drive toward the area where the people were gathered.

Alita saw faces looking at her, faces she could now see clearly. She went to them, hugging first one and then the next. None of them had known Victoria, and although they were there for Alita, they were there for her sister, too. She greeted friends and neighbors, and regular customers of the Sunriz Boutique. There were other shop owners from town. The mechanic who took care of her Miata, and her favorite bartender from the Treehouse Bar at Norwood's. Several of her former teachers from New Smyrna Beach High School were there. She gave a long hug to her old diving coach, Tony Stemble. The day she struck her head on the board, he was the one who pulled her out of the water, gave her first aid, and notified Marjo.

All of this was Meg's doing, and Alita could not have felt a deeper love for her friend and business partner.

She turned to Meg, who was still at her side. "How did you—"

"I just made a couple of phone calls and it took off from there. You have lots of people who care about you."

Alita saw Phil Krynak and was about to wave at him when her hand stopped in mid-air. Behind Phil, a man in a dark suit and sunglasses was making his way toward her. She felt her jaw go slack. *It can't be ...*

It was Luke O'Connor.

He came up to her and reached to take her hands, but she embraced him first.

"I can't believe you came all the way from Nashville," she said. "When did Meg get in touch with you?"

"Meg?" Luke looked puzzled.

"Yes, didn't she call you?"

"No."

"How did you know?"

"When I couldn't find an obituary online, I decided to call funeral homes down here. Phil Krynak gave me the details. I was going to let you know I was coming, but I knew you'd be busy. I hope you don't mind that I'm here."

"Mind? I'm glad that you came."

"Alita, it's time." Phil was beside her, and Alita's surprise at seeing Luke O'Connor faded as the moment was at hand.

Phil led them to the small opening in the ground, and the stainless-steel urn that rested on a pedestal draped in velvet. Alita was flanked by Meg and Luke, with her friends and neighbors around them.

Several hundred feet away, a white Lexus headed south on Ridgewood Avenue. It neared the entrance to Edgewater-New Smyrna Beach Cemetery. The right turn signal came on, then the brake lights, but instead of turning the car sped up and continued southbound.

Several minutes later the same Lexus passed the cemetery again, going north this time. There were two southbound lanes of highway and a median strip between the car and the cemetery, and like before, the car slowed, the driver seemingly drawn by activity that was taking place within the cemetery.

From the highway it was possible to see a group of people standing close together in the cemetery. Those same people, had they looked, could have seen a white Lexus passing by on Ridgewood Avenue. But no one would ever know what words might have been spoken between the driver of the car and one of the mourners, if the emotional distance that separated them had not been so great.

Meg put her arm on Alita's shoulder. "Are you sure you don't want to take one more day off?" she asked.

"I will see you in the morning," Alita said. "Now go get some sleep. It's been a long day." She gave Meg a hug. "Love you."

"Love you, too." Meg turned to Luke. "Thanks again for dinner, Luke, and I hope you'll come back to see us."

"I would like that. Good night, Meg."

The front door closed and Luke smiled at Alita. "She's like a mama bear to you, isn't she?"

"Yeah, she's more of a mother to me than my own mother was."

"Oh, I'm sorry."

Alita remembered she had never mentioned Marjo to Luke.

"She's not dead. She lives here in town. It's just … a long story."

Maybe it was because she was still reeling from burying her sister's ashes that morning. Maybe she was simply exhausted from everything that happened over the last nine days. Or maybe it was because she felt a growing bond with Luke O'Connor, the man who found Victoria's body, offered to help her find her sister's killer, and even flew down from Nashville to attend the funeral. Whatever it was, she felt a sudden need to share one of her family's most guarded secrets.

"You up for a glass of wine?" she asked. "Red?"

"Sure."

"Give me a sec. I'll be right back."

Alita went to the kitchen and returned with two glasses and a bottle of wine which Luke opened. They retired to her lanai and sat in the wicker rockers with a small table between them. The six-foot privacy fence on her property's back and side boundaries shielded them from her neighbors' view.

They sat without speaking until Alita was ready.

"I'm going to tell you something that now only three people on earth know about," she said. "Me, Meg, and my mother. It can't go beyond you. Please."

"Of course."

"Victoria was nine when I was born. When I was growing up, I worshipped her. She was my big sister, and she always looked out for me. Despite the age difference we were really close. But life wasn't easy for her because Marjo—that's my mother's name—gave me all of the attention. She had this crazy idea that I was going to be a famous model. She always made such a big deal out of dressing me up and showing me off. Victoria was a teenager and had to watch me go to pageants and get new clothes all the time. Our parents made good money so it wasn't like she had to dress in rags, but Marjo never fussed over her, you know what I mean?"

"I can see how that would upset an older sister. Or any sibling, for that matter."

"I'm sure it bothered Victoria, but she never took it out on me."

"Your father. Couldn't he see what was happening, what your mother was doing to your sister?"

"Well, my father was always closer to Victoria than he was to me, like she was his favorite. He always called her 'Daddy's little lady.' I don't know if I really thought about it all that much. If I did, I probably thought he was just making up for how Marjo treated her."

Alita paused for another, longer taste of wine. It wasn't easy when she told her family's history to Meg, and it was just as hard telling Luke now.

"But something changed," she continued. "Victoria was acting out, getting in trouble at school, shoplifting, stuff like that. She hid it, but she was cutting herself, too. For the first time there was tension between my father and Victoria. He had never gotten on her case about anything, but he started to come down on her really hard. He would just explode over the littlest things."

"How old was she then?"

"Just turned seventeen. I know because they had a big fight on her birthday. It was the first time I ever saw him hit her."

"Wow, that's terrible." Luke was shaking his head.

"They were yelling at each other and I was terrified, but Marjo just stood there without saying a word. When he slapped Victoria, she finally grabbed my hand and took me outside to the car. We went to the mall, can you believe that? Just left Victoria with him and we go shopping."

Alita closed her eyes. For a moment she was once again a little girl, with her hands over her ears as her sister and her father shouted at each other a few feet away. And then the slap to Victoria's face.

"Things got really bad after that. I was stuck in the middle because I loved my father and I loved my sister. I didn't want them to fight, but I couldn't stop them. Then late one night it was the worst ever, so loud it woke me up. I was sitting in bed just shaking and feeling helpless. It got quiet for a while and I thought it was over, but then my father started cursing at her. Vile, nasty things, and I heard banging on the walls and stuff breaking. I got up and came down the hallway just as Marjo was coming out of their bedroom."

Alita felt her mouth go dry. "This is so hard to say."

"You don't need to go on." Luke reached over the table between them and squeezed her hand. "It's okay."

"No, I have to do this. I need to get it out, I want you to know." Her lips tightened and she took a breath. "My father came staggering out of Victoria's room. He was holding his hand on his chest, and I saw blood on his pajama top and dripping down his arm. He took a few steps toward us and then fell down on the floor. Marjo was shrieking and ran over to him. That's when Victoria came out of her room and into the hallway. She had a knife in her hand. Marjo screamed, 'you killed him, you killed him!' I ran to my father and held onto him. With the blood, his blood, on my face and my hands."

Alita couldn't keep another montage of images and sounds from her mind ... people in uniforms rushing up the stairs and into the hallway, one of them kneeling to work on her father, pushing repeatedly on his chest with his hands. Marjo in hysterics, being restrained by two of the men. Victoria crumpled in the corner, the knife still in her hand until someone took it from her. And finally, that moment their eyes met as her sister was led away.

Alita swallowed hard. She noticed the pain on Luke's face.

"I had to stay with our neighbors while Marjo rode to the hospital in the ambulance. My father was still alive when he got there but he died about an hour later. When Marjo came back home and told me he was gone, that was when I went from worshipping my sister to hating her. And for a long time I wished she would die for what she did to our father."

"I can't begin to imagine what that was like. What you went through, what Victoria went through." Luke looked as drained as Alita felt inside. "What did they do with her?"

"She was in a juvenile detention center for a year. They released her when she turned eighteen. She left and never came back home again."

"A juvenile facility? Didn't they charge her as an adult for ... well, it would be a type of murder charge, wouldn't it?"

"It wasn't murder. It was a heart attack. My father died from a heart attack."

"But the knife, and the blood. I thought she stabbed him in the chest?"

"That's what Marjo and I thought at first, too, that she stabbed him. But Victoria had just cut him on the arm. Not bad, but deep enough that it was bleeding quite a bit. He was holding his arm when he went into the heart attack. The blood on his pajamas came when he grabbed his chest. Once they knew it was a heart attack that killed him, whatever Marjo said to them was enough to keep Victoria from facing serious charges. That kept everything out of the newspaper, which is what Marjo wanted. She knew Victoria wasn't going to talk to the police or anyone else."

"About?"

"About what had been going on in our family." Alita turned to face Luke. "My father sexually assaulted Victoria for years. I didn't know it. I was just a kid and I wouldn't have understood it anyway. But Marjo knew, damn her. She knew all along, and yet she did nothing to stop it."

"How could she just let that happen and look the other way?"

"Well, now you know my mother."

Another breath, shallow this time, and another sip of wine. Alita heard loud laughter coming from down the street, and closer, the soft tinkling of her bamboo wind chimes.

"I later found out from Victoria that she was seven when he first came into her room at night. She grew up with it, thinking that it was normal. But when she was older, she wanted it to stop. He threatened her, and convinced her that she couldn't tell anyone because no one would believe her. Their fights began when my father thought he was losing control of her. The night she cut him, she hid the knife before he came into her room. She wasn't going to let him touch her anymore."

"But he still tried?"

"Yes. But in the end, she wasn't defending herself." Alita's voice cracked. "She was protecting me."

"You?"

"Victoria told him that she was leaving home and was going to move in with friends. And you know what he said to that? He told her to go, that she was getting too old for him anyway, and that ... I was getting to be just about the right age."

Luke sagged in his chair. "That's so sick."

"She sacrificed herself for me out of love, and in return I hated her, because I thought she killed our father. But I just didn't know. She sent me letters and gifts from the detention center, but I threw them away without opening them. I wrote terrible letters back to her. Marjo even helped me write them."

"But you were able to get back together, to be sisters again?"

"Well, Marjo and I moved here to New Smyrna Beach. I think she was running from the past and wanted to go where no one knew her. She would never talk with me about Victoria. Ever. And that was fine, because I still hated my sister then. After high school, I enrolled at the University of Florida. I worked part-time, and Marjo sent me a check each month to help out. I was home on break during my sophomore year. She started an argument when I told her I was going to major in Art. She said I was being stupid and would always struggle if I went that route. I said she could just keep her money, that I'd pay my own way. She laughed and told me that she had never sent me a single cent. The money was coming from Victoria, not her. Victoria would send her a check, then Marjo would write a check for the same amount and send it to me. That floored me, you know? I mean, why would my sister, whom I hadn't heard from in years, send me money for college? But it also upset me, because I wouldn't have accepted it if I had known where it was coming from. Another check came in the mail while I was home on break. I saw the envelope and wrote down Victoria's address. She was living in Jacksonville, and two days later

I was knocking on her door."

"That was a shock for her, I'm sure."

"Oh, yeah. I was about to tear up the check right in front of her when she hugged me. I broke down crying. We talked for hours, and she told me the whole story, the truth about what had happened. I think you can understand why I've felt so guilty since then. My sister went through hell to protect me, and tried to help me, while I was hating her. I just wish I had known the truth all along."

"You did the best you could with what you knew at the time."

"Maybe so. At least I hope I did."

"Her last name was LaRue … her marriage didn't last?"

"She never married. She was never even in a serious relationship, at least not with a guy she'd want to marry. She legally changed her last name to LaRue. Maybe to build a wall between what was her old life and what she hoped her new life would be." Alita shook her head. "But changing her name didn't change her demons."

Luke refilled their glasses and Alita told him more details about Victoria's struggles with drug addiction and her years in the sex trade. She also told him about the many times she tried to help Victoria make a fresh start.

"It was like she was doomed to fail every time, no matter what she did," Alita said. "She had no real control over her life, ever. And all that goes back to the horrible things our father did to her. And Marjo, too, by doing nothing about it and treating Victoria like she didn't even exist. To this very day."

"So your mom and Victoria—"

"No. They were never together again. And today she didn't even come to her funeral."

20

SEE was Winston Dawdy's acronym for his victim process: Selection, Education, and Elimination. *SEE.*

The Elimination of his victims was always the most pleasurable part of *SEE*. A simple gunshot to the back of the head was too boring. His kills required creativity, which he had in ample supply. The more creative the kill, the better.

Selection was the easiest part of the process. Unlike many serial killers, he was not drawn to a certain type of victim, nor did he seek them out. They would just appear—a woman playing fetch with her dog in the park; an elderly man talking to a cashier at the grocery store; or even a soccer mom's Facebook rant that caught his attention. Wherever it was, whoever it was, at that moment he knew that someone needed to die.

But Education was by far the most critical and challenging component of *SEE*. Education involved learning everything about his potential target by using an arsenal of electronic tools, conducting extensive research, and engaging in surveillance until routines and patterns were both established and predictable.

When Dawdy went online he always used a Virtual Private Network, or VPN, to encrypt his web activities and conceal his identity. A gifted and resourceful hacker since his teens, Dawdy found that most firewalls were no challenge for his keyboard skills, and the backdoors he left behind on network servers gave him easier access on future visits. For the lowest hanging fruit he scoured social media sites and gleaned photos and personal details that people share far too freely.

With the general public's nearly every move monitored by security cameras and enhanced facial recognition software, Dawdy often wore some type of disguise when researching a target—wigs, facial hair, dark glasses, skin coloration, body padding, orthodontic devices, cheek plumpers, latex lumps, bumps, and scars, prosthetic ears, even full-face masks. Growing up in community theatre, immersing himself in the BFA Actor Training Program in college, and endless hours watching and studying the great masters of cinema made him adept at accents, dialect, and alteration of posture and gait. Winston Dawdy was an ever-changing chameleon who could walk without leaving a footprint, and stalk without casting a shadow.

The Education process could be as short as a few days if the victim existed modestly on the fringe of society and wouldn't be missed. Or, it could extend for months for someone with a busy social life and a constantly changing schedule whose routines were harder to predict. Independently wealthy and with no close relatives, Dawdy had the resources and freedom to take whatever time was necessary. Once he locked on a scent he never let it go, and like the stealthiest predators in the animal kingdom he would always stay downwind from his prey.

Something, he didn't know what, had drawn him to Nashville. On his second day in Music City he saw a woman get into a car ahead of him as he was driving past the Hard Rock Café. That old familiar feeling set in, and he just *knew*. Education began when he tailed her to her apartment complex. He soon learned that Victoria LaRue was a drug-addicted hooker. An easy target.

After ten days of Education he walked up to her on a Broadway sidewalk in The District. He knew the lure of two grand would be too much for her to turn down, and by freelancing for the night she wouldn't have to turn over a chunk of the cash to her escort agency. It also meant she would be alone when she met him, because she would not have the protection of the "muscle" that Satin Dolls sent with her on outcalls.

Dawdy stayed in Nashville for a week after the Elimination of Victoria LaRue. The police were tight-lipped about the case, so the local media mostly ignored the story. All according to his plan.

The seven days also gave him time to write the chapters about Victoria LaRue's Selection, Education, and Elimination. Creative writing was in his genes and came easily to him, but his current book-in-progress didn't involve much creativity. The events happened in real life and real death, and he was simply writing down the details.

Before he left Nashville he stopped by the post office and paid cash to send a package to a remailing service in Florida that asked for no information from its customers and kept no records. Upon receipt, the remailing service would open the outer package, find payment in full—also in cash—and send the enclosed, sealed nine-by-twelve envelope to Potter Literary Associates in Los Angeles, California. The return address label in the upper left corner of the envelope was also that of Potter Literary Associates—by design, not a mistake. Each step in the process was calculated, efficient, and untraceable.

He was at a Wendy's in Glendale, Kentucky, when he overheard two men in business suits laughing and talking about a mutual friend and his experience with a Mistress Sasha in Speedway, Indiana. He didn't catch all of the conversation, but he heard enough to know that someone needed to die.

Once he was home on his secluded twenty-acre estate in farm country outside Johnstown, Ohio, Dawdy dove into the Dark Web and found the website of "Mistress Sasha and her Dungeon of Pleasure and Pain."

Education had begun.

21

The busiest Labor Day weekend in the Sunriz Boutique's five-year history kept Alita's mind on her work instead of what was happening, or not happening, in Nashville. But after the holiday, with kids going back to school, came the annual brief lull in tourists to New Smyrna Beach, which meant fewer customers. Meg and Alita alternated days to give each other some time off.

When she wasn't working, Alita retreated to her home studio to refocus on her art. With brush in hand, she stared at a blank canvas until her arm grew tired. Defeated, she would pour a glass of wine, open a bag of chips, and curl up on the couch. She never had her mother's fixation on weight, but she didn't need to step on the scales to know that comfort foods and alcohol were adding pounds to her frame. She would find time to care another time.

She called Detective Blate regularly. When she was able to catch him in his office his response was always a variation of "nothing new to report." With each passing day the lack of progress was soul crushing. Alita felt the likelihood that Blate would find Victoria's killer grow smaller as her need to return to Nashville and *do something* grew larger.

By the last day of September business had picked up again and both Alita and Meg were in the shop at the end of a long day. Alita locked the front door of the Sunriz Boutique and turned the sign in the window to "Sorry We're Closed."

"I thought today was never going to end," she said.

"I know. My feet can use a break." Meg folded and replaced a beach towel a customer considered but didn't purchase.

Alita opened the cash register and removed the drawer. She hit several keys and the register spat out a tally receipt. "You have time for a little wine?"

"Sure. You get the deposit ready and I'll tidy up a bit. Where do you want to go?"

"Let's just have a glass in the back. There's a bottle on the shelf underneath the coffee maker. And don't worry about tidying up. I'll come in early tomorrow."

"I could tell all day that something's on your mind," Meg said.

"Yeah, but I wanted to wait until we closed."

They retired to the rear of the shop. Meg opened the wine while Alita counted the bills and coins.

"Mostly credit card sales today," Alita said. "I'll make out a deposit slip in the morning before I go to the bank."

They pulled chairs next to Alita's desk and clinked their glasses together in what had become their new ritual.

"To Victoria," they said in unison.

"You know I hate to leave you alone," Alita began, "but I just have to go back to Nashville, Meg. This Friday it will have been two months. That's long enough. Detective Blate keeps telling me he has no new information. I don't know if they're doing anything at all. He says they are, but who knows? I just feel that if I don't go there and shake things up, nothing will ever happen. They will just forget about Victoria."

"Go, for as long as you need. You want me to book your flight?"

"No, I'm taking my Miata this time. I can make it in a day, and I won't have to worry about flights or rental cars."

"Are you going to stay at the same hotel? I can reserve a room."

"I should have told you this before now, Meg, but I just … couldn't. I called Jamila last week, the manager where Victoria lived.

She's going to let me rent the apartment month to month. A month's rent there is actually cheaper than a few days in a hotel."

"No," Meg said. "Not a good idea. I don't think it's safe for you to stay there."

"I'm locked in, I already mailed her a check." Alita hoped the firmness in her voice would end debate but not cause offense.

Meg shook her head. "I know you feel the need to be there, but if the police don't have anything after all this time, what can you do?"

"I don't know. I just know I have to go. Being down here with nothing going on up there is driving me crazy. I would like to leave Friday morning and stay a few days. If that's … okay."

"I'm on your side. Whatever you need to do."

They sipped their wine as Meg gave Alita time and space for her thoughts. What *was* she going to do in Nashville, other than continue to prod Detective Blate from a closer distance? She had no ideas at all, just a deep belief that she had to go there. For Victoria.

19 Crimes Red blend was Alita's favorite everyday wine. At home in a kitchen drawer she had a collection of all nineteen corks, denoting each of the crimes that several hundred years ago could get British criminals banished to Australia. She rotated the bottle that sat between them and looked at the label, at the image of the convict with a vacant stare on his face. She picked up the cork to see which felony was printed on it:

13.

ASSAULTING,

CUTTING, OR

BURNING CLOTHES.

The coincidence was not lost on her.

22

A lita left before sunrise on Friday morning. It was seven hundred miles to Nashville and the fastest route would take over eleven hours, including the white-knuckle stretch through the heart of Atlanta. With the hour she would gain from the time zone change she would arrive at Hunting Creek Apartments around four o'clock.

She stopped for gas in Valdosta, Georgia. Before hitting the highway again she dropped the top and tucked her hair under her Florida Gators ball cap. Tuned to Classic Vinyl on SiriusXM radio and the volume cranked up, she was ready to rock 'n' roll the rest of the way to Music City.

On the entrance ramp to I-75, a lifted pickup truck with Bull Nuts dangling from the hitch sped past on her left, horn blaring. A guy in the passenger seat leaned half out the window to gawk down at her and yell words she couldn't make out over the sound of their horn and Alice Cooper on her radio. She learned long ago that her best reaction to such characters was no reaction at all, so she stayed easy on the gas pedal until the pickup became a speck in the distance and faded from sight.

I-75 offered an endless stream of northbound 18-wheelers, many flying by at eighty miles per hour or more. She stayed in the right lane and checked her rearview mirror often as she would be nothing more than a speed bump for those forty-ton behemoths. Interstate driving otherwise bored her, with miles of long, straight highway made even more monotonous by cruise control and bland scenery. When she bought her Miata she chose a six-speed manual transmission because she loved shifting gears and tracking a tight line through curves. There would be no time on this trip, going or returning home, but one day she would detour to Deals Gap, North Carolina, to test the Tail of the Dragon—three hundred and eighteen curves in only eleven miles.

She thought about letting Luke O'Connor know she was coming to Nashville, but decided against it. He was an in-demand record producer and would have no time to get together. Besides, if she had not formed any course of action, how could he help her?

That last thought, her lack of any real plan, haunted her. She brought her notes from the many nights she spent searching the web for anything she could find, along with her list of new questions for Detective Blate, but she found no reason to think that her notes or her questions would change anything. She was on the sidelines in the hunt for Victoria's killer and she wanted to take direct action, be involved, do something that would make a difference. But what? She kept drawing blanks.

With nothing to do but keep her car between the lines as she drove, she again thought about everything that had happened, everything she saw, heard, and did the last time she was in Nashville. She pictured the peaceful setting in the cemetery with no traces of the horrific, brutal crime that took her sister's life. None of it made any sense, none of it pointed to any avenues to pursue. If Victoria was the victim of a cunning serial killer, perhaps Blate was right—*they would be damned lucky to catch him*. She couldn't bear to allow that thought to rent space in her head.

Alita didn't know how long Victoria worked for Satin Dolls. Although her sister would share brief stories about her more unusual clients and experiences, she kept the actual business end of her profession from Alita.

She did have the phone number for Satin Dolls but couldn't find an address during any of her web searches. That matched what Blate told her, that the escort agency was outcalls only and did not have a physical location. A thought came to mind—Victoria once told her that several preachers used her services. The upside-down cross that was placed between her legs ... *what if her killer was one of the preachers?* A man of God who was a regular customer would be someone Victoria trusted, a man she might willingly meet in a cemetery at midnight for whatever reason the preacher gave her. *Finally, something ... but would it lead to anything?*

"Damn." Alita banged a fist on the steering wheel. She forgot to bring the Ziploc storage bag with the business cards and the slips of paper with names and phone numbers she found in Victoria's apartment. None of them were listed as Preacher, Reverend, or whatever— that would have jumped out at her. Detective Blate made photocopies. She would make sure he cross-checked the names and numbers with every "holy man" in the Nashville Metro area. She would do the same as soon as she was back home in New Smyrna Beach.

She was road weary when the trip meter hit seven hundred miles and thankful when she pulled into the parking lot of Hunting Creek Apartments at ten minutes before four o'clock. Despite the warm, sunny, early October afternoon, no one was in the small pool next to the office.

"Here she is," Jamila Crockett said with a warm smile. "I wasn't expecting you for another hour."

"I thought Friday traffic would be worse than it was but I made good time. Thanks for sticking around."

"No worries, I'm still on the clock. But you have to be exhausted driving all that way. Would you like a bottled water? That's all I have in the office."

"No, I just want to get to the apartment and kick back a bit."

"I can imagine. Let me get you the key." Jamila opened the cabinet mounted to the wall behind her desk and ran her fingers along a row of hooks. "Ah, here we are. B202." Jamila handed the key to Alita. "It's not real comfy because … well, you've been in it."

"It's fine. I'm just glad you let me rent it. Do you need another deposit? Do I need to sign anything?"

"Just pay rent when it's due and you can have it for as long as you want. Saves me paperwork and having to screen a new tenant. But no wild, drunken parties, you hear? We have enough of them already."

Alita laughed. "Okay, I can agree to that if I have to. But seriously, I truly appreciate it, Jamila."

"My pleasure, girl. By the way, we went through the fridge and cabinets and tossed anything perishable. There are a few canned goods, but I'd pitch them, too. You'll want to do a little grocery shopping right away. And something else I need to tell you … we had to spray the entire building for roaches yesterday, so there might still be a slight odor."

"I'm a Florida girl. We spray for bugs all the time down there."

"Glad you understand. I didn't want you to freak out if you saw a dead roach. Oh, and just so you know, I'm taking a three-day weekend and won't be back until Tuesday. Yolanda will be in the office eight-to-five while I'm out. She's a sweet kid, you'll like her. But you have my personal cell number if you need to get in touch with me. Don't hesitate to call."

"I wouldn't think of bothering you on your time off. Are you doing anything special?"

"Going to Memphis. Heading out right after work. Some great barbecue there."

"Enjoy it, I'm sure you will. And I need to get out of here so you can get going."

"One other thing," Jamila said. "I know you could use access to the internet while you're here." She picked up a pen and wrote on a piece of paper she handed to Alita. "Don't share this with anyone, and don't tell Yolanda I gave it to you. It's the office Wi-Fi login and password. The previous manager added a Wi-Fi extender, so you should be able to get on the network from the apartment."

"I wouldn't share it or say anything, of course, but I can't take this if there's any chance you could get in trouble."

Jamila laughed. "Don't you worry about it. They wouldn't know what to do around here without me."

"I'll get my own Wi-Fi as soon as I can but this will really help for now. See you when you get back."

With a wave goodbye, Alita was out the door.

She moved her car to a space in front of Victoria's building and raised the top on her Miata. She looked around, at the other three buildings in the complex and the pitted and patched blacktop parking lot. *My new home away from home*, she thought. She popped open the trunk and grabbed her small suitcase.

A man was headed down the interior stairs as she was going up to the second floor. He ignored her greeting and stared at her as they passed. Her mind couldn't block the thought—*could it have been him?*—but if she looked with suspicion at every man in Nashville she would soon be too bogged down to do anything.

She needed to jiggle the key in the lock just as Jamila had done. When she opened the door the musty smell that hit her on her initial visit was gone. She did detect an odor from the roach spray.

Jamila felt bad about the roaches so Alita didn't tell her that in Florida most people hire a service to spray quarterly for large cockroaches commonly called "palmetto bugs." They live mostly outside in flowerbeds and mulch, but one will sometimes find its way into the house only to soon go legs up after crossing the chemical barrier. Alita visited Victoria in another Nashville apartment complex a few years ago, a place that was infested with a smaller variety of roach that could swarm in walls by the hundreds or even thousands. She would take a random palmetto bug over those roaches any day.

She opened the fridge and found it empty, the same for the cupboards save a couple of canned goods that she put in the trash. She was not a fan of Walmart, but a nearby Supercenter would have food and other items she would need for the apartment. However, even though she was tired and hungry, she had a stop she wanted to make before Walmart.

It was seven miles to the cemetery. She parked and walked to the spot where Victoria was murdered. She had not visited Victoria's grave in Florida—the grief was still too close to the surface to go there. But here, where Victoria's life ended, there was no pain, no grief, no emotions at all, for reasons she still could not understand. She sat on the ground as time seemed to stand still. Instead of thoughts and plans and questions, her mind was blank. She felt nothing more than the gentle breeze on her face and the soft grass beneath her.

She wandered the cemetery, her thoughts coming back into focus as she read inscriptions on grave markers and took in uniquely shaped stones. The Lyft driver dropped Victoria off at the front entrance and she was found almost at the back end of the cemetery. How did she get there? Did she walk, maybe on the same paths that Alita was now following? Did she see the same grave markers?

Alita left the cemetery shortly before sunset and drove straight to the Walmart Supercenter. She was now dead on her feet, so she bought things that would tide her over until she could return when she felt like shopping—snacks, coffee, Diet Coke, a frozen pizza for dinner, donuts for breakfast. She was happy to see that Walmart sold 19 Crimes Red, so she picked up several bottles and a wine opener. She bought new sets of sheets to drape over the couch and chair in the living room, and an inflatable Airbed, more sheets, and two pillows for the bedroom. Cans of Lysol and Febreze were among her most needed items.

Back at the apartment she popped the pizza in the oven and opened a bottle of wine, filling a glass that she rinsed first. While the pizza was baking she grabbed her phone to FaceTime with Meg.

"Hey, I was wondering when you were going to check in," Meg said. "What's up?"

"I was just at Walmart, believe or not."

"I know you were. And the cemetery before that. You shouldn't go there by yourself, Alita."

Meg had been tracking her with the "Find My" app.

"I can take care of myself," Alita said. "I'm a big girl, Meg, and I'm about to get bigger because I have a pizza in the oven. But you wanted to see the apartment, so let me give you a fast tour."

"Yes, please."

Alita tapped the icon on her iPhone to switch to its front camera.

"Here's the uh, dining room. Dinette table, only three legs." With her free hand she pushed on the top of the table to make it wobble. "I will obviously have to eat only balanced meals here. Oh, and just one chair," she pulled it out from the table, "so no dinner guests for me."

Alita panned to the living room. "Jamila said this stuff was stacked by the trash dumpster when someone moved out. But it's not that bad."

"My god, Alita! You're not going to sit on those things, are you?"

"It's okay, I bought sheets to put over them." Now sorry she had started the tour, Alita pulled back the curtain to the sliding glass doors. "It's dark so you can't see much, but there's a cute little balcony here. And down there's the parking lot."

Meg was silent as Alita closed the curtain and moved to the kitchen.

"Not much to see here. Small and basic, but everything seems to work." Next was the bathroom where she flipped on the light.

"Shower tub, sink, toilet. What else does a girl need?" She turned off the light. "And finally, the bedroom."

"There's no bed. Alita, you can't sleep on that mattress. It looks terrible."

"I bought an Airbed. And more sheets. But it's not like I'll be living here full-time. If I keep poking the bear, otherwise known as Detective Blate, maybe he'll do his job and I won't have to come back again."

Alita was relieved when she heard the timer on the oven go off.

"Pizza's ready, Meg. I'll check in tomorrow, okay?"

"Be safe."

If a sadness meter existed, Alita knew it would have maxed at one hundred percent in the tone of those two simple words that Meg said to end their conversation. She should never have given Meg even a glimpse into the way that Victoria had lived, the way that she would now be living when in Nashville.

She applied a coat of Lysol to the decrepit couch and topped it with Febreze to make the smell bearable. She spread a new sheet over it and sat in semi-darkness, munching on her pizza. The seven hundred miles, the glass of wine that turned into two, and the overwhelming loneliness she felt took their toll. By ten o'clock she had inflated the Airbed and placed it close to Victoria's mattress on the floor, seeking a sanctuary that only sleep could bring. She had just closed her eyes when she had a chilling thought.

If Victoria's killer was someone she trusted, that person could also have a key to the apartment!

She hurried to the front door to secure the chain lock.

Disguise our bondage as we will,
'Tis woman, woman, rules us still.
    —Thomas Moore

The Education process for the Elimination of Mistress Sasha took five weeks and involved web research, surveillance, a hidden GPS tracker, remote hacks of her cell phone and computer, and three phone calls with Mistress Sasha herself from Winston Dawdy's latest burner phone. The Education process also yielded a surprising but welcome twist—a bonus victim. Multiple targets meant multiple variables and more chances for something to go wrong, thus Dawdy preferred to eliminate just one person at a time. But this time would be different, and the risk minimal.

Dawdy's Education found that Pamela Dobbins was thirty-eight, divorced for ten years, and employed as an office temp for a local staffing agency. Both of her parents were dead and she had no siblings. She lived alone in a modest brick ranch home on Rosewood Drive in Speedway, Indiana, and drove a blue Honda CR-V. She was a member of the nearby United Methodist Church but did not attend during the time Dawdy was shadowing her. Although a "Beware of Dog" sign was planted in her front yard, she did not have any pets. Her credit card records showed that she bought a ticket last year to the Indianapolis 500—the famed Brickyard oval was only two miles from her house. She went to gentle yoga once a week and did most of her shopping at Kroger, Meijer, and Whole Foods Market. Although registered to vote, she didn't cast a ballot in the last two general elections. Pamela Dobbins seemed to lead a normal, perhaps even dull, life. But several times a month she became "Mistress Sasha, the Ravishing Ruler of the Night." Her ad on the Dark Web listed the services she offered to a select clientele: "bondage & discipline, dominance & submission, sadomasochism." Her location was the Indianapolis Metro area and sessions were in her Dungeon, by appointment only, with no outcalls. Identity checked in advance, cash paid upon arrival, five hundred dollars for an hour's worth of pleasure or pain.

Dawdy's initial plan was to pose as a client seeking Mistress Sasha's services, but the deeper his research took him into the world of BDSM, the more he realized he would lose control of the action once the role-playing began. He could never allow that to happen. Simply moving on to another victim didn't cross his mind—Mistress Sasha needed to die. It didn't take him long to come up with a new plan.

Dawdy called Mistress Sasha and told her he had a Peeping Tom fetish. He didn't want his own session, he wanted to secretly watch her with another customer. Mistress Sasha replied that she had too much integrity and respect for her clients to allow such a thing. Her response was the same the second time he called to say he would pay her three hundred dollars more than her usual fee. When Dawdy phoned a third time to raise his offer to fifteen hundred dollars, in cash, her integrity and respect for her clients were not quite as important anymore. She did stress there could be no photographs, video, or audio recording. Mistress Sasha apparently followed that rule herself, as Dawdy's hack of her home Wi-Fi network found no security cameras, at least not any that were on the network and uploading to a cloud. When his fun was over he would still use his bug detector to sweep for hidden cameras and listening devices.

Mistress Sasha told him that she screened her clients by verifying names, addresses, and phone numbers. Although she ran a cash-only business, she also asked for a credit card number when booking appointments and processed a hold charge—a necessity because she was inviting strangers into her home. "I mostly have loyal, repeat customers who trust me with their deepest secrets," she told Dawdy on the phone, "but if a client ever crosses me, I have enough information to make their life a living hell."

He told Mistress Sasha he was a dentist who practiced in Indianapolis and lived in the suburbs. "Just call me Tooth Doc," he said, once he convinced her that he couldn't tell her his real name because of his profession. Or maybe it was the fifteen hundred in cash that swayed her. Either way, after she called back to confirm the cell number he gave her—his burner phone—Mistress Sasha trusted him enough to waive her screening requirements. An hour later she called again to say that she had a ten o'clock appointment that evening if he was ready to "peep."

She gave Dawdy her street address—which he already knew— and told him he must arrive at precisely nine-fifteen, "not a minute early, not a minute late," and bring the amount of cash they agreed upon. Her detached garage was behind the house and she would raise her garage door when she saw his car turn into her driveway. He was to pull in and park beside her car, then wait until she lowered the garage door again. She explained that a strange car in her driveway would spook her ten o'clock appointment, who was a long-time client.

His plan required only minimal research of the second victim, whom Dawdy viewed simply as collateral damage. By hacking Mistress Sasha's cell phone he had access to her contacts, calendar, voicemail messages, and texts, so he knew about Robert Slotten's standing ten o'clock appointment every other Friday night. Having Slotten's name and phone number made it easy to search the web for all the information he needed. Dawdy was confident that Mr. Slotten did not tell his wife or anyone else about his regular sessions with Mistress

Sasha.

Dawdy went past her house a second time. He drove at a speed that was neither too fast nor too slow, to not draw attention to the car or to himself. He continued up the street, looking for anything that seemed amiss from the multiple times he cruised the neighborhood over the past few weeks. He rented a different car for the night using forged identification and a stolen credit card whose absence would not be noticed by its owner. If trouble still found a way to present itself, the Sig Sauer P365 concealed in his ankle holster would serve him well, as it had on prior occasions.

Although it was dark and the only people who would see his face would soon be dead, he still used prosthetics and makeup to alter his appearance. His attire was casual, dentist-on-the-prowl, topped with a scally cap.

Dawdy made the loop on Sandalwood Drive and was back on Rosewood. He checked the time again. Without putting on his blinker he turned into Mistress Sasha's driveway. He eased into the garage at the back of the house and saw the garage door descend in his rear-view mirror.

Dawdy put the rental car in park and shut off the engine. He grabbed the canvas banker's pouch on the passenger seat and was half out of the car when the garage utility door swung open. Mistress Sasha stood in the doorway.

"Tooth Doc, I presume?"

"Right on time." He shut the car door. "Just as you wished."

"I didn't wish. I commanded. There is a big difference, as you will soon see."

He saw her eyes drop to the banker's pouch in his left hand.

"No worries," he said. "I have your money, just as you … demanded."

"I need to see it. And count it, of course."

Dawdy took a step toward her.

"Stay right there. Show me the money first."

Dawdy suspected that Mistress Sasha was packing her own concealed weapon. She stayed in the doorway as he unzipped the pouch. He took out the hundred dollar bills and spread them in his hands.

"Okay, come," she said.

Dawdy handed over the bills and watched her mouth move silently as she counted them. When she finished she went to hand the pouch back to him.

"No, you can keep it."

"Thank you, Tooth Doc." Mistress Sasha took the pouch and zipped it shut after stuffing the bills back inside.

The tiny tracking device that Dawdy hid behind the liner would help him locate the pouch when it was time to leave.

This was Dawdy's first chance to see Pamela Dobbins up close, and she fell well short of being "Mistress Sasha, The Ravishing Ruler of The Night." The photos in her web ads had to be several years old and filtered. Her face was puffy and plain. Her eyes seemed off-center, torqued to the right. From a distance he had seen her short, curly blonde hair; tonight, she wore a wig with long, flowing auburn tresses. Dressed in slacks and a blouse, she was five-six and her bones carried at least twenty pounds more than her driver's license weight of one hundred and thirty pounds.

"Follow me," she said. "We have forty-three minutes before my appointment gets here."

The back door of the house opened into a small, tidy kitchen. Dawdy watched Mistress Sasha put the money pouch in a drawer next to the stove. *Well, that makes it easy.*

"Sit down." She pointed toward the kitchen table. Dawdy took an end chair and she sat to his left. A piece of paper and a pen lay on the table.

"Tooth Doc, I don't judge people on how they get their kicks. If you get off watching and not participating that's your business and I'm fine with that. To each his own. But I don't know you from Adam, and since you won't give me your personal information I have no way to verify who you really are. So first, if you're a cop, by you contacting me that is entrapment. Plus, nothing I do here is illegal. I—"

"Relax, I'm not a cop. I'm a dentist, just like I told you."

"Then you shouldn't mind me asking … how many teeth do people have?"

"Thirty-two. Eight incisors, four canines, eight premolars, and twelve molars, including wisdom teeth. Humans are diphyodonts. As children we develop twenty deciduous teeth which are gradually replaced by permanent teeth. Wisdom teeth are usually—"

Mistress Sasha raised her palms. "Enough! Enough! I only looked up the number of teeth. The way you rattled all that off, and the part about the diphyo-whatever, you have to be a dentist. But still, I do need you to read and sign this." She slid the piece of paper and pen in front of him. "Just for my protection. Loose lips sink ships, as they say, and I can't put my business at risk."

Dawdy scanned the list of statements to which he was to attest or agree:

I am not involved with law enforcement in any capacity … I am not a journalist or any type of reporter … I will not share anything I observe tonight online or with any other person … I will remain completely silent for the duration of the session, and so on, for a total of ten clauses. And at the bottom: *by signing this document using my alias of "Tooth Doc" in lieu of my real name, I hereby agree that I will pay you $10,000 for any violation of these terms.*

"I'm risking more here than you are," Dawdy said. He took the pen and scrawled "Tooth Doc" at the bottom of the page. "Actually, I should have you sign something, too." He slid the paper back to her.

"Satisfied?"

Without answering, she rose and put it in the same drawer on top of the money pouch.

"This way," she said.

Mistress Sasha opened a door just off the kitchen and led him down a stretch of bare wooden stairs to a lower level that was half basement, half crawlspace. The furnace, water heater, washer, and dryer were against the far end. Closer to the stairs, a couch, chair, and coffee table sat on an orange area rug, with a flat screen TV mounted on the wall. The half basement was finished in knotty pine paneling except for the narrow opening to the crawlspace.

She pulled a black bandana from her pocket. "Turn around. I need you to put this on."

"That's not part of our arrangement. I'm just here to watch. I can't with that across my eyes."

"It's just for a second or two. There's something you can't see."

He turned and let her tie the bandana around his head.

"Now don't move."

Dawdy heard a metallic click followed by the faint creak of a door swinging open. Mistress Sasha moved only a couple of steps, so he knew that a release mechanism was hidden in the wall. A fake "knot" in the knotty pine, he guessed.

She turned him by the shoulders and took off the bandana.

"Welcome to Mistress Sasha's Dungeon of Pleasure and Pain."

The wall hid a secret room in what Dawdy now knew was more than a half basement. A thick door covered by a section of paneling had rotated open 90 degrees.

"Ingenious," he said. "This looked like just a crawlspace. No one would ever know this room is down here."

"That's the whole idea." She extended her arm. "After you."

The Dungeon was about the same size as the finished half basement. Thick black carpeting on top of a spongy pad covered the floor. The walls had wedge-style, sound-deafening foam panels, and acoustic tiles were fixed to the ceiling.

"So, this is it. What do you think?" Her words seemed to disintegrate in dead air as soon as she spoke them.

"I'm blown away. Totally. How did you do all this?"

"I didn't. The house belonged to my ex. He built the Dungeon before I met him. He was a master carpenter, great with tools. The son-of-a-bitch could do anything. He walled off this part of the basement and added the fake crawlspace." She pointed. "See how the ceiling is two feet lower there? What you think is the crawlspace opening when you come down the stairs is really just six inches of dirt. And it's completely soundproofed down here."

"You said ex. No longer in the picture?" Dawdy already knew the answer.

"I met him as I was just getting into the lifestyle, so when we married this became our little playground. But it turned out he had too many other playmates for my liking, so our marriage didn't last. He split about ten years ago."

"And you kept the Dungeon."

"Yeah, but I'm sure he built another one wherever he is now. Money's never been a problem for him."

Dawdy looked over the rest of the room, at a long table covered with an array of items: whips, chains, and paddles; leather hoods, harnesses, ropes, and various handcuffs; collars and nipple clamps; vibrators, dildos, and other sex toys of various shapes and sizes; and devices he had never seen before, even in his extensive research. In the center of the room was a circular bed with an electric hoist above it, and against the end wall, an armoire.

Mistress Sasha glanced at her watch. "Come on, I need to show you where you're going to be."

She led him to the tall, double-door armoire. Each door had a full-length mirror and a keyhole. Instead of unlocking one of the doors, she pressed a recessed button on the side of the armoire and the doors sprung open together.

"Interesting." Dawdy took a closer look.

"Another one of my ex's little creations. Get in and sit down so you can see how this will work when my client gets here."

There was a bench seat inside the armoire. Dawdy also saw an electrical outlet. Once he was seated, Mistress Sasha closed the doors. A six-inch by six-inch square had been cut out of each door panel.

Ah yes, one-way mirrors—just as he thought. From his vantage point he had a clear view of the entire room. The bench and the electrical outlet implied that others had watched the action in the past, and maybe filmed it as well.

"Now feel around in the upper left corner," she said. "You'll find a button. Press it."

Dawdy did as she said and the doors sprung open again. He stepped out of the armoire.

"That button's only for your peace of mind so you won't feel trapped and panic. Do *not* press it. Repeat, do *not* press it. Now, do you want me to get you some lotion, tissues, disposable wipes?"

"Sure. Whatever is handy." Dawdy wanted her to think he did.

"I also have to run upstairs and change. Do you need to go to the little boys' room? This is your last chance until the session's over."

"No, I'm good. Do you mind if I look at your toys while you're gone?"

"As long as you don't touch anything. I mean that. Anything."

Dawdy waited until her footsteps reached the top of the stairs before he pulled out the iPhone he carried in addition to his burner phone. He went to the armoire, sat on the bench, and pulled the doors shut. He shot ten seconds of video through the six-inch square behind one of the mirrors and played it back to check the quality. *Perfect.*

He exited the armoire and went to where Mistress Sasha's bindings were laid out. There were several rolls of duct tape. He knew she wouldn't notice the short strip he tore off. He returned to the armoire and stuck the strip underneath the bench.

He checked out the electric hoist mounted to the ceiling. It was plugged into an outlet, also in the ceiling, and had a large brass hook that hung from the pulley system. A remote control was fixed to the wall.

Dawdy heard Mistress Sasha coming back down the stairs. He almost laughed when he saw her in a black corset dress cross-laced in front, black fishnet stockings, black boots, and black gloves.

"It's almost time. Here." She handed him a packet of body wipes and a tube of lotion. "I don't care if you jerk off, but you cannot make a sound."

"No worries. I'll be a good boy."

"You better be. If you do anything to cause me to lose this client, I will find out who you really are, Tooth Doc, and I'll tell all your patients about your little visit tonight. Plus, you'll owe me ten grand. Or more."

"I said no worries and I meant it. I'm just here for the show."

"I don't know what you're expecting to see. It's just harmless role-playing between consenting adults."

"Maybe I'll see something I might want you to do to me sometime." He smiled.

"One never knows." She looked at her watch again. "Okay, final instructions. Once you're in the armoire, you stay there until I let you out. Don't get out on your own, even after the session is over and I take him back upstairs. Do not use that button."

"You've made that more than clear."

"Everything is precisely timed. During the first fifteen minutes I will make him comfortable. To you it will look *un*comfortable, but that's what he … never mind. Then I will begin disciplining him. That will go on for another fifteen minutes. At the half-hour mark you will hear *Bolero*, the version by the Boston Symphony. It is thirteen minutes and forty-nine seconds in length. While the song is playing I get creative and can do whatever I want to him. That's followed by one minute and eleven seconds of silence and stillness. That leaves exactly fifteen minutes. I spend that time unbinding him, which makes him uncomfortable again. He's in harmony when he's all bound up and in distress when he's not. I'm sure that doesn't make any sense to you, so don't even try to understand. Just watch, that's what you paid me for."

"Tell me, I'm curious. Does he have a safe word?"

Mistress Sasha broke character with a laugh and a shrug. "Yes. His safe word is 'more.'"

"Seriously?"

"Seriously. Now, after he's dressed, I will take him upstairs and he'll be on his way. I'll come back down and open the armoire doors, then you can be on your merry way, too. Tips are appreciated. Any questions?"

"Yes. Your client clearly gets something out of this. What do you get out of it? Or do you just do it for the money?"

"I don't do it for the money at all. And I get more out of it than he does." She gave him a coy smile. "And speaking of, he's at the door now."

"How do you know?"

"Because he knows better than to be late and disappoint Mistress Sasha. Now let's get you inside, Tooth Doc. Time to hide and peep."

***

Dawdy pulled the strip of duct tape from underneath the bench.

He tapped the record button on his iPhone and used the tape to secure it to the back of the mirror, in landscape mode. In less than a minute he heard two sets of footsteps coming down the stairs.

Robert Slotten, an advertising executive from Muncie, was a short, flabby man who was easily north of two hundred pounds. Head bowed, he looked timid and weak when he took off his clothes and stood naked before Mistress Sasha. It was hard to believe that Slotten owned one of the largest advertising agencies in the Midwest. Dawdy's research found that men like Robert Slotten paid for sessions with women like Mistress Sasha to atone for the power they held over their female subordinates. Being dominated in this manner by a woman somehow evened the scales for them. It was too weird, too much for Dawdy to fathom.

He watched as Mistress Sasha put a leather hood over Slotten's head and tugged on it until the holes were aligned with his eyes. She helped him into a leather harness with straps that ran between his legs, on each side of his testicles, and across his chest before being fastened in the back. She adjusted each strap and tested its tautness. The pair worked in tandem, as if each movement was a ritual they had performed many times in the past.

With a shove from Mistress Sasha, Slotten pitched forward onto the circular bed and rolled until he was on his stomach in the center. She went to the long table of toys and came back with a length of braided rope and a pair of handcuffs. She looped one end of the rope around his feet and tied it, then looped the other end around his neck, tying that end as well. Although she hadn't glanced even once at the armoire, she seemed to always position herself so that Dawdy had a clear view.

Slotten obediently put his arms behind his back as Mistress Sasha placed the handcuffs on his wrists and locked them into place. To this point neither had said a word.

She went back to the table and returned with a shiny metal ring and a short length of cable with carabiners at each end. She ran the cable underneath the loops of rope and his cuffed hands before clipping both ends of the cable to the metal ring.

Mistress Sasha pointed the remote control at the hoist above the bed. A thick cable with a brass hook at the end descended. When the hook was resting on Slotten's back she pressed the remote to pause the hoist. She slipped the metal ring over the hook, pointed the remote again, and the hoist began to reel in its line. Robert Slotten rose from the bed and slowly twisted in the air. Mistress Sasha started and stopped the hoist several times. With two or three seconds between cycles, each start and stop caused the line to jerk, inflicting a pulse of pain. Or pleasure? Dawdy couldn't see Slotten's face because of the leather hood, and he could only see his eyes when Slotten rotated toward him.

The leather harness dug into Slotten's flesh. The two straps that ran between his legs pinched his testicles together. The loop of rope around his neck, running under the handcuffs and around his feet, was pulled tight by the weight of his body, forcing his pudgy torso into an unnatural arc. An old Guns N' Roses song popped into Dawdy's mind. Slotten was tied up all right, but he wasn't pretty.

"Comfortable?" Mistress Sasha asked, at last breaking the silence.

Ah, discipline time!

"Yes," was the muffled reply.

"But you don't deserve to be comfortable, do you?"

"No, Mistress Sasha." The voice from behind the mask was more whine than anything else.

"What do you deserve?"

"Punishment. I deserve to be punished."

"Say it again! Louder!"

"Punishment. I deserve to be punished."

"And why is that?"

"Because I am nothing but worthless scum."

"You are scum, and for that you *will* be punished."

Their exchange sounded like poorly written dialogue from a bad porn movie, but Dawdy was mesmerized by what was unfolding before him. He was used to being in control in any situation, and it was fascinating to watch Mistress Sasha at work, totally in command of her chubby, pathetic client. She was not a kindred spirit—she was far too amateurish for that—but Dawdy wondered what it would be like if they formed a partnership, where he would Select a victim and conduct the Education. Together they could perform the Elimination in Mistress Sasha's Dungeon. But of course, that could never happen. Life taught him long ago that no one could be trusted. Ever.

Dawdy watched as she used a feather tickler on Slotten's genitals. Next, a leather slapper on his buttocks. She continued to insult and humiliate Slotten, but Dawdy grew tired of their verbal exchange and tuned it out. He was zeroed in solely on the physical interaction.

Mistress Sasha put down the slapper and tore into Slotten with a leather flogger. Dawdy had come across some of these items for sale online, even on Amazon.

Slotten must have said something that upset Mistress Sasha, or maybe she was just playing her role, because she pulled the leather hood halfway up his face and inserted a muzzle gag into his mouth. She pulled the hood down again.

Dawdy heard the opening notes of *Bolero* and guessed the mood was about to change. Other than light genital tickling, there had been no hint of anything overtly sexual, at least not in a physical sense. Slotten might be getting off in his head, but his body wasn't responding in that manner. Mistress Sasha picked up a butt plug from the toy table.

As the music rose in intensity, the butt plug was inserted, nipple clamps were put in place, and her various tools focused more and more on Slotten's penis that was no longer flaccid. Slotten twisted faster at the end of the cable as Mistress Sasha pushed on his feet each time they came around again. She flogged, she paddled, she tickled, she pinched, as Slotten rotated in the air, against the constant, rhythmic beat of the music. Mistress Sasha's back was to Dawdy, and she seemed consumed by her duties.

Halfway through *Bolero*, Dawdy pulled his Sig from its holster and reached to press the button in the upper corner of the armoire. The doors sprung open.

Dawdy saw Robert Slotten's eyes widen in confusion and terror as he crept closer. Whether Mistress Sasha was aware of him in the split second before his Sig smashed against her skull, Dawdy would never know. She crumpled to the floor, leather flogger still in her right hand.

By the time *Bolero* ended, Mistress Sasha's hands were cuffed behind her and a muzzle gag filled her mouth. Slotten made frantic, high-pitched noises muffled by his own muzzle gag. He strained against his bindings, but Dawdy had stopped him from turning at the end of the cable. Slotten could see everything that Dawdy was doing.

Dawdy pointed the remote at the hoist and lowered Slotten to the bed. He took the metal ring off the hook, which might have given Slotten a glimmer of hope that his ordeal might finally be over. Dawdy couldn't tell by the guttural sound that replaced the whining.

"Are you trying to say 'more'?" Dawdy asked. "I can give you more."

Mistress Sasha was still out, and she was dead weight as Dawdy wrestled her onto the bed next to Slotten. With an extra piece of rope he lashed them together by their feet. He ran the cable with the carabiners under that rope, clipped both ends to the metal ring, and secured the ring on the brass hook. He took his iPhone from the armoire and angled it to get a much closer shot. A press of a button and Slotten and Mistress Sasha rose together from the bed.

Dawdy had a "contract" and a money pouch to retrieve from a drawer upstairs and a GPS to remove from Mistress Sasha's car. He also had a bit of housekeeping to do, to erase all physical traces of his visit on the main floor after doing the same in the Dungeon. Contrary to folklore, Dawdy knew that being suspended upside-down did not result in a rapid death—it can take hours. He had to be finished before morning, so when he returned to the Dungeon he would speed up the process. But not too quickly, and with the proper amount of pain, of course. He just hoped that Mistress Sasha had regained consciousness by then.

He would love to see the look in her eyes.

24

E d Potter listened to the soft, rhythmic breathing that was the only sound in the darkness. He eased out of bed, hoping she wouldn't stir. He had been in her bungalow, her bedroom, enough times that he could navigate around her furniture with his eyes closed.

He pulled on the pants he left on the floor, then felt around and found his cigarettes and lighter on her dresser. He passed down the hallway, through the living room and out the sliding glass doors to the small, rear patio where he sat in a sling chair and lit a cigarette.

He had been his own boss for decades and could set his workdays and hours as he wished, but he remained traditional with a Monday to Friday, nine-to-five schedule. Still, he never lost that feeling of working for the weekend: Friday nights were the pinnacle; Monday mornings were the pits. When a Friday night included sex, it was a good week.

He never wasted much time analyzing their relationship—it wasn't there, and then one day it just was. Not that there was much to it. He had no one else in his life, so he welcomed the occasional intimacy despite the baggage that came with it. A lot of baggage.

She swung both ways, a trait that intrigued him as it would many men, but she leaned so far in one of those ways that her elbow nearly touched the ground. She hid her bisexuality from her female lovers. Or maybe she just hid him. Either way, he didn't care.

The most important person in his life right now was Winston Dawdy, a thought that was both absurd and perfectly reasonable to him. The mysterious writer was ever present in his mind. He didn't know if Dawdy would actually finish his book. Even if he did, would Potter ever hear from him again? But something about Dawdy's chapters, his correspondence, and their brief phone conversation told him a cosmic alignment was at work. His path and Dawdy's path were not only going to converge, they were meant to converge. He was certain of that, but not certain why. Winston Dawdy was such a departure from convention that Potter knew he had already lost the upper hand that agents maintain over new clients. Dawdy was the one setting the terms, he was already in control. But if Dawdy came through, if he finished the book and it was as good as the chapters he already sent, Potter could be on top of the publishing world again, and this time it wouldn't be followed by a rapid fall to the bottom.

He picked at a scab on his chin, the remnant of an errant pass with his safety razor the day before. He wondered where Dawdy was at that hour on a Friday night. He could be anywhere, as Dawdy provided no contact information and Potter's web searches yielded nothing. Dawdy said his book was almost finished and that it was practically writing itself. Maybe he was doing last-minute research. Maybe he was even writing the final chapter. Potter could only wait and hope.

He was about to light another cigarette when he heard the sliding glass door open. He turned to see her standing in the doorway, wearing nothing but a smile.

"Hey, is that little blue pill still working?" she asked. "I could go another round."

Potter let out a sound that was half sigh, half groan.

"C'mon, Sam. At my age, even Viagra has its limits."

25

Alita's sleep was fitful as the thin walls of Victoria's apartment did little to mute the laughter and loud voices in the interior hallway, or the clomp-clomp of people climbing or descending the stairs right outside her door. Perhaps a party was going on, or maybe it was just a typical Friday night in the building. Eventually the pedestrian traffic and clamor died down.

In the wee hours she thought she heard someone turning her doorknob. She held her breath and stayed still, straining to hear anything that might suggest an intruder was about to break into the apartment. The security chain gave no comfort as a strong shove would pull the screws from the door frame. The seconds stretched into minutes with no further sounds and she drifted off to sleep again.

Just before six a.m. she was startled by the pounding on a door down the hallway. She couldn't go back to sleep so she grabbed her phone and texted Meg her plans for the day—scrubbing the apartment, more shopping for essentials, and compiling questions to prepare for her meeting with Detective Blate on Monday. She didn't want to worry Meg, but she did end her text by saying someone might have jiggled her doorknob overnight.

Victoria's housekeeping efforts had always been sporadic—she kept a tidy house when she was off drugs, but when she was using she didn't care about herself or her surroundings. The apartment also needed a thorough scrub just by being vacant for weeks. Alita found cleaning supplies in the cabinet under the sink and went about her tasks the next several hours while listening to classic rock streaming from her iPhone.

The pest service did a good job of zapping the roaches but a few dead comrades were left behind—and they were the small, swarming kind that she hated. She picked up the disgusting bugs with tissues and tossed them in the trash. She was in the bathroom wiping down the mirror when she heard a knock on the door.

Alita looked through the peephole and was shocked to see who was standing there. She unlocked the safety chain and opened the door.

"Luke!"

"Hey, Alita."

"How in the world did you find me here?" she asked.

"Meg gave me the address. She said you could use a little help. I would have been here sooner but I had to make a few calls first."

"It's good to see you, but … help? I don't know why she told you that. I don't need any help."

"Meg said you'd say that. And this is coming from her, not me. You don't have any choice."

"Choice about what?"

"May I?"

"Oh, I'm sorry. Come in, come in."

Alita stepped back so Luke could enter, but he stopped to look at the door frame and both sides of the door, tapping on it.

"What are you doing?" she asked.

"Just checking."

"For?"

"Meg said you're going to be staying here whenever you're in Nashville, so she's getting you a new doorknob and lock, plus a deadbolt."

A woman walked toward them in the interior hallway so Alita closed the door behind them.

"I don't know what Meg is thinking," she said. "This is a rental apartment. I can't change locks or put in a deadbolt."

"Jamila is aware we're changing the locks and she's perfectly fine with it." Luke gave her a grin that showed he knew much more than she did about what was happening.

"Okay, how do you know Jamila? And how does she know about the locks?"

"I called the office and spoke with a nice young woman named Yolanda. She said she couldn't approve this and she wouldn't give me Jamila's cell number until I mentioned your name. And maybe promising her and Jamila a couple of tickets to the Opry helped a little, too."

"I can't believe you did that."

"Actually, she gave me the number as soon as I said it was your apartment. I threw in the Opry tickets as a little bonus. I called Jamila and told her about your uneasiness. Or Meg's uneasiness, if that makes you feel better. Her maintenance man doesn't work weekends unless it's an emergency, so she gave me the okay to change locks and do whatever was needed to make you more secure. I'm not handy, so I called a local locksmith guy I know who also happens to be a songwriter. He'll be here within the hour. But again, Meg set all of this in motion for you so don't blame me."

"All I said to her was that I thought I heard someone messing with my doorknob last night. I don't know, maybe I just imagined it. But I didn't mean for her to go overboard, to call you and do all this."

"She was worried that Victoria might have given keys to other people."

"I thought about that, too, which is a bit scary. I know it's a good idea to change the lock. But still."

Alita watched Luke's eyes scan the small apartment with its few pieces of battered, scarred, and once or twice discarded furnishings now covered with sheets.

"You know, you don't have to stay here when you come to Nashville," he said. "I could call some people who have—"

"Thanks, Luke, but no. It might sound strange, but I'll feel closer to Victoria if I stay in her apartment. That will keep my focus on why I'm here."

Luke nodded. "I understand. But if you ever change your mind, just call me."

Alita poured two cups of coffee and offered Luke a donut. He held up his hands in protest.

"Not for me. If I eat one, those miles I ran this morning would have been for nothing."

She couldn't bring herself to ask him to sit on fabric furniture that came from the dumpster, so she moved the single dinette chair to the living room. She sat on the couch, and they made small talk until they heard a knock on the door.

"That must be him." Luke went to the door and opened it to a chubby, bald man. "Hey, Andy. Thanks for coming on short notice."

"Anything for you, Luke." The locksmith paused to inspect the door frame and door, just as Luke had done.

"Andy, this is my friend, Alita. This is her apartment."

"Hi, Andy," she said.

"Pleased to meet you, ma'am. Do y'all have any preference for what kind of lock you want?"

Alita turned to Luke. "It should match the finish of what's here now, don't you think? Beyond that, I don't really know."

"Andy, give her something secure so she won't have to worry about anything. Whatever it takes. And stay with the polished brass."

"Sure, Luke."

They watched as Andy installed a new doorknob and deadbolt, both locks bump proof with re-key technology. While he worked, Andy talked nonstop about recent songs he had written, and his dream of still making it in the music business despite being just a year away from the senior discount at Denny's. When he finished, he gave Alita three keys and instructions for both locks. She handed one of the keys to Luke for safekeeping.

"How much do I owe you, Andy?" Alita asked.

"Ah, don't worry about it. I had extra locks on my truck and I wasn't doing anything this morning anyway."

"I can't let you do that."

"Tell you what. If Luke will listen to my latest songs, we'll call it all square." Andy hurriedly fished a USB flash drive from his pocket.

"Uh, sure," Luke said. "How many songs are on it?"

"Not many. Maybe twenty or so." Andy handed him the flash drive. "Be sure to let me know what you think."

"The first chance I get," Luke said.

He walked Andy to the door, and Alita saw him press several bills in the locksmith's hand. "Just a little something for coming out on short notice," she heard him say.

When Andy's footsteps faded on the stairs, Alita turned to Luke.

"Wow. He started at 'free' and ended up with you listening to twenty of his songs. I wish he would have taken my money instead of imposing on you like that."

"Don't worry about it. Occupational hazard, happens to me all the time. And who knows, maybe I'll find a diamond in the rough."

"You think?"

"No. I've heard his songs before."

Alita laughed. "Will you at least let me reimburse your tip? I saw that."

"It's no big deal." Luke looked at his watch. "Hey, it's almost lunchtime. You want to go get a bite to eat?"

"On one condition. You let me buy."

"You don't give up, do you?"

Alita felt a sense of security when she closed the apartment door and locked the new deadbolt. For good measure she checked the door-knob lock and pushed against the door. It didn't move in its frame.

"Better?" Luke asked.

"Much."

They walked out of the building into the sunshine. Alita paused when she saw the silver metallic Porsche 911 parked next to her Miata.

"Wow. Yours?" she asked.

"Yeah."

"Carrera 4 GTS Cabriolet. Sweet."

"Impressive. You know your cars."

"I know some cars. Yours is on my list of dream machines. What year?"

"2014. Have you ever ridden in one?"

"No."

"Always a first time."

Luke opened the passenger door and Alita eased in. When he was behind the steering wheel she leaned back against the seat. "Ahhh," she exhaled. "Nice."

"It is, but it's not really practical around town with all the crazy drivers. I take my SUV most of the time but it's in the shop right now. A tourist was stargazing and rear-ended me on Music Row a couple of weeks ago."

"Why would someone try to look at stars with all the lights in the city? He should've driven out in the country for that."

Luke laughed. "It happened in the middle of the day. He was cruising up and down the Row thinking he might see a country music star. We call it stargazing."

"Oh, so he was looking for stars and actually ran into one."

"I'm far from being a star. I'm more like an asteroid. I just help the stars make good music."

The engine came alive and Luke pumped the accelerator several times.

Alita absorbed the luxury, the scent, and especially the sound. "Now *that* is music to my ears."

"Top down?" he asked.

"Always."

On the way to the restaurant, over the low whistle of the wind, their conversation was relaxed and came easily. Alita felt comfortable with Luke. For all of his wealth and success, he seemed to be a down to earth, genuine, nice guy.

Luke pointed out Tootsie's Orchid Lounge and told her he had some good stories about the famous watering hole.

"And that's the Ryman Auditorium," he said. "The Grand Ole Opry was there for thirty-one years. When you have time I can give you a private tour."

Alita looked at the large, brick building as they drove past. "I'm not really into country music but I would love to see the inside of that."

"Count on it."

Luke turned into the Library Garage on 6th Avenue North and parked in a reserved spot on the first level.

"Well, here we are." He pushed a button to raise the convertible top. "The place I'm taking you is just up the block. You'll love it. Best burgers in town. Also, great Buffalo Wings, chicken, beef tacos, whatever you want. If you haven't heard of Copper Branch, they're all over Canada and now they're expanding into the States. Nashville was their second U.S. location."

Alita felt a twinge of anxiety. She forgot to tell Luke she was a vegetarian.

"Uh, no, I haven't heard of them." Alita hoped for at least one vegetarian offering on the menu. Just one. Maybe she'd settle for a salad, the meal of last resort for any vegan or vegetarian dining out.

"They have a Songwriters Showcase several nights a week, so I dropped in to check out new talent. I fell in love with the food and I'm a regular now."

Alita's anxiety continued to rise until she saw the protruding round sign that read "COPPER BRANCH" in a semicircle at the top, with "PLANT-BASED POWER FOOD" at the bottom.

"Wow, that's a relief. You don't know how worried I was. I'm a vegetarian."

Luke laughed. "I know, Meg told me. All the things I mentioned are plant-based."

Alita gave Luke a soft punch to his arm as she realized he was teasing her all along. Her life turned far too serious since Victoria's murder and she welcomed a moment of light-heartedness.

Once they were seated Alita looked over the menu. She was not used to so many choices, and each one was vegan, not just vegetarian.

"I highly recommend the Copper Burger Deluxe." Luke pointed at the menu. "It comes with caramelized onions and the Copper Sauce is out of this world. You get Cape Cod kettle-cooked chips, too. You won't have to eat again until a week from Tuesday."

She dropped the menu on the table. "Sounds good. Copper Burger Deluxe it is."

"And if it's not too early for you, they carry a great New England IPA from Southern Grist Brewery located right here in town."

"I'm liking this place more and more."

While they waited for their food Luke talked about a few of the performers who graced the stage on the Copper Branch's Songwriter Showcase nights.

"There's so much talent in this town it's crazy," he said. "Every other person you run into is an aspiring songwriter, or singer, or picker."

"Like Andy."

"Yeah, like Andy. That really does happen to me all the time. But I understand it. He is just trying to get someone to listen to his songs. There is an upside for me … that's how I was able to get a locksmith to come out right away on a Saturday morning."

Alita tilted her head and smiled. "Yes, that was impressive. So how did you become a record producer, anyway? Is there a school for that?"

"We do have Belmont University here. You can get a great music business education in a number of areas, including music production. They even offer graduate degrees."

"That's where you went to school?"

"I didn't go that route. I'm Nashville born and raised, so I started writing songs as a kid. I picked up the guitar and became a fairly decent picker. I'm not much of a singer, though, so I knew early on that a record deal wasn't in my future. But I was always hanging around the music scene, and I met a lot of people who helped me along the way. I worked for BMI, a couple of record companies, a music publisher. Let's see, what else. I was an assistant engineer—running the board in a recording studio—which gave me more experience in the creative process. I learned from every record producer I ever met. My goal was to figure out what it was that made some songs a hit while others flopped."

"Wow, you're really able to do that?"

Luke laughed and shook his head. "No, that's an art no one can fully master."

"I need to ask. Your secretary—"

"Marika."

"Yes, Marika. She spoke to you in Japanese. How did that come about?"

"First, I'm not that fluent, but I can get by. When I was a senior in high school I fell in love with an exchange student from Kyoto named

Suki. I begged my parents for money so I could study Japanese, but of course they said no. I worked odd jobs and mowed grass, did everything I could to earn enough to pay for language lessons and a private tutor. I was hoping to go back with her to Japan after graduation, but at the end of the school year she essentially told me to get lost. In perfect English."

"Ouch. That began as such a sweet story!"

"With a sour ending, unfortunately. But I hired Marika a few months ago—her dad's in the auto industry here—and she has helped me brush up on my Japanese."

Their food arrived and Alita dug into her Copper Burger Deluxe. It was even more delicious than Luke described.

"How long will you be here this trip, and what are your plans?" he asked.

"I drove so I'm not tied to a return flight. I'll just see what happens. But I hate to keep asking Meg to run the shop by herself. I'll probably head back to Florida on Thursday."

"And in the meantime?"

"I'm not sure. I do have an appointment with Detective Blate on Monday morning. I've been working on a list of questions for him. Not that I expect he'll tell me anything new or helpful. But beyond meeting with him, I don't know. I'm just hoping that something will come to me."

"What time is your appointment on Monday?"

"Nine-thirty."

"You want company? If there are two of us, we'll have him outnumbered."

"Really? That would be great, if you can get away."

"I'll be in the studio working on a new project on Wednesday, but Monday is free. I'll have to run first, so I'll just meet you there."

While they were eating, several people passed their table and said hello to Luke. Alita saw other diners sneaking glances in their direction.

After a decadent dessert of Copper Branch's non-dairy New York Cheezecake, they headed back to the Library Parking Garage.

Alita was about to open the passenger door when Luke said, "Wrong side."

She looked up to see him holding out his key.

"You're driving."

"You can't be serious," she said.

Luke shrugged. "Hey, I already have one car in the shop. Why not two?"

"But I can't … I shouldn't … I … give me the key."

Alita rushed around the front of the car and snatched the key from Luke's hand. He was still laughing as she slid behind the wheel and inserted it into the ignition.

"Hey, I'm doubly impressed now," he said. "Most people wouldn't know the ignition is on the left side of the steering wheel. I thought I was going to have a little fun watching you try to find it."

"Not a chance. But do you know why it's on the left?" she asked.

"Uh-oh. No, I don't. Something tells me that you know."

It was Alita's turn to laugh. "Way back in the early days of racing, the 24 Hours of Le Mans, the drivers used to have to line up and run to their cars. The Porsche car builders found that by putting the ignition on the left, drivers could use their right hand to get into first gear as they're starting the engine. That second or two they saved could make a difference in the race."

"Mind blown. How in the world did you know that?"

"I told you I've never ridden in one, but I've sat in several, at dealerships. Just dreaming. A salesman explained to me why the ignition was on the left. I thought he was making it up, but I later googled it and he was right."

"I don't know if I can ever start my car again without thinking of that."

Just as Luke finished his sentence the engine again roared to life.

"Promise me one thing," she said, trying to make her face look serious.

"Sure. What?"

"Warn me if you see any stargazers."

26

The Carrera 4 GTS Cabriolet was everything Alita thought it would be, and more. With so much horsepower at her fingertips she kept an eye on the speedometer to keep from going ten miles per hour over the limit. Or twenty. Despite falling in love with Luke's car, she turned down his offer to tackle the hills and curves outside Nashville. She was comfortable behind the wheel, but not *that* comfortable. Besides, she was on a mission, not a vacation.

Alita drove through the Hunting Creek Apartments parking lot and slowed to a crawl for the speed bumps. Several people—residents or visitors, Alita didn't know—stared as they went by.

She parked and turned off the engine. With a contented sigh, she leaned back against the seat and gripped the steering wheel with both hands a final time.

"That was amazing," she said.

"You drove her like a pro."

Alita put her hand on Luke's forearm. "Thank you. For taking care of the locksmith, for letting me drive your car, for lunch, and—"

"You bought lunch, so like Andy says, we're all square." Luke grinned. "I'll see you on Monday?"

"Nine-thirty, meet you there. Blate won't know what hit him."

Alita waved as she watched Luke drive away. She also noticed the handful of people in and around the parking lot were still watching her.

There were no good hiding places in Victoria's small apartment, so Alita stowed her laptop beneath the mattress whenever she didn't take it with her. The new locks gave her peace of mind, as the only other people who would have keys to the apartment were Luke and Jamila.

Alita set her laptop on the dinette table and powered it on. She was careful not to put extra weight on the corner with the missing leg to avoid the table toppling over. She clicked on the Wi-Fi icon and entered the network name—"Office" and password—"Titans" that Jamila gave her. *Using your city's NFL team nickname as a password is not a good idea,* she thought.

She searched the web for anything that might be the first clue to finding Victoria's killer. She typed in scores of words and phrases that included everything she could think of about the murder—Victoria's profession, the setting, the burning of the body, the posing, the roses, the upside-down cross. She googled escort services—starting with Satin Dolls—and was shocked at how easily sex could be bought and sold with a few keystrokes. She jotted down notes and questions for her meeting with Detective Blate. The roses that were found in Victoria's hands—did Blate know if they were taken from a grave in the cemetery, or could they have been purchased at a Nashville florist, something Blate could trace to a credit card and a murderer?

Blate told Alita that Victoria's cell phone was never found. What Alita didn't tell Blate was that she reached out to Victoria's carrier to keep the service active. She hadn't called her sister's number, worried it might affect the investigation in some way—but now she couldn't think of one. *To hell with Blate.* She reached for her phone.

The call went straight to voicemail. Alita thought she had cried so many tears over Victoria's death that the well was dry, but at the sound of her sister's voice on the recording she broke down in heavy sobs.

With her eyes still stinging, she thought of another call she wanted to make. Another item on her to-do list to check off. She didn't know where it would lead, if anywhere. Blate tried and didn't get much.

He was a cop, but she was Victoria's sister. Maybe that would make a difference.

She punched in the number.

"Satin Dolls," a female voice purred. "How may we please you?"

"Hello, I'm calling about Victoria LaRue. I'd like to speak with—"

The call dropped.

"Okay … that's not very pleasing." Alita hit redial.

"Satin Dolls, how may—"

"Please don't hang up. My name is Alita King. Victoria LaRue was my sister. I'm in Nashville and I'd really like to talk with—"

The call dropped again.

Alita's finger hovered over the redial button as she debated whether to try one more time. Satin Dolls didn't have a physical address, so the only way she could ever reach them was by phone. She had nothing to lose.

She tapped the redial button. A single ring and she heard a recorded message that the subscriber's mailbox was not set up yet. Satin Dolls had blocked her number.

By early evening she still wasn't hungry, thanks to the Copper Burger Deluxe and dessert she ate for lunch. She was headed to the refrigerator for a soda when she heard a light knocking on the apartment door. She looked through the peephole and saw a scrawny, scruffy man, maybe late twenties, rocking side to side. She slid the safety chain in place before unlocking the deadbolt and the doorknob, keeping a narrow space between the door and the frame.

"Yes?"

"I'm Bobby. You just moved here, didn't you?" His voice was high-pitched and childlike, and his open mouth held few teeth. Those that remained were broken and carious.

"What do you want?"

"You sure are pretty."

"Uh, Bobby, I'm kind of busy right now, so maybe another time, okay?"

"Okay!" His large grin again showed the multiple gaps in his teeth. "I'll be back."

Alita closed the door and listened to the sound of his footsteps going down the interior hallway. She left the safety chain in place and relocked the deadbolt and doorknob.

Twenty minutes later Alita heard the same light knocking on her door. Through the peephole she again saw Bobby standing there. This time she unlocked the safety chain as well and opened the door with a hand on her hip.

"I'm back, like I said I'd be!" He sounded proud of himself.

"Yes, you are." She stood rigid and folded her arms in front of her, but doubted he would pick up on her body language. "Bobby, I have work to do. Please don't come back tonight, okay?"

"Okay!" With that, he wheeled around and was off again.

Alita closed the door. The poor guy clearly had mental challenges, and another night she might have chatted with him for a few minutes. But not tonight.

Her back was tight from the kitchen chair so she took her laptop and moved to the couch, aware that the only barrier from the grimy fabric was a bed sheet and thin coatings of Lysol and Febreze.

More web searches led nowhere and she was out of questions for Blate. Defeat was creeping in. She thought a pep talk from Meg would help.

"Hey, stranger," Meg answered.

"I didn't know if I would catch you. Am I interrupting anything?"

"No, I just pulled into Publix."

"I'll let you go then, but call me when you get home."

"Now is good. I haven't gone into the store yet. How's it going?"

"I meant to call you earlier to thank you for getting the locks changed, but I knew you might be busy at the shop."

"I was worried about you after what you said. So how much was it? I'm paying you back."

"It was free."

"What?"

"Yeah. Luke knew a locksmith who's also a songwriter. The locks and installation were free. He just asked Luke to listen to his songs in return."

"Luke really is a big wheel up there, isn't he?"

"Yeah, Meg. It seems like everyone in town knows him. Oh, and he let me drive his Porsche today. What a fantastic car. He's even going with me to see Blate on Monday. He wants to be my wingman."

"It sounds like he is interested in you," Meg said in a singsong voice.

"No, it's not that way between us. He just wants to help because he feels a connection to Victoria. Finding her that way was really hard on him."

"Alita, he's a nice guy, great-looking, and seems to be rather wealthy. Just sayin'."

She heard a knock on the door—*Bobby again*—and welcomed a reason to end the call. A fine line divides encouragement from meddling, and Meg was close to crossing it.

"Someone's at the door, Meg, I need to go. Love you."

"Love you back."

Alita put down her phone and headed to the door muttering about Bobby. The knock repeated, louder this time. She pulled open the door.

"I told you—"

It wasn't Bobby. Before her stood a red-haired, ruddy-faced man well over six feet tall, with a bull neck, arms like tree trunks, and a body sculpted like it rarely left the gym. Alita couldn't believe she had been so careless, so stupid to open the door without checking the peephole first.

"Yes?" She hoped that someone, anyone, would come down the hallway.

She saw his eyes track her body to her feet then up to her face again, where his gaze fixed.

"That your Miata out there? With the Florida tag?" he asked.

"Why?"

"Your right rear tire looks low. Might want to add some air."

"I'll do that." Alita tried to close the door but he blocked it with his foot. She was seconds from yelling for help.

"How much do those little things go for, anyway?"

"I don't think you'd fit in one. Now please, I have something on the stove."

The large man pulled his foot back.

"I'm Big Red, by the way. I didn't get your name."

Heart racing, Alita closed the door, locked the doorknob and deadbolt, and slid the safety chain into place. She didn't hear any footsteps on the stairs, but when she looked in the peephole he was gone.

27

Winston Dawdy swept Mistress Sasha's house for electronic bugs, detached the GPS from her car, took the money pouch and the contract he signed from the kitchen drawer, and erased all traces of his visit upstairs and down. He wore a hairnet, shoe coverings, and gloves as he worked so he would not to leave any new evidence behind.

When he went to the Dungeon for the final time he opened the camera app on his iPhone and tapped record. With his other hand he checked Robert Slotten for a pulse. Slotten was dead, literally bound for his eternal destination. Being harnessed and suspended upside-down for several hours, combined with obesity and sheer terror, likely led to a fatal heart attack or cerebral hemorrhage. Not the happy ending that Slotten was hoping for that evening.

Mistress Sasha, however, was still very much among the living. She was turned away from Dawdy and he watched as she struggled against her bindings. It was futile, like a blue marlin after a five-hour battle, beyond exhaustion but still fighting rod, reel, and hook to the inevitable end.

He stepped around so he could see her eyes behind the black hood he placed over her head earlier, and more importantly, so she could see him. He kept the iPhone camera trained on her. The whites of her eyes were marked by red splotches and striations from broken capillaries, but instead of fear Dawdy saw rage. He would have been satisfied with either emotion.

Mistress Sasha was trying to speak, but the sound was muffled by the muzzle gag in her mouth. He thought about removing it just to hear her last words, but he needed to jockey cars before daylight and the clock was ticking. Time to hurry things along.

He propped his iPhone on the table of toys so it had Mistress Sasha in frame. He took a length of rope from the table and looped it twice around her neck. She seemed to surrender at that point as she stopped thrashing and her body sagged at the end of the cable. The rage left her eyes as she blinked several times, then kept them closed.

Dawdy leaned close to speak quietly in her ear.

"You should have had your own safe word, Pamela. Sweet dreams."

He jerked the rope and held it taut for several minutes.

Dawdy found Robert Slotten's keys in one of his pants pockets. He removed the license plate from the rear of Slotten's car and replaced it with a plate he had stolen two days earlier. He drove Slotten's car to the Indianapolis International Airport and parked in the long-term Economy Lot. With the different license plate, it could be weeks or even months before the car was discovered.

He rode a shuttle to the Transportation Center. From there he took a taxi to the Hardee's just off W. 25th Street. The restaurant stayed open all night on Fridays and Saturdays, so the destination was not unusual at that hour. He declined small talk with the cab driver and paid the fare in cash.

He walked less than a mile from the Hardee's to Mistress Sasha's house. With his head tilted downward, the darkness and the scally cap set low on his brow would ensure that any security cameras along the way would not catch a good view of him.

An hour before dawn he backed out of Mistress Sasha's garage. He closed the overhead door with her remote.

He dropped off his rental car at the airport and took a shuttle back to the Economy Lot. He exited the shuttle two rows from where his own car was parked and waited until the shuttle moved on. In the unlikely event anyone took notice of him, he would look like any other weary traveler, suitcase in hand and about to head home.

Dawdy hadn't slept in over twenty-four hours, but he made the two-hundred-mile drive home to Johnstown without stopping for rest or refreshments. The Selection, Education, and Elimination of Mistress Sasha unfolded flawlessly from beginning to end, just like the *SEE* process for all of his victims. Robert Slotten was a bonus, and Dawdy enjoyed their brief time together. He planned to download the Boston Symphony's *Bolero* track once he was home, and it would trigger a warm memory whenever he heard it again.

As he clicked off the miles he outlined the latest chapters of *Stay Downwind* in his mind. When he told Ed Potter his book was practically writing itself he meant it. *If Potter only knew.* Dawdy was going to give himself a well-earned, rare night off. He would rise early on Sunday morning and spend the day at his keyboard. He would write the Mistress Sasha chapters over two days, devote another day to editing them, then send his latest work to Potter via his remailing service in Florida. Not only did he want to keep Potter intrigued, which was not a real challenge, but in a world full of potential victims another *SEE* was always on the horizon.

He lost an hour changing time zones and it was one o'clock in the afternoon when he turned into the long, winding lane that led to his country estate set well back in the woods. His home for the past five years, he picked the property for its location, its variety of mature trees, its half-acre pond, but most of all, its privacy. As much as he wanted to know everything about everyone around him, he wanted no one to know anything about him.

Dawdy opened an app on his iPhone and turned off the array of security cameras that blanketed the interior and exterior of his home, including cameras located throughout the woods and overlooking his pond. He would turn them on again later, but he didn't want even his own cameras to record the clothing he would toss on the bonfire he would soon build, or the suitcase he would carry into the house.

Dawdy changed clothes and went back to the garage to get a big scoop of fish pellets. His pond was stocked with largemouth bass, catfish, and sunfish, plus a few grass carp to control vegetation growth, and he enjoyed feeding them daily when he was home. Standing at the edge of his pond, he slapped his hand against the side of his leg three times and watched the surface of the water ripple as scores of fish swam to him. The two largest bass were named Bonnie and Clyde.

His travels prohibited him from keeping a traditional pet. Two years back, he paid twenty-five thousand dollars for a female Bengal cat, an exotic domestic breed that looked like a miniature leopard. He named her Tana. He boarded her once when he was gone for six weeks to carry out a Selection, Education, and Elimination, but later realized that the boarding records could be used to prove he wasn't home if he ever came under suspicion. That was unlikely to happen, but he couldn't take the chance—nor could he bear to never see his beloved pet again. Tana was now stuffed and on permanent display in his great room.

Dawdy lit a bonfire at sunset. He sat in an Adirondack chair sipping a cold beer as he watched the flames dance and grow in height and intensity. He tossed the shirt, pants, and scally cap he wore in Speedway into the fire along with his hairnet, shoe coverings, and gloves. He added Mistress Sasha's garage door opener and the empty banker's pouch. The last item was the contract he had signed. He laughed as he scanned the terms again by the firelight. If he were one to keep souvenirs the contract would have held a place of honor in his collection, but souvenirs were far too risky. He dropped it into the bonfire.

He would always have one memory, the video recordings he made with his iPhone. His phone was set to never upload photos or videos to the cloud, so he Airdropped the video files to a 256-bit AES encrypted disk image on his Mac that would forever be for his eyes only.

He sat by the fire as it burned down to ashes. One more beer and he would head back to the house to watch his latest movie before bedtime.

28

L uke was waiting under the Metro Police Headquarters portico when Alita arrived. She parked two spots down from his
Porsche and trudged toward him.

"Ready for battle?" Luke made a fist and extended his arm.

Alita gave him a fist bump that lacked conviction. "I don't know
what I'm ready for."

"Is everything okay?"

"It's a Monday, I'm tired, and I just … I'm okay. I'm fine."

"No, you're not. Tell me. I know something's wrong."

Alita stopped and turned to Luke. "I had a visitor on Saturday
night who rattled me a little bit. Actually, a lot. Then I spent all day
yesterday on my laptop which was totally unproductive and wiped
me out. And now I have to face Blate and I'm just not ready for it."

"What happened Saturday night? Who was the visitor?"

"A huge guy. Creeped me out. Called himself Big Red."

"What did he want?"

"I don't really know. He came to my door to tell me one of my
tires needed air. But I checked yesterday morning and all four of them
were fine."

"Have you seen him before?"

"No."

"How did he know which car was yours?"

Alita shrugged. "I don't know that, either. Maybe he lives in one
of the apartments and saw me."

"Or maybe not. I think you need to mention this to Blate."

Alita checked her watch. "We better go inside."

Detective Blate was twenty minutes late for their nine-thirty appointment. When he walked up to them, he looked at Alita. "Is there a reason he's here?"

"A pleasure to see you again, too, Detective," Luke said.

Blate scowled and motioned them to follow him. He led them down the same corridor to the same small room as Alita's first visit. They sat down and he closed the door.

"Okay, I'm all yours," Blate said.

"Standard question," Alita began. "Is there anything new?"

Blate shook his head. "Nothing, same as the last time we talked on the phone, and the time before that, and the time before that. You know, I'll take all your calls and I'm willing to meet you in person like this, it's part of my job, but it seems so pointless when not one single thing has changed."

"That is precisely the point, Detective. Nothing has changed. Nothing."

"Miss King, we've been down this road more times than I care to count. No witnesses. No evidence at the scene. Nothing in your sis- ... Victoria's apartment that gave us any direction to go. Unless we get a lucky break, a tip from someone who knows something, or a piece of evidence just falls out of the sky, there isn't anything else we can do."

"Have you thought about offering a reward for information?" she asked. "That could bring tips in."

"The department won't be doing it, but there is Crime Solvers."

"How much of a reward?" Alita hadn't researched Crime Solvers but that was now on her to-do list.

"Up to a thousand dollars unless they've changed the amount recently. But it doesn't have to be set up, it's in effect now. If someone has information about Victoria's murder, or any crime for that matter, they can contact Crime Solvers. Anonymously, if they want. If the tip leads to an arrest, they could be eligible for a reward."

"But you haven't released anything to the public. Someone might have seen something, but they might not even know a murder took place in the cemetery that night. You need to put the word out there."

"Now is not the time," Blate said. "That's not how a homicide investigation works. Maybe down the road."

Alita knew that road was blocked, and there would never be a time. Not only was Victoria's life not worth a penny to them, the police didn't want any information about her murder being released to the public. She looked at her list of questions.

"The roses they found. Did you check florists, or grocery stores with floral departments, to see if anyone remembered anyone unusual buying roses?"

Blate grimaced and rubbed the bridge of his nose with a thumb and forefinger, clearly bothered by Alita's questions or maybe just her presence. "We can't check with every clerk in every flower shop and grocery in Nashville to see if any of them remember something about a routine sale that took place weeks ago. And that's assuming the roses were even bought locally. You can't be serious about that."

Alita felt deflated. *Maybe it was a stupid question.*

"Okay, I should have asked before … you said the Lyft driver dropped her off at the cemetery. Where did he pick her up?"

"Hunting Creek Apartments," Blate said. "Right outside her unit."

"Any stops along the way?"

"No. From her place directly to the cemetery."

"Did they talk? Did she say anything to him about why she was going to the cemetery that late at night?"

Blate shook his head. "He remembered her, of course, because it was an unusual destination. But she didn't say and he didn't ask. He said he doesn't get into people's business."

"Did you check to see where her cell phone pinged?" Luke asked.

Blate scowled again at him. "I have already told Miss King that Victoria's cell phone last pinged off a tower consistent with the Mount Olivet Cemetery location, and also appropriately along the way. I'm not going to repeat any information to you that I've already told her, so maybe you ought to just sit there and listen, and catch up from her later."

Alita saw Luke's jaw clench. She placed her hand on his arm, hoping he wouldn't respond to Blate. He gave her a slight nod.

"I should tell you that I'm paying to keep her cell phone service active," she said.

"I knew that, and that's your choice, but there's been no activity on her phone since that night … other than your call. I think her killer took it and it's in a thousand pieces by now. We did obtain her cell phone records and went through her calls and texts. Nothing jumped out."

Alita paused to again refer to her list of questions. She wanted to get Blate out of his comfort zone, hoping he might slip and reveal something he shouldn't like he did their last time together. But not only was he rock steady today, perhaps the well of information was dry.

"So, anything else?" Blate asked.

"Yes. You know the business cards and slips of paper with names and numbers? I took them back to Florida but I didn't bring them with me this trip. You made photocopies. Would you mind making a copy for me?"

"I can't. It's evidence."

"But the first time I was here you said it wasn't evidence, that's why you just copied them."

"I changed my mind."

"Come on, Blate," Luke said. "You don't have to be such a jack-ass. All she wants is—"

"Luke, it's okay." Alita again put her hand on his arm. "Just let me talk." She looked back at Blate. "Forget the copies, I have the originals when I get home. But the upside-down cross that was between her legs. You said before that you thought the cross meant something to the killer. Victoria once told me that several local ministers used her services. Did you check the names to see if any of them were ministers or preachers?"

"Yes, we did. No known ministers or preachers, at least not with a brick-and-mortar church and a flock of followers. Could it be a mail order holy roller who has a small cult that meets in his basement? Yeah, but we have no way of knowing. And as I told you before, we can't track down every one of those names."

Luke turned to Alita. "Tell him about the guy on Saturday."

Alita nodded. "I'm staying in Victoria's apartment and—"

"You're what?" Blate asked. "Why there?"

"I'm not going to rest until Victoria's killer has been caught, so I'm renting her apartment for when I come up from Florida."

Blate crumpled in his chair. He interlaced his fingers behind his head, looking as if a debilitating migraine just struck him.

"Okay," he said over a sigh. "Again, it's your money. But what's this about a guy on Saturday?"

"He knocked on my door and told me one of the tires on my Miata needed air, but I checked the next morning and they were all fine."

"And?" Blate's eyebrows raised.

"Well, that's it, but he just seemed ... weird."

"Did he threaten you in any way?"

"No."

"Touch you at all?"

"No."

"Did you let him in the apartment?"

"Of course not."

"And he left? He walked away?"

"Yes."

Blate shrugged and held up his palms. "Then I'm not sure what you want me to do."

"You have to admit it's odd, Detective," Luke said.

"Maybe, or perhaps he's just a helpful kind of guy. None of that is criminal behavior. Did you get a name?"

"He called himself Big Red. That's all I know."

"What did he look like?"

"Red hair, short and straight. Large man, about six-three and weighs maybe two-fifty, real muscular. Ruddy complexion, with one of those tear tattoos under his right eye. Had a hook-shaped scar on his left cheek. Diamond stud in his left ear lobe."

"How long was he there?"

"Uh, maybe a minute."

"And you got all that in a minute?"

Alita nodded. "I didn't know if he was going to attack me or not. I thought his description would be important if he did."

"That's impressive," Blate said. "If he comes back and bothers you, be sure to let me know. But right now there's nothing we can do based on what you've told me."

Alita moved on to ask more questions about Satin Dolls, the Lyft driver again, the autopsy, and the crime scene. Blate answered each question but shared no information that he hadn't already told her. There was no reason to continue.

Blate walked them to the front entry where he surprised Alita by shaking hands with both her and Luke.

"Mr. O'Connor. And Miss King, I'm sure I will be seeing you again soon."

"I don't think so, Harold." Alita didn't know if the shock on Blate's face was from her use of only his first name or her entire sentence.

Either way it didn't matter, for she was at a fork in the road and just chose her path. "But thank you for your time."

"Can you believe that guy?" Luke asked, once they were outside the building.

"Actually, I think I can."

"What do you mean?"

"Blate did check out her apartment and copy all those names. He talked to someone at Satin Dolls, he talked to the Lyft driver. He found out where her cell phone pinged that night and has followed up with the cell phone company to look into her calls and texts. He even knew I had called her number—I just wanted to hear her voice. I had doubts at first when he was withholding information from me, but I can now accept that he is actually working on her case. Problem is, like he said, there's nothing else he can do unless they get a tip or lucky break. But I'm not going to just keep waiting for something to happen."

"You have a plan?"

"Not yet. But I will."

***

Alita did a web search on her iPhone. A Staples office supply store was only a few miles away. She shifted into gear and left the Metro Police building in her rear-view mirror, along with any confidence that Detective Harold Blate would solve Victoria's murder on his own. Except for a handful of people, no one in Nashville was even aware of what took place in Mount Olivet Cemetery that night, and she needed to change that. *But how?*

Serendipity by definition cannot be planned or expected, but Alita was wishing for any sort of sign as to what her next step should be when there it was, right in front of her. A sign. She couldn't believe she hadn't thought of it before.

Yes! That's it! It worked in other cases, maybe it would work for Victoria. It was worth a try. But first, some shopping to do.

Alita loaded her cart with pens, felt tip markers, highlighters, index cards, sticky notes, pushpins, and a small bulletin board. She added scissors, tape, rubber bands, a stapler and staples, paper clips, binder clips, and several legal pads. She had brought her laptop with her from Florida but she still needed a printer. She found a Brother copier/printer/scanner that was on sale. She added a flash drive, then tossed in a second one. By the time she pushed her cart up and down every aisle in the store she had enough supplies to set up a small office. And a Murder Board. Victoria's apartment would become her remote headquarters, her own homicide investigation unit. If Detective Blate and the Metro Police Department couldn't find Victoria's killer, she would find him on her own.

Back at the apartment, she used thumbtacks to hang the bulletin board on the wall behind the dinette table, adding a few pushpins for future use. Empty kitchen cupboards became makeshift storage cabinets to organize the supplies she purchased. Following a few failed attempts and a recheck of instructions she was able to print a test page with her new Brother printer. She inserted one of the flash drives into a USB port on her laptop, reformatted it, and copied the folder named VICTORIA from her laptop's hard drive to the flash drive. She wanted a backup copy of the VICTORIA folder in case something happened to her laptop. The folder contained files of all of her research, all of the questions she asked Blate and the answers she received, except for that morning's exchange. She typed a summary of her conversation with him and copied that file to the flash drive, too.

She spent over an hour researching and reading FAQs on both the Nashville Crime Solvers website and the national website for Crime Solvers USA. She was about to close her browser window when she answered a call on her cell phone.

"Hope I'm not interrupting anything," Luke said.

"No, I was on the web learning all the details about Crime Solvers but I just finished. What's up?"

"I know your time is tight and you have a lot you want to do while you're here, but is there any chance we could get together in the morning for a couple of hours?" he asked. "From say, about ten until noon?"

"Sure. Where do you want to meet?"

"I'll drop by. I need to talk about something, but I don't have time to go into it now. So, you'll be there for sure, at ten?"

"I'll be here."

"See you then."

As Alita set down her phone she wondered what was on Luke's mind. Although there were a number of things she wanted to do while she was in Nashville, her schedule was more flexible than his. Besides, he had done so much for her already. But what would he want to discuss for two hours? And the day before he would be in the recording studio working on a new project? *It must be really important to him.*

She sat at the three-legged dinette table and returned to her laptop to act upon the serendipitous moment that struck her earlier. A Google Search yielded several possibilities and a clear choice, one that not only listed information about the entire process, it also included price ranges, a clickable map with locations and site-specific details, and a design spec sheet she could download. Excited, she called Meg.

"Have customers?" Alita asked.

"Not at the moment. Everything all right?"

"I came up with a great idea. I just checked it out online and I'm pretty sure I can make it happen."

"Okay, now I'm intrigued," Meg said. "Details."

"Blate wants to keep a lid on the investigation but I think it's time to blow that lid off. And if he's not willing, I am. I've decided to rent a billboard to ask for the public's help in solving Victoria's murder."

"Oh, like that movie a few years ago?"

"Yeah, sort of."

"That sounds like a big step, Alita. But isn't it too soon? Don't they do that as a last resort?"

"Please don't be like Blate. If not now, when? Six months? A year? If nothing turns up, I've lost all that time and she will have just been forgotten. If people see the billboard now, maybe somebody with information will come forward. I've looked all of this up online. Billboards work, Meg, and I believe the sooner the better."

"Then I believe it, too. Is it expensive?"

"I'll have to contact them to get the exact price because it depends on location, size, how long I rent it, and a few other things. But based upon the rates I found online, I can afford it. The location I want has four billboards together, two side-by-side facing one way, and behind them are two side-by-side facing the other way. I would take any of them. I used Google Earth and actually saw the signs from both directions. And get this, Meg … it's right across the road from Mount Olivet Cemetery."

"That is the perfect location! And you know I can help out with the cost."

"No, you've done plenty already. But I want that location so bad."

"By the way, have you heard from Luke?" Meg asked.

Alita found the pivot a bit odd as Meg knew that Luke was with her to meet Blate that morning. "He called me a little while ago. Why?"

"Hey, a customer just came in. Talk later. Bye."

Alita shook her head. She loved Meg, but her partner and friend had her quirky moments and that was one of them. She let it go because a more pressing matter was on her mind.

Volunteer State Outdoor Advertising was open until five o'clock. She could make it there in about twenty minutes, which should give her enough time to find out all she needed to know about billboards and hopefully reserve the location she wanted.

Just before the Fesslers Lane exit off I-40 she made a short detour that would add only a few minutes to her travel time. Fesslers Lane took her to a right turn on Lebanon Pike, and she was soon in front of Mount Olivet Cemetery. The four back-to-back billboards she saw online using Google Earth were on her left. She swung into the cemetery entrance, turned around, and looked at the other side of the billboards that were now on her right. Any of them would work.

She cut back to I-40 from Fesslers Lane and in less than fifteen minutes pulled into the Volunteer State Outdoor Advertising parking lot.

Bryn Wolda, an account executive, greeted Alita. Although Bryn's clientele was almost exclusively high-volume repeat customers, she was sympathetic when Alita told her why she wanted to rent a billboard, and patient as she walked her first-time customer through the entire process.

"Do you have a general area of the city in mind?" Bryn asked.

"Actually, I have a specific location I've already picked out. Online."

"Good. Where are you looking?"

"It's on Lebanon Pike, opposite Mount Olivet Cemetery. There are four billboards together, two facing each way."

"I know exactly where you mean. Let me check the availability."

Bryn swiveled to her computer and entered a series of keystrokes and mouse clicks.

"Ah, here we go. Lebanon Pike." She leaned closer to the screen. "I have good news and bad news. All four are currently rented—that's the bad news—but there is one that will be available November first. That's uh," Bryn looked at her calendar, "a little over three weeks from now."

"I'll take it!"

Bryn laughed. "You didn't give me time to tell you which one. It faces east, so that means it would be visible to traffic headed toward downtown. It would be on their right. There are two billboards side by side that face east. It would be the one to the left, closest to the road." Bryn continued to peer at the screen. "It's illuminated, so you have all-night visibility. And it looks like it's rated at over seventy-five thousand impressions a week. That's motorists driving by who see it."

Alita had no clue how that number was calculated, but it didn't matter. She secured a billboard in the location she wanted. "Whatever it is, I'll take it."

"Then it's yours. It's what we call a poster billboard. It's ten feet, six inches by twenty-two feet, nine inches in size. And if you're into the environment, it's printed on PosterFlex which is a recyclable material."

"I am, so that's good. Can I start with a three-month term?"

"Sure. Your term will begin the first of November. Our crew installs seven days a week so Saturday is not a problem. You pay for the rental now, that way your billboard is reserved for you. When you come for the design process you can pay for that plus the printing and installation. There are variables we won't know until you make your choices. Color printing, things like that. And if you want to extend the term we'll need at least thirty days' notice. And another payment in advance, of course. Could you come in tomorrow, say two o'clock, to meet with our graphic designer?"

"Sure."

"Okay, great. Be thinking about the message you want to convey, the general layout you want, what graphics, and so on. But don't worry, she'll help you with everything. Her name is Ruth Stile. Any questions?"

Alita already had a credit card in her hand. "No, it all sounds good."

Bryn drew up a contract which Alita signed, initialed, and dated.

When the paperwork was finished and Alita had her copy of the agreement, Bryn stood and shook her hand.

"We'll see you tomorrow at two o'clock," Bryn said. "And one more thing … I really hope this helps you find the guy who did it."

"It has to, Bryn. Right now it's the only hope I have."

29

A lita found Jamila in the office when she stopped by Tuesday morning.

"Welcome back," she said. "How was Memphis?"

"The music was hot and the barbecue was out of this world. You need to go there sometime, girl. By the way, I heard you got new locks on Saturday."

"I'm sorry Luke bothered you on your mini vacay, but thank you."

"Bother me? Shoot, I got Opry tickets out of it."

"You're a country music fan?" Alita asked.

"Hell no. But I'm going to the Opry!"

Alita laughed. "I do feel safer with the new locks." She fished the third key from her pocket. "This is for you. It fits both the deadbolt and the doorknob. I gave one to Luke, too. I'll be sure to get it back from him whenever I move out. But I did want to ask you something."

"Sure, what?" Jamila hung the key on the key rack.

"Do you know a guy named Bobby? He came to my door twice on Saturday night."

"I should have told you about Bobby. It's a sad situation. When he was a kid he was skateboarding and got hit by a car. He has brain damage, a plate in his head and everything. Mentally, he's about eight. He lives at the other end of your building with his mom. I'll have her talk to him about not coming around, but he's harmless."

"I thought so. I'm not worried about Bobby. But there was this other guy who stopped by. He calls himself Big Red. Do you know him?"

"Not by that. What's his real name?"

Alita shook her head. "He didn't say. Just Big Red. And his nick-name fits. He's a big, muscular guy with short red hair. Maybe in his thirties."

"What did he do?"

"He just said something odd about my Miata. I'm starting to think it was nothing."

"Well, he's definitely not a renter. I know all of them because they have to come to the office to sign the lease. But people have friends and relatives move in and out, and I never know about it or even see them. I'll keep my eye out for a big guy with muscles and red hair."

Alita went back to the apartment to work on the billboard design she began the night before. She sketched several drafts until she was happy with the text and general layout, but still needed to add a photo. As she scrolled through the thousands of photos on her iPhone, it hurt her to see how few of them were of Victoria. Of the ones she found, it was easy to see whether Victoria was clean or strung out on drugs when the photo was taken.

She scrolled to a photo from three years ago, when her sister was briefly off drugs and feeling happy and carefree. Victoria was on her way to the Keys and had stopped in New Smyrna Beach to spend a couple of hours with Alita. They were eating lunch at The Breakers, sitting on stools at the bar overlooking the beach and the ocean. The windows were open, and the breeze was gently caressing Victoria's hair. She looked stunning, and Alita took a photo of her. That was the one she would give to Bryn. That was how she wanted the world to see her sister.

Alita heard a knock at her door. She checked the peephole before unchaining and unlocking it.

"Good morning," Luke said. "I think I'm a bit early."

"Come on in. Can I get you a cup of coffee?"

"I'm good." He stopped by the three-legged dinette table. "You bought a new printer. Is that MacBook Air new, too?"

"It's the one I brought with me. I'm setting up my own little office here."

"I'd say. And what is this?" He stepped over to check out the bulletin board that was half-covered with pinned notes.

"Just something I'm putting together to help me keep track of things. You know, a timeline, people I've talked to. Stuff like that."

"Good plan. And these?" He pointed at the drawings on the table.

"I'm going to put up a billboard about Victoria's murder. Those are just basic layouts I came up with."

"A billboard? I think that's a great idea. Have you contacted anyone yet? I have connections."

Alita laughed. "You and your connections. I already rented one, yesterday. I'm meeting with their graphic artist today to put together the design. She wanted me to bring something to get us started."

"Oh … I didn't know you had someplace to go. What time is your appointment?"

"I made it for two o'clock. I knew you were coming here and I want to focus on you. You said between ten and noon, but if you need longer I can reschedule."

"We should have enough time. But do you mind if I take a peek at your layouts?"

"Sure. This is the one I decided to use."

She picked up the drawing from the table and handed it to Luke. He studied it for a few moments.

"I like it," he said. "People driving by, they don't have time to read too many words. They're on their cell phones, anyway. You want the message to jump out and grab them. Where will your billboard be?"

"On Lebanon Pike, across from the cemetery. It's on the right, facing traffic headed downtown."

"You will get a lot of attention there."

"That's the plan."

"What's this circle for?" Luke pointed again.

"I want to put a photo of Victoria there. Let me show you the one I want to use." Alita brought up the photo and handed her iPhone to Luke.

"Victoria was lovely," he said. "Where was this taken?"

"New Smyrna Beach. The Breakers, one of my favorite hangouts."

Luke handed the phone back to Alita. "But you're putting her photo in the middle of the billboard. I think you should move it to the left side. That way it's closest to traffic as they go by." He picked up a pencil from the table. "Do you mind?"

"No, go ahead. But shouldn't we be talking about … whatever it is you wanted to talk about?"

"That can wait." He rotated a blank sheet of paper to landscape mode. "Say this is the billboard. I'd put the photo here." He drew a circle in the upper-left corner. "I'd put her name in bold, all caps, to the right of her photo. You have it too small on your sample."

"Okay, I can see that."

"Be sure to use a strong font. And here … I would put all of that in red. And because the billboard is across the street from the cemetery, I would have a thick arrow under that line, pointing at it. That's emphasizing that it happened right over there."

"Great touch," Alita said. "I didn't think of that."

"It says you're offering a reward for information that leads to an arrest. I think you should include the amount."

"Crime Solvers is going to handle the reward process for me, but I'm putting up a ten-thousand-dollar reward on my own."

Alita heard the "beep-beep" sound of a truck backing up. Luke went to the sliding glass doors and opened the curtain.

"They're here," he said.

"Who's here?"

Alita hurried over to look for herself. A large furniture delivery truck was backed in and a man was pulling out the loading ramp.

"I don't understand," she said. "What is going on?"

"Meg, your guardian angel, wasn't going to let you stay in this apartment with furniture about to fall apart. She was appalled that you're sleeping on an air mattress on the floor. She called a company yesterday to lease a one-bedroom furniture package. They offer next day delivery, so she set it up for ten this morning. She called me and asked if I could make sure you were here when they delivered."

Meg's moment of quirkiness now made sense. "I can't believe she did this." All Alita could do was just shake her head at Meg's latest generous gesture.

They turned at the same time when the door opened.

"Knock, knock," Jamila said.

Luke shrugged at Alita. "Yeah, she knew about this, too. I called her this morning."

"You need to clear the table, Alita," Jamila said. "And empty the dresser. I'll strip the bedsheets off the mattress. Let's hop to it." She sounded like a drill sergeant barking orders. "All of Victoria's furniture needs to go to the dumpster before they bring in your new things."

Alita was so overwhelmed she didn't say anything, she just did as Jamila directed.

The deliverymen carried Victoria's recycled furniture to the dumpster—first the dinette table and single chair, then the easy chair with a broken arm, the soiled couch, the small table that once held the crystal glass butterfly she had given to Victoria, the mattress on the floor in the bedroom, and the now-empty ancient dresser.

They carried in the leased furniture—a round, glass dinette table with four chairs for the eating space; a taupe sofa with matching contemporary armchair, cocktail table, end table, and table lamp in the living room; and a queen bed and headboard with a pillow top mattress, dresser, mirror, nightstand, and table lamp for the bedroom. Jamila told the men where each piece of furniture should go. In less than two hours, the drab, depressing apartment turned into a warm, comfortable, welcoming living space.

Alita saw Luke give the men an envelope.

"No, you're not going to do that," she said. She went for her purse in the corner, on top of the stack of items that came from the old dinette table.

"It's already been taken care of." Luke shook hands with both of the men. "Thank you guys, much appreciated."

After the men left, Alita turned to Luke.

"What did you mean, it's been taken care of?" she asked.

"Meg thought of everything. She paid them extra to carry out the old furniture. She also tipped them. She asked me to give them cash and said she'll mail a check to reimburse me." Luke shrugged again. "Hey, I'm out of that loop. You'll have to take it up with her."

Meg was that one in a million friend, and Alita owed her so much. She went over to the couch and ran her fingers across the fabric. "I would have been fine with what was here, but this is just amazing. I still can't believe it."

"Meg leased everything for six months," Luke said. "That was their shortest term. It can be renewed, but hopefully you won't need to. She also said to tell you she added the damage waiver, so don't worry if you spill any wine."

Alita laughed. "That is so Meg. And so me."

"Oh, another thing. The company also rents electronics and Meg was going to get a TV for you. I told her not to because I have several TVs at home I never use. I'll drop one off."

"Thanks, but I don't need it. I'll be working whenever I'm here."

"You say that now, but you'll want some distraction. You're getting one of my TVs and we'll get streaming set up for you. I insist."

"You're as bad as Meg, you know that?"

"I'll let you two iron out those details," Jamila said. "I need to get back to the office. The apartment looks lovely, Alita. I'm really happy for you."

"Thanks so much, Jamila."

Alita moved everything she had stacked in the corner to the new dinette table. It was a relief to no longer worry about the old, creaky, three-legged one toppling over.

"You're not leaving any space to eat," Luke said. "And aren't you getting hungry?"

She looked at her watch. "I don't have time to be hungry. I need to be ready to meet with the graphic designer. I want to use all of your suggestions, so I'm going to redo this sample before I go."

"Whoa, wait a minute," Luke said. "You need to listen to the graphic designer. Don't follow any of what I told you. I was just making stuff up to buy time until the furniture got here."

"Seriously? That's funny. But I thought your ideas were great and I'm going to use them. I loved the arrow pointing at the cemetery."

"I actually did like that one, too," he said.

"Want to hang around and help me finish?" she asked. "Do you have time?"

"You have a chair for me now, so how could I refuse?"

-30-

Winston Dawdy wrote the chapters about the Selection, Education, and Elimination of Mistress Sasha and Robert Slotten in two days, just as he planned. Tuesday was set aside for a full day of editing, but the chapters were so easy to write and so clean that he finished editing before noon.

Research told him that using thin latex gloves didn't rule out the small chance of leaving latent fingerprints on receptive surfaces. The odds were remote but precaution was second nature to him. He donned disposable polymer gloves before taking the pages from his printer. He slipped them into a nine-by-twelve mailing envelope along with the cover letter he printed. He added a mailing label addressed to Potter Literary Associates in Los Angeles, California, and a return label in the upper-left corner with the same address. He closed the self-seal envelope and put it in a larger envelope along with enough cash to cover the postage and the fee his remailing service would charge. He sealed that envelope and stuck on a label addressed to Secure Remailing Services in Old Town, Florida.

Dawdy didn't grocery shop or buy gas in Johnstown. Or use the local post office. The Columbus Metro area was less than twenty minutes away, so he would drive to the city and use a different post office whenever he sent a package to his remailing service. The postal clerks never gave him a second glance.

He took less than an hour to disguise his appearance with facial prosthetics, make-up, a hairpiece, and thin driving gloves before setting out for the post office in Dublin, on the northwest edge of Columbus.

Ed Potter would soon receive more chapters of *Stay Downwind* from Winston Dawdy.

31

A lita met with graphic designer Ruth Stile at Volunteer State Outdoor Advertising at two o'clock. She told Ruth what happened to Victoria, where it happened, and the purpose of the billboard. They went over the mock-up that she and Luke created so that Ruth could get a general idea of what Alita wanted.

Alita used AirDrop to share the photo of Victoria she hoped to use. She sat across from Ruth, watching on a separate monitor in front of her.

"I know this photo is special to you," Ruth said. "The resolution's fine, so we're good there, but there's too much going on in the background to put on a billboard. I think a one-quarter headshot with a transparent background would be better."

Alita dabbled in image editing on both her laptop and her iMac at home, but not with Ruth's speed and skill. The photo of Victoria sitting at the window bar at The Breakers, with the ocean and a beach filled with people in the distance behind her, soon became a closeup image of just Victoria, cropped at mid-chest with no background.

"Wow, you're good," Alita said.

Ruth looked up with a smile. "Part of it's me, part of it's AI."

Ruth adjusted the color and resized the photo. She began the design by filling the entire billboard with a bright yellow background. She added a red rectangle that stretched across the top.

"These colors will make the message pop," Ruth said. "We can always change if you don't like the final product, but I think you'll see what I mean."

"Oh, I already like the colors. They will definitely stand out."

Ruth dropped in Victoria's photo on the left side of the billboard, with a small space above and below the photo. "I thought I might have to resize it, but that balance looks good, don't you think?"

"I do. In my first design I had the photo in the middle. My friend told me that I should move it to the left."

"Your friend gave you good advice."

Adding text came next. In the red rectangle at the top, in large white capital letters with a thin black outline: "WHO KILLED VICTORIA LARUE?"

Below that, in black letters on the yellow background, in sentence case with no period at the end: "Murdered in Mount Olivet Cemetery on August 3rd"

Although Ruth liked Luke's suggestion of having an arrow pointed toward the cemetery, it didn't work when she placed it because it looked like the arrow was just pointing at Victoria's photo.

Next: "Her killer is still at large." in black letters, with a red line underscoring.

Left of center, Ruth added in black letters: "HAVE A TIP? CALL:"

And below that, in larger red letters: "Nashville Crime Solvers"

And across the bottom: "352-357-3878"

In the lower right corner, framed top and bottom with black bars, a large red rectangle with white letters: "CASH REWARD!"

And below that: "$10,000"

Once Alita saw the final product, with the fonts and colors and all of the elements spatially arranged, the design took on a life of its own—and that was just looking at a computer screen. On a billboard, the power of that message would grow, and reach someone who knew something about Victoria's murder. At least she hoped.

Ruth printed a color copy of the layout and gave it to Alita. "The deadline for final approval of the design is ten days prior to your install date, so live with it a few days and make sure it's exactly what you want."

"I can't imagine any changes, but I'll let you know. I think you did a great job."

Alita paid the balance due for design and installation. Before she left, she had a final question.

"Am I allowed to use this layout on other things? Like flyers or whatever?"

"You can't take our design to another billboard company," Ruth said. "That's in the agreement you signed. But otherwise, you can do whatever you want with it. Once you've given final approval I can email you a digital file. Do you have an InDesign subscription?"

"Yes. Both InDesign and Photoshop."

"Great. I'll send an InDesign file so you can make any changes you want."

Another way to raise awareness about Victoria's murder was already forming in Alita's mind. That would have to wait, because she was going to do something that evening she hadn't shared with Luke, or even Meg. It was possibly dangerous and definitely against the law, but it might get her closer to answers she desperately needed.

32

Alita took I-65 South to the Thompson Lane exit and turned into the parking lot of the Walmart Supercenter on Powell Avenue. Despite her only law enforcement "training" being binge-watching true crime shows, the minute she left Detective Harold Blate's office on Monday she knew she had to seize control of the mission to find Victoria's killer. She would no longer defer to whatever course of action, or inaction, Blate thought was appropriate. But as she thought about the purchase she was about to make and what she was going to do that evening, she wondered if she was wading into water that would soon be over her head. There was only one way to find out, and it would begin with a phone call.

Alita knew what a prepaid phone was and she had heard of burner phones from movies and TV shows. When she asked the young clerk in Walmart's Connection Center to explain the difference between the two, he gave her a strange look but also the information she wanted.

She chose a Nokia phone that was under forty bucks, including tax. It was likely she would make only one call with it.

When she was back home in Victoria's apartment she went online and reserved a room for the night at a hotel near Vanderbilt University. She was hemorrhaging money lately, so it was just one more charge on a credit card nearing its limit.

Alita grew more nervous with each passing minute as the clock inched closer to the time she would leave to drive to the Comfort Inn. In a sarcastic nod to her mother, she would pose as an out-of-town real estate agent, in Nashville to attend a seminar. She wondered if her false narrative was necessary, as perhaps in the end the only thing that mattered was the money that would change hands. She had no idea what the cost would be and hoped the four hundred twenty-two dollars in cash she carried would be enough.

The veggie burger on her plate went untouched. She wrapped it in foil and put it in the refrigerator for a late-night meal once she was back home. *If I get home tonight.*

Second thoughts arose on the way to the hotel, but they were not strong enough to make her turn back. As she ran the various scenes through her mind she became more comfortable with what she was about to do. Not completely comfortable, but better than she felt earlier. She would be in a hotel with dozens, or perhaps scores of people within earshot, so the chance of physical harm was low. Her phone call could technically be viewed as a crime, but that would mean the police made great effort just to catch a small fish in a small pond. Even if that happened, they likely wouldn't charge her with a crime once they knew who she was and what she was trying to do. *Or would they? Probably a "yes" if it came to Detective Blate's attention.*

Alita checked in and was given a third-floor room overlooking the pool. Once inside the room, she closed the door and sat on the bed.

She took the Nokia burner phone from her purse. About to press the first digit, she had a disturbing thought: *what if they're not open tonight and I did all this for nothing?*

She placed the call.

"Satin Dolls," a woman answered. "How may we please you tonight?"

It's her ... disguise your voice, disguise your voice!

"Yes, I am interested in your, uh, services ... if you can accommodate me." Alita panicked. *Accommodate?* The script she rehearsed multiple times was gone from her mind. "I mean, I prefer to be with, uh, I like women instead of men. Do you have women you send out for, you know, other women?" Alita knew the answer, as Victoria once mentioned going out on such appointments.

"Just relax, dear. I know what you're asking and yes, we do. But you realize this is for companionship only, right? You're paying to have a friend for the evening."

"Yes, I understand that. Can I ask what you charge?"

"Depends on travel time and how much companionship you want. Where are you located?"

"The Comfort Inn, near Vanderbilt. I'm in town because—"

"It's two-fifty for the first hour, and one-fifty for each additional hour. Cash up front, and you are expected to tip."

"I have enough for an hour. With a tip."

"And you have the cash? We don't take anything else."

"Yes."

"What's your first name?"

Alita was caught off guard by the question. She paused before saying, "Hope."

"Okay, Hope. She'll be there in about half an hour. What's your room number?"

***

Alita counted out two hundred fifty dollars plus twenty-five dollars for a tip. She placed it on the dresser and put her purse in the bottom drawer. She felt flushed, and when fanning herself brought no relief she went to the bathroom to splash cold water on her face. She wondered if she should have told Meg or Luke what she was about to do. In case things went horribly wrong.

When the knock came, it was too late for a change of plans. She unlocked and opened the door.

"I'm Crystal. Are you Hope?"

"Yes," Alita said. "Come in."

The slender girl looked like she should be working her first job at McDonald's instead of turning tricks for Satin Dolls. Her chestnut hair with purple highlights was cut in a long pixie, crowning a pretty face discounted by heavy makeup and bright orange lipstick. She was dressed in white shorts, a black crop top T-shirt with "MÖTLEY CRÜE" printed across the chest, and charcoal pointed-toe ballet flats.

"I need the money first," Crystal said.

"Sure." Alita went to the dresser to get the cash. "There's two-fifty, plus a twenty-five-dollar tip."

Crystal counted the money before stuffing it in a pocket in her shorts. "Is there anything special you like to do?" Her tone was one of disinterest.

Alita hated herself for the thought that entered her mind—*Victoria would have been so much better at this than Crystal.*

"Look, I just want to talk," Alita said. "I don't want anything else from you."

"Dirty talk? I'm down for that, if that's what turns you on."

"No. Just talk … talk. I'd like to ask you some questions."

"Wow. Okay, I guess. About what?"

"A coworker of yours. Victoria LaRue."

Crystal stared blankly at her. "I don't know who that is."

That was a possibility that had escaped Alita.

"How long have you been with Satin Dolls?"

"Three weeks. A month. I don't know."

"And you've never heard the name Victoria LaRue, or a Victoria who used to work there?"

"No. They call me when there's a job and a guy swings by and picks me up. I know there are a couple of other girls but I've never met them and I don't know their names."

"Do you know about a woman who worked for Satin Dolls getting murdered?"

"Murdered? Hell, no." Finally, a touch of emotion in Crystal's voice. "Look, you're starting to freak me out. I think I better leave."

Alita couldn't be sure, but she felt that the girl was telling the truth.

"Crystal, please don't go. I'm sorry if I've frightened you. Victoria was my sister. She worked for Satin Dolls, just like you, and she was murdered two months ago."

"Damn." Crystal plopped on the bed. "That's really bad. I'm sorry."

"I called Satin Dolls twice hoping to get information, but whoever answered the phone hung up on me when I mentioned Victoria's name."

"That'd be Lavodis. It's her cell phone. That's the only number."

Lavodis. Alita finally had the owner's name.

"And my name isn't Hope. It's Alita."

"Alita," Crystal said, pausing on each syllable. "I like that name."

"Look, I paid for an hour, and even though you can't tell me anything about Victoria I would still like to talk. I'm curious about you. How old are you?"

"Eighteen."

"Close to nineteen?"

"Just turned eighteen."

"How far did you go in school?"

"Tenth grade."

"Is this your first time doing this kind of work?"

"Nope. I been on the streets since I was sixteen. My mom kicked me out of the house. Gotta get by somehow."

"I can't imagine what you've gone through," Alita said. But she could, because Crystal's story had parallels to Victoria's life. "Are drugs a problem?"

"Maybe."

Alita sat down beside her on the bed. She put her hand on Crystal's shoulder.

"You remind me so much of my sister. Drugs were a problem for Victoria, too. Have you ever thought about getting off drugs? Quitting this business and doing something else?"

She saw a flash of irritation in Crystal's eyes as she pulled away from Alita's hand.

"Easy for you to say."

"It is, I know it is. My life has been easy compared to yours. But there are programs to get you off drugs. You can get your GED, get job training. You could have a whole new life and leave this one behind."

"Why do you even fucking care?"

"Because I tried to help my sister, but I couldn't. She was too far gone. But you're a lot younger, you can still change. Let me help you. Please."

"Won't do any good."

"But maybe it could. Hold on." Alita went to the dresser and took her purse from the bottom drawer. When she opened it to get a business card and a pen, she saw the rest of the money she had tucked inside. She jotted down her number.

"Here's my business card. I put my cell number on the back. I want you to call me if you ever need to talk."

Crystal looked at the front of the card. "You live in Florida?"

"Yes, New Smyrna Beach. Please, think about what I said, okay? A better life is out there, and I'm willing to help you find it." On impulse, Alita reached into her purse again and took out the remaining one hundred forty-seven dollars in cash. "I want you to take this. On one condition. Buy food with it, buy clothes, buy anything you want except drugs. Can you promise me that?"

Crystal didn't reach for the money, she didn't say anything.

Alita put her arms around her and was surprised when Crystal hugged her as well.

"It's going to be all right." Alita held her close a few moments longer. "But promise me?"

"Yeah, okay."

Alita pressed the money into Crystal's hand. Instead of putting it in her pocket as before, she slipped off a shoe, placed it on the insole along with Alita's business card, and put the shoe back on.

"Why did you do that?" Alita asked.

"Because I have to turn over all the money you gave me up front, including my tip, to the security guy who brought me here. He'll give me fifty of that back. But what you just gave me I hid it in my shoe so Big Red won't see it."

Alita froze. "Big Red is here?" She heard the disbelief in her voice.

Crystal nodded. "Yeah. He's the guy who usually drives me around. Why, do you know him?"

"We've met." Her fear came roaring back, now mixed with anger and confusion. "Where is he?"

"He's outside somewhere, keeping an eye on the door to make sure I'm safe. Some guys want to get rough, some guys don't want to pay. And even though you're a woman, he doesn't know who else might be in the room."

Alita went to the window and parted the drapes just enough to peer down at the pool area. In the muted light she could see Big Red sprawled on a lounge chair facing her room.

She weighed her options. She could let fear win and watch Crystal walk out of the room and into the night with Big Red. Or, she could meet him again in the safety of a public setting and try to get answers from him.

It really wasn't a choice.

If she walked down to the pool he would see her coming and she'd lose the element of surprise. She had to lure him to the room.

"Crystal, if you're in trouble with a customer, how do you let your security guy know?"

"I'm supposed to turn the room light on and off several times."

"Listen to me," Alita said, locking eyes with Crystal and hands firmly on the girl's shoulders. "I don't want to put you in a bad situation, so if Big Red asks you about this later, you tell him you were uncomfortable with me."

"Why?"

Alita pivoted to the light switch and rapidly flicked it on and off several times.

Crystal let out a shriek. "Oh, shit! Why did you do that?"

Alita held a finger to her lips when the thump of heavy footsteps grew louder. She whispered to Crystal to sit on the bed. The doorknob jiggled.

"Crystal? You okay? Open up."

Alita swung the door inward. Eyes wide, Big Red took a step back.

"What the hell?" he said. "Alita? What are you doing here?"

How does he know my name?

"Hello, Big Red." She fought to keep her tone even, her face blank.

She saw his gaze move to Crystal in the background.

"Crystal … did you know about this?" he asked.

"No, she didn't, so just leave her out of it. But it's time that you and I had a little talk."

Big Red squinted, as if his brain was short-circuiting from trying to fathom what was happening. He was silent until the wires sparked again.

"Okay," he said. "But Crystal, you go wait in the car first."

She rose and padded toward the door without looking at Alita, but Big Red blocked her exit. He stuck out his hand.

Crystal reached into her pocket and pulled out the money she put there earlier. She gave it to Big Red, who counted it before stuffing it into his own pocket.

"I'll be down in a minute." He swiveled to let Crystal pass. "Stay off your phone."

Big Red doesn't look so imposing tonight.

"Sit over there." Alita pointed to the queen bed farthest from the door. She stood just inside the room, the door half open for a rapid exit if needed.

Big Red sat down on the bed.

"What are you doing here?" he asked again.

"Answer my questions first. Why did you lie to me Saturday night?"

"I didn't lie to you. I thought your tire looked a little low."

"Are you going to play games or are you going to level with me? I have a Nashville cop on speed dial and I know he'd be interested in what you do for a living. I think it's called human trafficking."

Big Red grunted. "No, it's not. Crystal is a willing participant and can walk away anytime she wants. Trust me on that. I just drive her around, that's all."

"I can still call my cop friend and let him decide."

Big Red sighed. "All right, I lied about your tire."

"Why?"

He shrugged. "I just wanted to see you. Up close, face to face. The tire thing was the best I could come up with."

Alita had not even known there were dots before they connected in that moment.

"Victoria ... you knew my sister, didn't you? You drove her around on appointments just like you do with Crystal."

"Yeah. On both counts."

Alita closed the door and sat down on the other queen bed, anger gone but endless questions lingering.

"Can I call you something other than Big Red? Like, your first name?"

"Eric."

"Okay, Eric. How do you know my name?"

"From Victoria. She talked about you all the time. Showed me your pictures, read me your letters. She was so proud of you."

Alita dug her fingers into the sides of her legs. She could not let herself get emotional. Not now.

"That doesn't explain how you knew I was staying there," she said. "Or my Miata."

"I have a friend in your building. She told me a young blonde chick took over Victoria's old apartment. She saw you in the Miata with the Florida plate. When my boss lady told me you called and said you were in town, it all added up. I just had to stop by to see if it was really you, Victoria's kid sister. And it was. But I've answered your questions, now it's your turn to answer mine. What the hell were you doing here with Crystal?"

"It was my version of your low tire story," Alita said. "I wanted to talk with someone from Satin Dolls who knew Victoria, to see what information I could get."

"Information about what?"

"Anything that might lead to the person who killed her. That was the best that I could come up with. But just my luck, they sent someone who didn't even know Victoria."

"Crystal said that?"

"Yes, why?"

Alita saw Big Red's gears shift. "Victoria told me you have a business in Florida that does really well," he said. "Why move to Nashville, and her old apartment?"

"I'm not living there, I just stay there when I come up to meet with the detective working on the case. But Eric, how long did you know my sister?"

"Four, maybe five years. When she started working for Lavodis. Our boss lady. That's how we met, I drove her on her first appointment. But your sister, she was …"

Big Red lowered his head. She saw what passed for sadness on his face when he looked up again.

"Go on," she said.

"She was more than just a chick I worked with. I mean, we were on again, off again, but she was … special to me. I should have just told you that when I stopped by."

Alita nodded, understanding but not wanting more details of their relationship.

"Do you know how she died?" she asked.

Big Red shrugged his massive shoulders. "Just that she was murdered. The cops told Lavodis it happened in Mount Olivet Cemetery. And I'm tight with Lavodis. She doesn't know anything more."

"Please be honest with me, Eric. Was Victoria working for Satin Dolls that night?"

"Absolutely not, I know that for a fact. I swear."

"Could she have been working for another escort service on the side?"

"Victoria only worked for Lavodis."

"She went to the cemetery alone, late at night. Why would she do that?" Alita asked.

Another shrug. "No idea at all. It's crazy."

"I've spent a lot of time talking with the police," Alita said. "They brought up the possibility of a drug deal that went bad."

Big Red huffed. "Those cops are watching too many cop shows. Drugs are so easy to get there's no reason for her to go to a cemetery, especially at midnight. It wasn't a drug deal."

He just echoed Blate's words and Alita's thoughts.

"You drove her to appointments, you were with her often. Did she ever have trouble with any of her customers? Any of them try to hurt her?"

"We had the occasional drunk who got out of line, guys who weren't going to pay, or the ones who like it a little too rough. But nothing we couldn't handle. Everybody loved Victoria."

Not everybody, Alita thought.

Big Red's phone buzzed. He pulled it from his pocket and looked at the screen. "I need to go. We have another job to get to."

"Eric … would you give me your number? In case I have more questions."

"For Victoria's sister, anything." He took a pen from the small desk and jotted down a number on a piece of hotel stationery. He handed it to Alita.

"Thanks," she said. "But one other thing, Eric."

"What's that?"

"Please look out for Crystal. She's just a kid."

-34-

Alita checked out of the Comfort Inn and headed back to Victoria's apartment. She believed enough of what Big Red said to cross Satin Dolls off her list, as Detective Blate had done. Victoria wasn't working for Satin Dolls the night of her murder and there was no reason to suspect Lavodis, the woman who ran the escort service. As for Big Red, Alita didn't think he was involved in Victoria's death, either. Her sister wouldn't have a Lyft driver drop her off at midnight to meet Big Red in a cemetery when she saw him whenever he drove her to meet a customer. Once again, nothing made sense. Despite all of her efforts, she was back to square one.

She was finally able to relax when she got home and changed into her pajamas. There was enough wine left in the bottle for one glass, and she settled on the new couch with her reheated veggie burger.

Alita couldn't get Crystal off her mind. *Just barely eighteen and maybe already too far gone to save.* She wanted to help her, but did Crystal want to help herself?

With the wine glass empty, she stretched out on the couch. Although she would have made do with Victoria's decrepit furniture, she was much more comfortable thanks to Meg. She wanted to text her and tell her again how grateful she was, but her eyes closed and she drifted off to sleep.

Wednesday morning found her more rested than she had felt in days. Maybe it was the full night of uninterrupted sleep, or maybe it was because she no longer feared a knock on her door. She now knew Bobby was harmless and Big Red had no reason to return.

She called Volunteer State Outdoor Advertising and told Ruth Stile she was satisfied with the billboard layout and didn't need more time to consider changes. Ruth promised to email files to her later in the day.

She was getting dressed when her iPhone signaled an incoming text. The number wasn't familiar but she knew the sender by the short message: "Thx for the xtra $$. Crystal."

Alita created entries for both Big Red and Crystal in her Contacts app and added their cell numbers. She didn't know their last names, but in the notes section for Big Red's entry she added "Eric."

It was her last full day in Nashville and there was only one stop on her schedule: Metro Forensic Services.

When she walked into the building a different woman sat behind the counter.

"Good morning," Alita said. "Is Dr. Carringer available? I don't have an appointment. I was just hoping he'd have a few minutes."

"Your name?"

"Alita King. I met with him in August when I came here to identify my sister's body."

"Let me check for you." After a short phone conversation the woman turned back to Alita.

"He'll be free in about forty-five minutes if you'd like to wait."

"I will, thank you." Alita sat down in one of the steel and fabric chairs that lined the wall, just like before.

As she waited and the time ticked away, she wondered how Luke's recording session was going. One day, once Victoria's killer was caught and all of this was behind her, she would take Luke up on his offers to sit in on a recording session, attend the Grand Ole Opry, tour the historic Ryman Auditorium, and have a cold beer at Tootsie's Orchid Lounge. And maybe take that sweet car of his to the hills and curves outside Nashville.

She thought about Meg—running the Sunriz Boutique by herself, checking on her house, getting the new door locks, and leasing furniture for the apartment. There would come a time when she and Meg would close the shop for a week and go to a vacation spot of Meg's choosing. Alita owed her that, and so much more.

Forty minutes later, Alita saw Dr. Carringer walking toward her. She gave him a wave.

"Hello, Alita," he greeted. "Good to see you again."

"I'm sorry to pop in without an appointment, but I'm going back to Florida tomorrow so this was my last chance on this trip. Do you have a few minutes?"

"I'll make time. Come on back."

He led her down a hallway but stopped at an office well short of the rear of the building, where she had seen the butterfly tattoo on Victoria's leg.

Dr. Carringer sat behind his desk. Alita took a chair in front.

"What can I help you with?" he asked.

"Several things. First, I would like to get a copy of Victoria's death certificate."

"That I can't help you with, not here. But I can tell you how you can get a certified copy. I don't recall, what was Victoria's family situation? I know you're her sister, but what about spouse, children, parents, other siblings? Is there an attorney representing her estate?"

"She didn't have an estate. No car, insurance, money in the bank, anything. She was never married, no children, no other siblings. Our father died years ago, and our mother … well, I don't want to go into their relationship other than to say they didn't have one."

"I'm sorry to hear that." He paused. "So there's no estate or legal reasons, you just want a copy?"

"Yes."

"Just so you know, it's not really going to give you much information." Carringer turned to his computer and entered keystrokes. "Do you want the death certificate to show cause of death?"

"Sure. I mean, isn't that always on a death certificate?"

"Not in Tennessee. Cause of death is released only to the immediate family or an attorney on behalf of the estate. Even then it's not automatically included. You have to check a box on the form to have the cause listed."

"I didn't know that. So yes, check the box."

A few more keystrokes and Alita heard the laser printer behind Dr. Carringer cycle on.

"I'm printing you a copy of the application. You can apply by mail, but since you're in town you might want to go there in person today if you have time."

"I do."

He swiveled in his chair and took a single sheet off the printer. He handed it to Alita.

"Vital Records is on Charlotte Avenue. The address is at the bottom. There's a small application fee. Take a minute to look over the form to see if you have all of the information you need to complete it. They will want to see your government-issued ID, and they might need documentation that Victoria was your sister."

Alita read over the form. "No problem, I can answer all this. I'll go there from here to get the death certificate. But can you give me a copy of the autopsy report, since you're the one who performed it?"

"I wish I could, but I can't do that, either. That has to go through the State Chief Medical Examiner." He turned back to the keyboard. "I can print you a form for that, too, but you can't pick it up today. You can apply online if you want, and receive the records electronically."

"Including the toxicology report?"

"That would be included, yes."

Dr. Carringer printed another form and handed it to Alita.

"Thanks," she said. "You know, I was in a state of shock when I was here before. I had questions, but I just couldn't bring myself to ask them."

"I wouldn't have been able to answer them at that time. Victoria's case was still pending."

"But you can talk about it now?"

"The police investigation is still open, but our case here is closed so I can talk about what you'll be getting in those documents."

Alita shifted in her chair. "I should tell you that I did see her at the funeral home that day. All of her. So you don't need to hold anything back from me."

Dr. Carringer nodded.

"She was ... not dressed when I saw her," Alita said. "Do you know what she was wearing?" Perhaps Victoria's outfit might be a clue to what she planned to do that night.

"I found no evidence of charred clothing or similar particles on her body."

"You're saying she was totally nude?"

"I'm not saying that for certain, but ... yes."

"Was she sexually assaulted?" Alita asked.

"That's difficult to answer, too. I found no semen in her vagina, where it would have been protected from the fire. There could have been semen on the exterior of her body, but we have no way of knowing due to the destruction of the skin. So again, I don't know."

Unlike Detective Blate, Dr. Carringer was at least trying to answer her questions.

"Was she dead when she was set on fire?" Alita hoped for an affirmative answer.

Dr. Carringer leaned back in his chair. Alita saw the breath he took, and slowly let out.

"She had redness, or burned mucosa in her trachea, which shows that she was alive when the fire started. There's no accurate way of telling exactly how long she lived after that. If it's any comfort, I don't think she suffered."

"How could she not suffer when she was burning alive?" Alita regretted the sharpness in her voice. "I'm sorry. I didn't mean it to come out like that."

"No apology is necessary. I know this is difficult. For both of us. I don't think she suffered because the tracheal damage was not severe. Victoria didn't die from being set on fire."

"What do you mean? I saw her. She was like … she looked just like charcoal."

"I need to take a step back here, Alita. I can talk to you about the autopsy results, the cause of death, but I can't get into why Victoria's body was in that condition. That falls under the police investigation, and I don't think they're going to talk about it, even with a family member. I will say this—the human body doesn't burn easily. I have to leave it at that."

Alita tried to deduce something from that comment but came up empty.

"So how did she die?"

"She was injected with a massive dose of heroin and carfentanil."

"I've heard of fentanyl, but what is carfentanil?"

"It's a synthetic opioid a hundred times stronger than fentanyl. At that dosage it would have rendered her unconscious and she would have succumbed rather rapidly. That's why the trachea was not badly burned. At some point she stopped breathing, well before the fire did the damage you saw."

Alita caught herself shaking her head. "Then what you're telling me is that someone injected her with heroin and carfentanil and then set her on fire? Why?"

"Someone injected her, or she injected herself. I have no way of knowing that answer, nor could I find an injection site because of the condition of the body. As to why the fire was set, again, that's beyond my jurisdiction."

Alita struggled to process the information she was just told.

"I just don't know what to think. You said she might have even injected herself. Could it have been an accidental overdose? Maybe she wasn't murdered. Maybe she went there to do drugs with a friend, she OD'd, the friend panicked and set her on fire for some crazy reason."

"No, Victoria's death has been ruled a homicide. But I've told you all of the information I can as a medical examiner. It's now in Detective Blate's hands. I hope one day you'll get answers to every one of your questions, Alita. And I hope those answers bring you closure and peace."

She wanted to tell him she wasn't going to rest until she found those answers, that she was willing to spend the rest of her life doing everything in her power to find Victoria's killer. But for the first time the tiniest sliver of doubt crept into her mind.

What if he's never found?

35

A lita thought she would face more red tape when she went to Vital Statistics to get a copy of Victoria's death certificate, but the process went smoothly. She gave the clerk the form that Dr. Carringer printed for her, showed her ID, answered several questions, and within ten minutes the document was in her hands.

As Dr. Carringer stated, there was not much to it. The top half of the certificate was filled out by the funeral home director and included information about Victoria that Alita vaguely recalled giving to them on the day she saw her sister's body. The bottom half noted the cause of death—"Combined toxic effects of carfentanil and heroin." In the section for other significant conditions contributing to death was listed "Thermal Injuries." In the section for manner of death, the checkbox for "Homicide" was marked with an "X."

There were entries for date of death, time of death—a three-hour window between midnight and three a.m.—and even a question as to whether or not tobacco use contributed to the death. The final question, the final space, asked for the location of the "injury." It read simply "Mount Olivet Cemetery."

The death certificate was signed by Dr. Rodney Carringer.

Back in the apartment Alita filled out the online form to request a copy of the autopsy report, which would be mailed to her home address in New Smyrna Beach.

She checked her e-mail and saw that Ruth Stile sent her the files for the billboard design. Ruth included both a pdf and an InDesign file, which gave Alita the ability to make her own changes if she wished to use the design for something else.

She walked down to the apartment complex office just before five o'clock and caught Jamila before she left for the day.

"Hey, girl," Jamila said. "I was wondering if I was going to see you again before you left. You're still leaving tomorrow, right?"

"Yes. I plan to be on the road at dawn to avoid rush hour. But I wanted to give you an update on Big Red, the guy who knocked on my door."

"About your tire going flat?"

"Right. Short story, it turns out he knew Victoria and just wanted to see who I was. Long story, I'll tell you the next time I'm here. But I gotta run for now, tomorrow comes early. And thanks again for everything."

"I'll watch the apartment while you're gone. Be safe."

Alita fixed a large salad for dinner and emptied her refrigerator of anything that might spoil while she was gone. Other than Meg, wine seemed to be her best friend of late as there was always an open bottle in her cabinet or on the counter. She would make sure the bottle was ready for the recycle bin before she went to bed.

She launched InDesign on her laptop and opened the file that Ruth Stile sent her. She rescaled the document and tweaked the elements, reducing it to business card size, and exported a pdf copy which she uploaded to her VistaPrint account. She placed an order for a thousand business cards that would look like a miniature version of the billboard. They would be delivered to the Sunriz Boutique well before she made her next trip back to Nashville.

She finished packing her suitcase and tidied the apartment so she could make an early getaway in the morning. She was in bed when she texted Luke to tell him goodbye, and that she hoped things were going well in the studio. She also sent a short text to Meg to let her know what time she hoped to make it home the next day.

She turned out the light and had just closed her eyes when her phone buzzed. It was a response from Meg:

"Have a safe trip. Please call me the minute you get home. I need to swing by."

36

W inston Dawdy was home on Wednesday night, at his computer and browsing the web. He was in a good mood, having just watched the Mistress Sasha Elimination video again.

He rechecked news outlets in Speedway, Indiana. In the five days since his night of fun and games, there were no reports of bodies being found in a house on Rosewood Drive. Poor Mrs. Slotten didn't know where her husband was or why he never came home last Friday night.

The Mistress Sasha chapters were due to reach his remailing service in Florida by Thursday, and should be on Ed Potter's desk by Monday, Tuesday at the latest. Dawdy would give Potter a few days to drool over them before he followed up.

He closed his browser and opened the Podcasts app on his iMac. A couple of clicks and he was listening to the latest episode of *Try To Imagine*, a true crime podcast hosted by Dr. Luminol.

During long drives across the country for another Selection, Education, and Elimination, Dawdy became hooked on true crime podcasts. His favorite was *Try To Imagine*, despite the host's contrived name.

Dr. Luminol's shtick was to get the listener to try to imagine what it was like to be in a victim's shoes. He would use the phrase "try to imagine" a dozen times or more in a sixty-minute episode: "Try to imagine you're a frail, elderly woman alone in your house. It's after midnight, you hear glass break and footsteps coming toward your room. Try to imagine what you would do." Dr. Luminol's podcasts seemed to always feature a murder that an author had already written about in a true crime book. Dawdy guessed that Dr. Luminol skimmed books to get details of cases, then sensationalized them in his podcast with his "try to imagine" angle. It was lazy pseudo-journalism, but it was entertaining, even amusing at times—when a CSI team used the chemical luminol to discover trace amounts of blood on floors or walls, Dr. Luminol would bellow, "They're spraying *me* all over the crime scene!"

Dawdy leaned back in his chair and propped his feet on his desk as the podcast began. The latest episode detailed the 2017 rape, murder, and dismemberment of a local news anchor in Aspen, Colorado. He was not familiar with the case, but he would not search the web to learn the outcome in advance. He would let Dr. Luminol unravel the story in his own melodramatic way.

Twenty minutes into the episode, after perhaps the fifth time Dr. Luminol said "try to imagine," Dawdy sat up in his chair. He paused the podcast.

He had followed Dr. Luminol's series since learning of it in April, and had listened to twenty-nine episodes so far. Not once during any of those podcasts did the thought come to mind, but it was in his mind now.

Dr. Luminol needed to die.

It would be a challenge. He did not know Dr. Luminol's real name or where he lived. He didn't know anything about him, other than he hosted the true crime podcast *Try To Imagine* and uploaded new episodes every week. Selection had just occurred. Education was next, and Dawdy would learn everything he needed to know about the man who called himself Dr. Luminol.

As for Elimination, he already knew how that would end.

37

It was almost six-thirty when Alita pulled into her driveway. She left Nashville before dawn, but three stops for gas, a break for lunch, and a forty-five-minute construction delay south of Atlanta made it a long day. She wanted just to grab a sandwich and unwind, but Meg had insisted she call the minute she was home. She tapped the name at the top of her list of Favorites.

"Hey, you made it," Meg said. "I was tracking you on the app. I'll be right over."

"Wait, Meg. I'm beat. Can't we do whatever it is on the phone? Or tomorrow?"

"I won't stay long, promise."

Ten minutes later Alita peered out the window to see Meg with a medium-sized cardboard box in her hands. Alita opened the side door for her.

"It's good to have you back," Meg said.

"What's this that's so important?"

"You had it sent to the shop." Meg set the box on the kitchen table. "I almost opened it before I realized what it was."

Alita was puzzled until she looked at the return address. She took a knife from the silverware drawer and carefully slit the shipping tape around the top edges.

Meg moved closer. "I hope it's as pretty as the one in the photo."

"We'll soon see."

Alita lifted an object out of the box and put it on the table. It was bound in layers of packing paper.

"She made sure it was protected," Meg said.

"Had to." Alita kept unwrapping.

The last piece of packing paper peeled away to show a thick fabric bag with a drawstring at the top. Alita untied the drawstring and pulled it wide. She gently picked up the object inside.

"Oh my," Meg said. "It's amazing."

"Yes … it's perfect." Alita cradled a custom, handmade ceramic urn topped with a hand-painted, glass and ceramic monarch butterfly. The talented artisan added an engraved gold plate with three lines of text on the front of the urn:

VICTORIA

FOREVER FREE

FOREVER LOVED

"Are you okay?" Meg put an arm on Alita's shoulder.

"It's just overwhelming, that's all." Alita set the urn on the table and gazed at it, hand on her chest.

"Let me clean up for you, then I'll head out of here so you can get some rest." Meg bent down to scoop up packing paper.

"You know, I'm really not that tired now," Alita said. "Please stay."

They sat down at the table, the ceramic urn topped by the beautiful monarch butterfly in front of them.

Alita rotated the urn, looking at the colors, the detail, the artistry. "I still can't believe how beautiful it is."

"Do you know where you want to put it?"

"I'm going to have my handyman build a niche in the wall in the living room, across from the entertainment center. I might have him add accent lighting."

"That would be nice," Meg said. "I didn't mean to be so mysterious about it. I just wanted to wait until you were home."

"I'm glad you did."

"Do you have time to tell me about Nashville?"

"Yes. But first, you crazy, wonderful woman, I can't believe all you did for me. I feel safe there now with the locks, and the furniture made it so comfy and cozy. I don't know how you did all that from down here. Thank you so much. But I'm going to repay you and—"

"Stop right there. Don't even say it. Because no, you aren't."

"Well, we're going to revisit that. But Nashville … it would take all night to tell you. Or longer. But I did find out something that totally floored me. I went back to the medical examiner's office yesterday. Dr. Carringer, remember?"

"He was the guy who was halfway decent to you, wasn't he?"

Alita nodded. "Right. I wanted to get copies of the autopsy report and death certificate. He told me Victoria didn't die by fire, Meg. She didn't burn to death. It was a drug overdose."

"What? It wasn't murder?"

"Oh, she was definitely murdered, just not by fire. She was injected with a lethal mixture of heroin and carfentanil."

"What's that?"

"I didn't know, either. It's like fentanyl, only way, way worse. Like a hundred times stronger. Dr. Carringer said she was still alive when she was set on fire, but for just a few seconds. She died from the overdose."

"There's no good news about any of this," Meg said. "But I am glad she didn't suffer any more than she did. What else did he tell you?"

"Not much. I mean, she ended up deep in the cemetery, and he thinks she was naked at that point. She's injected with the drugs, then set on fire. But why? I still have no answers."

"That's so bizarre," Meg said. "But the billboard. That could really help. When are they going to put it up?"

"The first of November. I hate to ask, but I'd like to be there if you wouldn't mind."

"I keep telling you, do what you need to do, for as long as it takes. I just wish I could be there with you."

"I know, Meg. I know."

"But it's time for me to scoot so you can get some rest."

They said their goodbyes with one last hug and Meg headed home.

***

Alita went to the linen closet to get the plastic container that held the rest of Victoria's cremains. She took it to the kitchen. What she was about to do called for a ceremony of some sort, but what?

She turned off the overhead lights, leaving only the soft glow from her under cabinet lighting. She fumbled in a drawer for a book of matches and lit a stick of incense.

The earthy-scented smoke curled toward the ceiling. The thin plastic container, looking cheap and brittle, sat next to the beautiful butterfly urn. There was a metaphor for Victoria's life in that image, but Alita didn't let it fully form. Her index finger followed the contours of the butterfly until she had touched every inch of it.

The red glow from the incense burned down until there was nothing left but residue. *Ashes to ashes.*

She took the black bag with Victoria's cremains from the plastic container and placed it in the monarch butterfly urn. She reset the lid and moved the urn to her bedroom where she placed it on her dresser.

Until her handyman could build the niche in her living room wall, Alita would keep Victoria's beautiful butterfly urn where it would be the first thing she saw each morning, and the last thing she saw each night.

E d Potter was in a foul mood. He disliked Monday mornings in general, and this one began with a visit to the dentist for a crown prep. He dropped his dental insurance nine months ago, so this would be one more bill he would need to squeeze into his already bursting budget. His regular dentist was ill, so he was treated by a new associate dentist who seemed indifferent to his pain.

After the dental appointment Potter was on San Vincente Boulevard halfway to his office when he heard the "whump whump whump" of a flat tire. He pulled into the Dunkin' Donuts parking lot to await the AAA emergency service truck. Ninety minutes later, an hour longer than quoted when he called, the technician finally arrived. The tech removed a roofing nail from the left rear tire and was able to plug the puncture. Potter tipped the guy the last ten bucks in his wallet, then drove off cursing the new dentist, himself for dropping his dental insurance, the person who invented roofing nails, and the Miami Dolphins. He had nothing against the NFL football team, the words just came out of nowhere when he muttered, "Fuck the Miami Dolphins." He knew it was going to be one of those Mondays.

Sam glared when Potter walked into the office at ten past noon. "And here he is," she said. "About damn time. I had lunch plans and thanks to you I'm already late."

Potter didn't slow down as he walked past Sam's desk, he just gave her a frown and waved her off with his hand. He sat in his squeaky chair, and opened the bottom drawer of his desk for his bottle of whisky. After pouring two fingers into a glass, he lit a cigarette and enjoyed his first moment of peace since climbing out of bed that morning.

He saw the short stack of mail that Sam put on his desk, probably the most useful task she would do all day. Opening the top envelope with his index finger resulted in a deep paper cut and another round of cursing. His injury came with insult when the contents of the envelope turned out to be a scathing letter from a now former client who said he "smelled a scam." *Some fish spit out the hook.*

Potter glanced at four pieces of junk mail and skimmed a query letter from a writer who lived in Wasilla, Alaska. He was down to the three large mailing envelopes that had been at the bottom of the short stack of mail. He picked up the top one and was about to open it when his eyes settled on the next envelope. The mailing address and the return address were the same: *his* address, Potter Literary Associates. Potter dropped the envelope that was in his hands. Only one person used his office address for both the recipient and the sender: *Winston Dawdy.* The envelope was postmarked Old Town, Florida, the same postmark as Dawdy's first letter.

Potter picked up the envelope and tore it open, not taking any precautions against the chance of a second paper cut. He read the cover letter first:

Dear Mr. Potter:

I am becoming comfortable with the thought of having Potter Literary Associates represent me, thus I am enclosing additional chapters for you to read. These chapters required challenging and extensive research, and I trust that you will find my writing continues to reflect my attention to detail.

I also want to assure you that I am nearing the end of my book with only a few chapters still to write.

I look forward to one day meeting you in person.

Regards,

Winston Dawdy

Potter thumbed through the pages. They weren't numbered this time, nor were there any chapter headings.

He stubbed out his cigarette and downed the rest of the whisky in his glass. He began reading the first page.

When Potter was about a quarter through the pages he paused, because at that point he *needed* a distraction from the intensity of what he was reading. He lit another cigarette and poured more whisky. The phone rang for the first time since Sam left for lunch. He let it go to voicemail.

Potter couldn't fit Dawdy into a pigeonhole as a writer. He had talent, he wasn't a hack or a wannabe who never would be. And although Dawdy was a proficient wordsmith, he was not on a level with legends like Thomas Harris, a true master of the craft whose every word deserved to be printed in gold ink. Dawdy's strength was in telling a story in a way that made people forget they were reading a work of fiction. He made the action and the dialogue ring true, and Potter credited much of that to Dawdy's writing style and research. Whatever the formula, it was working.

Potter returned to the pages in front of him, more riveted with each page he turned. He finished just as he heard Sam drop her keys on her desk, on the other side of the partition that separated the front of the office from the back.

"Hey, Sam," he yelled. "Before you get settled, come here a minute."

"You have to give me a minute first," she yelled back. "I have to pee so bad I can taste it."

"Yeah, yeah, okay." Potter picked up Dawdy's mailing envelope and looked at the postmark. He thought about what he would do once he had Dawdy's full manuscript. Odds were good it would need at least minor revision and polishing—every Stephen King best-seller had an editor and proofreaders—but Potter knew any issues could be fixed. Dawdy's book could be big. So big that he might interest multiple publishers, maybe even set up an auction. No matter how hard he tried, Potter could never totally push from his mind the catastrophe he created years ago with *The Devil's Finest Hour*. That debacle nearly cost him his career—*should* have cost him his career—but Winston Dawdy could catapult him to the top again.

"Ah, much better," Sam said through a relieved sigh. She sat down in front of Potter's desk. "Now, what do you want?"

"You didn't look closely at today's mail, did you? Our boy came through for us again."

"Don't tell me. Winston Dawdy?"

"Yeah, Sam. And what he sent is even creepier than the hooker in the cemetery."

"Oh, I can't wait to hear about it."

Sam was a loyal employee, and away from work they were casual friends with occasional benefits, but her sarcasm could sting like salt in an open wound.

"Sit down." Potter didn't try to hide his irritation.

"All right, I'm sorry. I know you think he's our meal ticket."

"Oh, so you don't like him now, but if his book hits big he's *our* meal ticket. Is that how it works?"

Sam laughed. "C'mon, Potter. You're dying to tell me about what he sent, so tell."

Potter shifted in his chair and leaned forward. "His serial killer does his whole *SEE* thing—that's Selection, Education, and Elimination, remember?" Potter's hands were moving in concert with his words. "He selects this dominatrix he found on the Dark Web. He calls her Mistress Sasha. She lives in Speedway, Indiana. I thought he made up the town, but it's where the Indianapolis 500 is. A suburb of Indy. She's nondescript, has a boring day job, lives on a quiet street, but nobody knows what her pastime is. He—"

"Wait a minute. You say 'he.' What's the serial killer's name? I don't remember you telling me from the first chapters he sent."

"I don't know. It's written in first person, from the serial killer's point of view. He doesn't name himself. At least he hasn't so far."

"Hmm. Okay, go on."

"He does his Education, learns all about Mistress Sasha, knows her routines, everything. Same as the Nashville hooker chapters. Hacks her phone and computer, finds out she doesn't have any security cameras. He—"

"Hold on," Sam said. "All this hacking … isn't that hard to do?"

"Dawdy has me convinced his serial killer knows how. That's what matters. Anyway, he books a session with Mistress Sasha. He pays extra so he can secretly watch her with a customer."

"Like a Peeping Tom."

"Don't interrupt. She takes him down to this dungeon that's hidden in a false basement in her house. She puts him in an armoire with a one-way mirror, thinking he's just a kinky guy who gets off by watching. Her customer arrives, and she binds the guy with ropes and leather and stuff, and then has this hoist apparatus that raises him up to the ceiling."

"This is really getting weird."

"Oh, it gets much weirder. Mistress Sasha is doing her thing to her customer while the serial killer is watching from the armoire. And all of this is going on while she's blasting the song *Bolero*. You know it?"

"Of course," Sam said.

"When her back is turned to him, he slips out of the armoire and knocks her out. Then he … well, I won't go into detail, but you wouldn't want to be the guy hanging from the hoist, let me just say that. He binds up Mistress Sasha—how's that for a plot twist—and hooks her up to the same hoist. She and her customer are hanging upside-down, back to back. And the Elimination, you need to read that for yourself. Actually, you need to read all of it. But are you ready for the real kicker?"

"No, but you're going to tell me anyway."

"The serial killer erases all traces of his visit. He leaves them in the hidden dungeon which is sealed air tight. She doesn't show up for her day job and the cops do a well person check. They find nothing. Her BDSM customers would think she just went out of business, and they certainly wouldn't come forward anyway. The bodies could be hanging down there for weeks, months, even years. Think about it."

Sam shuddered. "I don't want to. But don't you think that's a bit much? I mean, crazy shit happens in real life, but that sounds too Hollywood for me."

"Hollywood? Now you're talkin', Sam. We'll not only have a best-selling book, we'll auction the damn movie rights, too!"

-39-

Alita strolled the beach at ebb tide on Tuesday morning. The sun rose over a gently rolling Atlantic Ocean and a sky that was not threatening. It was mid-October, and if Florida's luck held, hurricane season would close in a month and a half without any major storms battering the coastline.

With some doing, she finally persuaded Meg to take a week off to make up for some of the time Alita spent in Nashville. Meg still didn't want to hear any talk of bringing on an employee.

Alita spent her days working in the shop, and her evenings sifting through the names and phone numbers she found in the drawer in Victoria's apartment. The men must have been some of her sister's customers—she could think of no other explanation. Slips of paper had first and last names, others just a first or last name. Half of the phone numbers were out-of-state area codes. Some men had given their business cards to Victoria, cards with not only their name but also their employer's name, address, and phone number. Was it drunkenness, sheer stupidity, or the cavalier mindset of an alpha male who thought there would be no consequences from his dalliance with a lady of the evening—from the police, his employer, or a significant other?

She set up an Excel spreadsheet and input all of the information she gleaned from the slips of paper and the business cards. She hoped for a sign from the universe, a subtle vibration as she held each one in her hand. A spark that would tell her *this is him, this is the man who killed Victoria!* When she put the last name and number into the spreadsheet there had been no vibrations, no sparks. *Was that itself a sign?*

It would soon be three months since Victoria's murder and still there were no suspects. No evidence. No motive. Detective Blate had only vague theories. In the deepest recesses of her heart and soul Alita knew the name of Victoria's killer was not in the spreadsheet in front of her. He was far too smart to leave any evidence behind him. She was defeated once again, and she now understood why Blate didn't undertake the task of tracking down each of these men who had likely paid for sex with her sister.

Alita was in the shop on Thursday when FedEx delivered a package. It was her order of one thousand "mini-billboard" business cards. She tore into the box and pulled out a card to check the printing.

"Yes," she said to herself. "Just what I wanted."

Although Alita vowed not to bother Meg on her week off, that didn't stop Meg from calling every day to see how things were going at the shop. When she called mid-afternoon, Alita invited her to drop by the house after work to check out the new business cards and the website she was building.

Meg pulled in the driveway before Alita could get out of her car.

"Somebody's anxious," Alita said.

"I've missed you, and I wanted to see what you've been doing."

"Come on in."

Alita retrieved the box of VistaPrint business cards and pulled one from the box. She handed it to Meg.

"What do you think?" she asked.

Meg slipped on her reading glasses and held the card up for a close look. "Nice. Just like the billboard, right?"

"The aspect ratio is not exactly the same, but it's close enough. So yeah, basically that's it. When I go back up to Nashville I'm going to blanket the whole town. Leave them everywhere. I'm going to design a flyer and post them around, too. Billboard, cards, and flyers. I want people talking."

"Does Detective Blate know about any of this?" Meg asked.

"No, but he'll find out soon enough. He chose not to release information to the public, but that's not my choice. I'm also going to blow up social media, and I've been working on a website, too."

"Do it all. Like you've said, the more you put the word out there, the better the chances the right tip will come in."

Alita nodded. "Exactly. I can see that, you can see that. Why is Blate so blind to the obvious?"

"Because he wants to be. But you're working on your website yourself? Why didn't you get Ethan to do it? He does such a great job on ours."

"I want to keep it real simple so I can update it and not have to rely on his schedule. Remember when you came to work for me? I was doing the website for the shop."

Meg laughed. "Yeah, and the first thing I suggested was getting someone else to do it. That's why we use Ethan."

Alita laughed, too. "Good point. But I'm happy with it. You have time to check it out for me?"

"Sure."

Alita got her laptop and set it in front of Meg. "It's on simulate, so navigate away."

Meg looked at the screen. "I like it already. You're getting better."

"That's only the home page."

"I know, but it jumps out at you. The billboard graphic looks great."

"I've been kicking myself for not thinking of doing a website earlier," Alita said. "I could have added the URL to both the billboard and the business cards."

"Have you thought about a domain name?"

"Already have it. Who killed Victoria LaRue dot com."

"Oh, that's good. That's really good."

"I haven't uploaded anything to the server yet. I want to wait until it's ready. So poke around a bit and see if you like the flow. See if you find any errors."

Meg clicked and scrolled through the pages of the website. She was unusually quiet, and Alita didn't know if that was a good sign or a bad one. She was about to speak, but Meg waved her off with, "Hold that thought. I'm concentrating."

Ten minutes later, Meg looked at Alita. "You nailed it."

"Really?"

"Really. I read every word, clicked every link, looked at every photo. So clean and easy to navigate. Enough information, but not too much. I loved the page you titled "My Sister." Touching on Victoria's struggles humanizes her, and people will love what you wrote about your relationship."

"I'm also working on a press release that I'll e-mail to every media outlet in Nashville. Say, how about a glass of wine and you check it, too?"

"Twist my arm."

Alita told Meg how to navigate to the press release on her laptop. She took two glasses from the cabinet and opened a bottle of 19 Crimes. She didn't look at the cork.

"This is good, too," Meg said. "Well written. You know, if you can find out what time the billboard is going up, you could invite the media to be there."

Alita paused in mid-pour. "That's brilliant, Meg. That would get the word out all over Nashville, all at once. I knew there was a reason I invited you over."

40

W inston Dawdy found great joy in the Elimination of a victim, but he kept an emotional flatline when it came to Selection and Education.

With one exception, Dawdy had never targeted a victim out of revenge, anger, disgust, fear, or any other cog of the human psyche. Someone simply had the misfortune of drawing his attention and triggering whatever it was in his brain that told him Selection had just occurred. His pulse stayed steady, there was no catch in the throat, no flush of excitement when the moment arrived. He felt nothing, other than the understanding that the person needed to die by his hand.

The Education process held the same absence of emotion. He learned the deepest, darkest secrets about people—Pamela Dobbins and her "Mistress Sasha" persona, for example—but nothing he discovered ever gave him pause. His sole objective was to learn everything he needed to know about a victim in order to carry out a successful Elimination without personal risk. Reacting with judgment to any revelation large or small would only cloud his focus.

Dr. Luminol's real name was Paul Winkleman. He was sixty-six and a retired autoworker turned true crime podcaster. He lived in Wyandotte, Michigan, on the outskirts of Detroit, until he moved to The Villages in Central Florida a year ago. He was tech-savvy enough to create and upload his *Try To Imagine* podcasts from home, but his computer skills did not include an ability to block hackers. Dawdy was able to gain access to Winkleman's home network and computer with little difficulty.

Dawdy searched Winkleman's internal hard drive to look for financial records—following the money usually led him to a wealth of information about his future victim. From Quicken files and electronic bank statements Dawdy learned that Winkleman was making over six thousand dollars a month with his Dr. Luminol podcasts in addition to his Ford Motor Company pension of nearly thirty-five hundred dollars. With eighty grand spread across multiple savings accounts and only small credit card balances, it was clear that Paul Winkleman was not missing any meals. Dawdy downloaded a number of files so he could research them in depth later, when he wasn't online.

He came across a list of expired ebook titles that Winkleman had checked out through his local library. Dawdy matched the titles to the content of some of Winkleman's podcasts, confirming his suspicions that Winkleman simply copied facts from true crime books and dramatized them as Dr. Luminol—and he didn't even buy the books, he just borrowed them.

Winkleman didn't use a password manager—he had a text file on his hard drive which included login credentials to every account he had on the web. Dawdy downloaded a copy, as the usernames and passwords would enable him to open doors to much more information about his target. He turned his attention to a portable drive that was connected via a USB port.

The first folder that Dawdy double-clicked to open was labeled "Angel Pics." The folder housed eighteen hundred and forty-seven images. He could tell by the thumbnails that the images were explicit photos of young girls being sexually abused by adult males. He closed the folder and opened the adjacent one labeled "Angel Vids." There were two hundred and sixteen videos in that folder. He didn't need to click on any of them to know their content.

Dawdy logged out of Winkleman's computer and leaned back in his chair to ponder this new complication. Paul Winkleman was so heavily involved in child porn that it was just a matter of time before the authorities came sniffing around. They might already be watching him, which would make Dawdy's Education process more challenging. If the cops were already on Winkleman's tail they could nab the pedophile and have him behind bars before Dawdy had a chance to carry out his Elimination. That would be a most unfortunate turn of events, but he was wary of taking any shortcuts that would speed up the timetable and introduce unnecessary risk.

Dawdy pushed the photos and videos on Winkleman's external hard drive to the back of his mind. They had not factored into the Selection of Winkleman as a future victim, nor would they interfere with his Education research other than the need for extra caution. But when the time was finally at hand, as it inevitably would be, Dawdy would remember those photos and videos, and he would take great pleasure in the slow and extremely painful Elimination of Paul "Dr. Luminol" Winkleman.

41

A lita stirred in the pre-dawn darkness. During the swing from slumber to awareness she didn't know where she was, or what day it was. It became clear as she rubbed the remnants of sleep from her eyes: she was in Victoria's apartment, and it was Saturday, November first. The day she had been awaiting for weeks.

Her last trip convinced Alita it was a waste of time and energy to drive back and forth when flying took just a couple of hours. Meg, doting friend that she was, had booked her flight and reserved a rental car.

She landed in Nashville on Thursday evening and spent most of the day on Friday—Halloween—going over all of her notes, all of her research, and planning what she would say to the reporters who would gather the next morning at Victoria's billboard.

Alita called the cemetery's office on Friday as a courtesy so they would be aware of the billboard when they saw it for the first time. June Wickliff wasn't in, so she spoke with a woman who said she appreciated the advance notice. Although she understood why Alita was renting the billboard, she wished it could have been in a different location. "But it is what it is," the woman said. "Right now our biggest concern is cleaning up the vandalism. You can't believe the damage that happens in a cemetery during Halloween season."

Bryn Wolda of Volunteer State Outdoor Advertising assured Alita that their workers would have the new billboard up before ten-thirty. Alita's emails to several dozen media outlets, including TV and radio station news departments, *The Tennessean*, neighborhood newspapers, online news outlets, and even two Nashville crime bloggers, said that she would be onsite for interviews and to answer questions from eleven a.m. until twelve-thirty p.m. She didn't state it in her emails, but she would stay until the last reporter left, even if it took all day. Her e-mails didn't go into great detail about the billboard and what had happened to Victoria, as she wanted to relay that information to reporters in person.

After a long shower she was toweling off when she paused to stare at her reflection in the mirror. She hadn't worked out in weeks and it showed. She was eating all the wrong foods. She was drinking too often and too much—lately she had no need for a wine stopper—plus staying up past midnight almost every night was also taking its toll.

"*You stupid, foolish girl,*" Marjo's voice whispered in her head.

"*Fuck off,*" her own inner voice answered.

She wondered why she hadn't crossed paths with Marjo in nearly three months. They shopped at the same Publix, dined at the same restaurants, drank at the same local watering holes, and drove the same New Smyrna Beach streets. Not a single sighting. Alita last spoke with Marjo, she last saw her, on the day she stopped by her house to tell her about Victoria's murder. Since then she rarely thought about her mother, and if she never saw her again she wouldn't lose any sleep over it.

It was a crisp, fall Saturday, with a predicted high temperature of only fifty-five degrees. Alita was glad she packed a light jacket in her suitcase. She would take it along in case her jeans and sweater weren't enough to block the chill from any wind.

Her stomach was rumbling despite a bland breakfast and she was already feeling on edge. She had freely talked about Victoria's murder a number of times to many different people, but never in front of cameras and microphones and strangers. She hoped she could rise to the occasion, but the jitters weren't helping her confidence.

A check of the clock showed the minutes were dragging by. Vanderbilt was hosting Missouri in a college football game that afternoon, but game day traffic wouldn't be much of a concern. Vandy's stadium was less than half the capacity of The Swamp, home of her beloved Florida Gators.

Traffic on I-24 was light, as expected. Her excitement grew as she took the Spence Lane exit. She could feel the dampness on the steering wheel beneath her palms when she turned onto Lebanon Pike. With the cemetery in view on her left, she could see Victoria's billboard on the right side of the road, towering above the pavement. The Volunteer State Outdoor Advertising crew had finished their work and were already gone. Ruth Stile's graphic design that looked good on a computer screen grew ten times more powerful when full-sized on the billboard. It took the blare of a car horn behind her for Alita to realize she had nearly come to a stop in the westbound lane of Lebanon Pike.

Alita pulled off the road and parked next to the fence outside the Goodyear Commercial Tire & Service Center. She had written talking points on index cards on the off chance her mind went blank while she was being interviewed. She got out of the car, leaving the index cards on top of the flyers and mini-billboard business cards she brought to hand out.

A sidewalk in front of the Goodyear Service Center went nowhere as it ended after eighty feet or so. Alita walked to the point where concrete met grass and stood facing oncoming traffic. She was close enough to the road to see the tilt of drivers' faces, even their eyes, and she was ecstatic to note drivers looking up at the new billboard. Passengers in several cars pointed up with their index fingers.

Satisfied, Alita returned to the rental car to wait for reporters.

She wasn't worried when no one showed up by eleven-fifteen, but each new quarter-hour of no-shows brought increasing despair, anger, and disbelief. She checked her sent e-mails to make sure she hadn't typed the wrong date or times. By one o'clock, thirty minutes past the time her event was scheduled to end, anger was all she felt. *Not one damn person!* A backup plan had been percolating but now it was in place. If they weren't coming voluntarily, she would make them come.

She went to the base of the column that supported the billboard and roughly gauged its circumference. A search on her iPhone yielded the nearest Home Depot store.

In less than an hour she again pulled off Lebanon Pike and parked next to the fence beneath the billboard. She took the flyers and the mini-billboard business cards along with a concrete paver she had purchased. She put the flyers on the ground with the paver on top so they wouldn't blow away, and stacked the business cards on the paver.

She locked her purse in the trunk and put her iPhone in her pocket. She took the combination padlock and the forty-foot-long stainless-steel passing link chain she had bought and walked around the billboard column five times with one end of the chain. Standing with her back to the column, she wrapped both ends of the chain around her body enough times to take out the slack. She inserted the shackle of the padlock through two of the chain's links, pushed the lock shut, and turned the combination dial. Her arms and hands remained free, but she was securely held against the column by the chain. The fence and her rental car mostly hid any view of her from the highway.

She took her iPhone from her pocket, did a web search for the number she wanted, and placed a call.

"WTVF NewsChannel 5," a female voice answered.

"Yes, I'd like to report something unusual," Alita said. "I thought you might want to know about it."

"Okay, what's going on?"

"I'm on Lebanon Pike, and just across from Mount Olivet Cemetery I saw a woman chained to a billboard pole. It's weird, she's all by herself with chains wrapped around her."

"And she's still there, she's there right now?"

"Yes, I just drove past. With those chains she's not going anywhere anytime soon."

"But it's a real person, right? It's not like an advertising dummy
or anything?"

"I saw her arms move."

"Okay, thanks for the tip. We'll check it out. Do you mind giving
me your name?"

"Victoria. Victoria LaRue. But I'm in traffic, so I have to hang up
now."

Alita couldn't believe what she had just done, but she didn't have
time to think about it. She looked up the number for WKRN News 2.
When she reached their newsroom she repeated the same story nearly
verbatim. The next call was to WSMV4. That station must have had a
news crew in the area, for their news van was the first to arrive minutes
later. The van pulled in behind her car, partially blocking the entrance
to the Goodyear Service Center.

A young Latino woman with a microphone in hand got out of
the van and came at a trot toward her, an older, heavy-set man with a
camera on his shoulder trailing close behind.

"Are you okay?" the reporter asked. "What's going on? Who did
this to you?"

"I'm fine, and I did this myself."

"Really?" She looked at the cameraman before turning back to
Alita. "I'm Camille Torres with WSMV4. May I talk with you? On
camera?"

"That's why I'm here."

Hesitation. "Okay … do you mind telling me your name?"

"Alita King."

"A-L-I-T-A?"

"Yes."

"Alita, why are you here? And why the chains? Are you protesting something?"

"No, I'm just trying to raise awareness."

"For what?"

"Look up." Alita pointed toward the billboard.

Torres raised her head and used a hand to shield her eyes from the sun. "Be sure to get a shot of that when we're done, Arnie," she said to her cameraman. "Alita, do you have a connection to Victoria LaRue?"

"She was my sister. And like it says, she was murdered right over there. On August the third."

"But I don't understand. Why are you chained like that?"

"The police have no suspects, no motive, no anything. I paid to put up the billboard because I thought if the media gave my sister's murder some coverage, it might lead to a break in the case. I sent emails to your station and a number of others to come here this morning for the unveiling of the billboard, but no one showed up. Not a single one of you. That's been the reaction every time to my sister's murder. No one cares. But I chain myself to the billboard and here you are, within minutes." Alita saw a WKRN van pull up to park next to the WSMV rig. "And speaking of, it looks like your competition just arrived."

Torres turned to look at the WKRN news van.

"Hey, I'm sorry," Torres said. "Your e-mail never made its way to me, otherwise I would have been here. I mean that. But I was here first. Can I have an exclusive on your story?"

"No, I want to spread the word as far as possible. Not just on one TV station. But I will let you interview me first."

Over the next thirty minutes Alita was interviewed separately by news crews from both WSMV and WKRN. The reporters also took flyers and a few of the mini-billboard business cards. An employee from the Goodyear Service Center came out to see what all the activity was about and to ask the WKRN van to move forward a few feet to open up their driveway. Traffic on Lebanon Road crept by and several cars pulled to the side, drivers and passengers now standing just beyond the news crews, watching. Alita was about to give a third interview, with the late-arriving WTVF reporter, when she saw the flashing blue lights of a police car followed closely by another.

The WTVF reporter and his cameraman stepped back as the two officers approached, but the cameraman kept recording.

"What's going on here?" the older of the two officers asked. Before Alita could respond he added, "Who did that to you?"

"No one. I chained myself to the pole because Victoria LaRue was my sister. Look up."

Alita saw both officers check out the billboard.

"But why the chains?" the younger officer asked.

"Long story."

"I go past here all the time," the older officer said. "This is new. When did it go up?"

"This morning."

"Ah ... so this was to get media attention. I understand now. But look, you're causing a traffic slowdown, onlookers are parked illegally on the side of the road and blocking the entrance to a business, and you're technically on private property. My sergeant's going to be all over my ass if I don't do something, so you need to get out of those chains and break up this little gathering."

Alita looked at the WTVF reporter. "Can we do this across the street, in the cemetery?"

"Absolutely. Can I help you get free?"

"No, I can handle it."

"Okay," the reporter said. "We'll move our truck over there and get set up. Thanks for sticking around for us."

"I wasn't going anywhere," Alita said. "If you want, I will—"

"The chains, lady." The edge in the older cop's voice showed he was growing impatient. He turned to the dozen or so onlookers on the perimeter. "And all you people with nothing better to do, get back in your cars and on your way. Bill," he gestured to the younger officer, "go keep traffic moving."

Alita read the code printed on the sticker on the back of the combination lock and turned the dial. At the last stop she pulled on the shackle but the lock didn't open. She pulled harder with the same result. She looked at the code a second time and repeated the steps. Once more she tugged on the lock's shackle, and once more the lock remained closed.

Alita looked at the older officer. "I'm sorry, it won't open."

With a sigh, the officer stepped up to Alita and turned the lock over to read the code himself. He rotated the dial to each stop and pulled on the shackle. Still locked.

"Chinese junk. You know, for all this trouble I should just run you in."

"Seriously?"

"Nah, too much paperwork." The officer finally smiled at her. "Just give me a minute. Hey, Bill, get the bolt cutters out of the trunk."

42

A lita went to the sliding glass doors and looked down at the parking lot. She saw a familiar car.

"But get this, Meg," she said. "After the third interview, the one in the cemetery, I went back to the apartment thinking that was it. But within an hour WKRN called and said they want me to do a second interview on their News 2 at 4 p.m. show on Monday. Live, in the studio. Can you believe that?"

"That's wonderful! But did you pack a decent outfit you can wear?"

Alita laughed. "You worry about stuff like that much more than I do. But remember, you talked me into bringing my big suitcase since I don't know how long I'm staying, so I'm good. But there's more, Meg. A reporter from *The Tennessean*, that's the major newspaper here, called me to set up an interview, too. I'm meeting her after the WKRN interview. It's crazy."

Alita heard a tapping on her door. "Dinner just arrived, I have to go. Talk later."

Before opening the door, she looked through the peephole just to be sure.

"I believe you ordered the OMG Vegan Pepperoni?" Luke stood there, a pizza box in his outstretched arms.

"The record business must be really tough if you have to deliver pizzas on the side," Alita said. "Come on in."

"Not yet. I have to run back to the car." Luke handed her the pizza box and headed down the stairs.

She was in the kitchen slicing the pizza when the door opened again. She came around the corner to see Luke carrying a flat screen TV.

Alita shook her head. "I can't believe this. Between you and Meg, I don't know which one is worse."

"Definitely Meg. But this is to watch your interview. I told you I had extra TVs I wasn't using. Where do you want it?"

"You're so sweet. I was just going to stream it on my laptop."

Alita cleared the dinette table of her research materials. "Just set it here for now. I can move it later. But we don't have much time before the news comes on."

Luke put the TV on the table and plugged it in. "Do you have Wi-Fi yet, or do you want to tether to your iPhone?"

"I'll get my own Wi-Fi soon, but Jamila is letting me use the office Wi-Fi for now. They have an extender, so the signal's strong."

Luke turned on the TV and navigated to the set-up screen. "What is their login?"

"The username is Office and the password is Titans."

Luke laughed. "That is so not good."

"I know. I'm almost afraid to use it."

Alita downloaded the Hulu app and set up a Hulu Live TV account. She and Luke relaxed at the dinette table with pizza and sodas in front of them, chatting and waiting for WSMV's early evening news. Just before five o'clock, Luke turned up the volume on the TV.

After an opening tease, the news team ran Alita's story, starting with a close-up shot of the billboard. Every pain, doubt, and fear that Alita had felt in her search for Victoria's killer was worth it when she saw the billboard on TV.

After the interview ended and the news moved to a piece about a mobile pet groomer who absconded with a customer's Standard Poodle, Alita pressed the mute button.

"I can't believe they led off with me," she said. "What did you think of it?"

"To be honest, because of the chains and all, I was worried about how they would cover it. How it might come across."

"You mean, like I was a crazy woman?"

"Well, I didn't want to put it that way." Luke grinned. "But that reporter did a good job, and you … it was clear that everything you said was from the heart. I don't think it could have been any better. And the billboard. I drove by it on my way here with the pizza. It is so powerful."

"You saw how it was a bit dicey for a couple of minutes with the cops, but they turned out to be okay."

"When will the other stations air their interviews?"

"WTVF is running it on their early news today, at six. WKRN has college football. But all three stations will have it on their ten o'clock news tonight."

Luke stayed to watch Alita's interview with WTVF. Their crew was the only one to record footage from both the billboard with Alita still chained to it and also from the cemetery where the murder had taken place—the latter a fact the reporter cited several times. The WTVF segment was nearly twice as long as the story that aired on WSMV. They showed a graphic that highlighted the reward, they included the number for Crime Solvers, and they even flashed the URL of the website Alita created.

Luke left early, having told a young country singer he would be in the audience for his set at the Bluebird Cafe. Alita lugged the TV to the bedroom and set it on the dresser. She changed into her pajamas and stretched out on the bed. Weary after the events and excitement of the day, she set an alarm on her iPhone to wake her for the late news in case she fell asleep. She soon drifted off.

At eight-thirty Alita snapped awake when she heard a knock on her door. *Please, not Bobby or Big Red.*

She put on her robe before going to answer the door, walking silently up to the peephole. Standing there was the last person in the world she expected to see. She unlocked the door and swung it inward.

"Marjo?"

43

Winston Dawdy was not one to shy from a challenge, but he knew the Education and Elimination of Paul "Dr. Luminol" Winkleman would be unlike any before.

To gather info about Winkleman he researched the area where the podcaster lived, a sprawling and ever-expanding Central Florida collection of 55+ communities united under the moniker "The Villages." He found a range of population estimates and differing boundaries on the web, but the development's own website stated nearly one hundred fifty thousand people resided in the assorted communities in Sumter, Marion, and Lake counties. He also learned that ninety-eight percent of the residents, known as "Villagers," are white; Republicans outnumber Democrats two to one; and the average age is seventy-two.

Although "golf car" is the correct term, most Villagers call the ubiquitous little machines "golf carts" and ownership of one is almost a requirement to live in The Villages. Many are customized, and the more they are tricked out, the better. Dawdy just shook his head when he saw a parked golf cart that looked exactly like a miniature UPS delivery van. If he killed simply to make the world a better place, that golf cart's owner would be next in line.

Dawdy noticed a strange phenomenon while scoping the area before zeroing in on Winkleman. Scores of automobiles and golf carts sported a loofah attached in some manner. Although tempted to ask a passerby on the street the significance of the loofahs, Dawdy didn't want to draw attention to himself by interacting with anyone. When he searched the web later he read that senior Villagers were still quite sexually active and even amenable to swapping partners. Loofahs were color-coded—there were seven colors in all— to advertise preferences ranging from just wanting to watch others to "anything goes" partner swapping. The bumper sticker he saw on the back of a golf cart that read "Old People Having Fun" could be interpreted many different ways.

He also saw online that The Villages was known as the "STD Capital of America," but other articles doubted the accuracy of that title. Dawdy didn't care to research further.

In addition to the geriatric Villagers' healthy sexual appetites, their per-person consumption of alcohol kept the area's beer, wine, and spirits distributors busy. The Villages has been called a "drinking community with a golf problem," where Happy Hour in bars and restaurants starts as early as eleven a.m., with doubles being served until closing time. Dawdy wondered if Paul Winkleman spent his days half-crocked with sex on the brain. He would soon find out.

Winkleman lived on Lakota Way in the Lake Sumter Landing area of The Villages. His modest white house with black trim, built in 2008, checked in at just under eighteen hundred square feet with three bedrooms and two baths. County records showed he paid sixty-eight hundred dollars a year in property taxes. None of the online real estate sites had photos of the interior of the home, but that didn't matter as this was a house that Dawdy would not be entering. It was too risky, as the street was narrow and the houses close together. He also knew that many senior citizens were either prone to hypervigilance or were just plain busybodies who closely watched the comings and goings of their neighbors. Dawdy drove past Winkleman's house one time, and that would be the only time.

He knew from Winkleman's hacked computer that he had an upcoming visit to his family doctor on Monday morning. He would seize that opportunity to view Winkleman from a short distance in the parking lot, and attach a tracking device to Winkleman's car—or golf cart, if that's how he arrived. Winkleman's house had a two-car garage, but Dawdy was unaware of what was parked inside.

Winkleman used his social media accounts only to promote his Dr. Luminol podcast, *Try To Imagine*. Each profile had the same photo, a headshot in which he looked straight into the camera, stern-visaged and perhaps trying to appear mysterious. None of his accounts included any other photos—of himself, family, friends, or pets. No photos of travels, or even just dining out. No glimpse at all into his personal life. Winkleman had never married and Dawdy's limited research to date had not uncovered any siblings or other relatives. Pedophiles come in all shapes, sizes, colors, and personalities—from popular, gregarious men who, once apprehended, are described by those who knew them as "the last person in the world you'd suspect to be a child predator," to stereotypical loners who shock no one when they are finally caught. Winkleman was somewhere on that continuum, and as Dawdy's Education progressed, he would learn where his target landed.

Dawdy thought about the folders he found when remotely searching Winkleman's computer, the ones labeled Angel Pics and Angel Vids. How had Winkleman acquired the disturbing photos and videos? With no known family members or any type of employment history around children, plus the sheer volume of images and videos, it was unlikely that Winkleman produced the content himself. Was he smart enough to avoid detection by using a VPN to wander the Dark Web in search of child porn, or was he just another naive pervert on a public file-sharing message board with the clock ticking until he's arrested? The possibility that law enforcement could also be tailing Winkleman was always in the front of Dawdy's mind. Attaching a tracking device to Winkleman's vehicle needed to be done without arousing the suspicion of anyone who might be watching.

Dawdy had much to learn about Winkleman, but the Education process involved more than just his future victim. An equally important part of his research would be to find the perfect location for Elimination. His plan for Winkleman's demise demanded a setting that had no chance of unexpected visitors, and was remote enough that no one would hear the sounds of Dr. Luminol's final moments as he recorded a podcast of his own murder.

The *SEE* process, from Education through Elimination, would take at least three weeks. Dawdy would spend a few hours at a time in The Villages, but he didn't want to rent a hotel room there—he wasn't a septuagenarian, and an "old man" disguise that would help him fit in with most Villagers required too much time in front of a mirror. He chose instead to stay in the resort town of Mount Dora, less than thirty miles from The Villages, where there would be no need to heavily disguise his appearance. Although snowbirds had begun their annual migration south to warmer climes in Florida, Mount Dora also attracted a younger crowd from Orlando, Winter Park, Sanford, and other nearby cities who flocked to the quaint, artsy little town known for its festivals, restaurants, shopping, and wine tastings. He had booked a two-week stay at The Lakeside Inn on Lake Dora. If needed, he would move on to the Hampton Inn until he completed his mission.

The Villages had live webcams in each of the four Town Squares, and Dawdy checked out the Lake Sumter Landing webcam when he was still in Ohio. Although Villagers like to party hearty in all its variations, they still rolled up the sidewalks at an early hour most week nights. Dawdy would check the webcam at ten o'clock and not see a soul in sight. But tonight was Saturday night, and the streets had a regular flow of cars and golf carts at the ungodly late hour of eight-thirty. He decided to stop in for a drink at the Lighthouse Point Bar and Grille on the southern edge of Lake Sumter.

For the first of November it was a warm night, with a gentle breeze blowing off the lake. He chose an open table on the deck at water's edge and ordered an IPA he hadn't tried before.

From his table he had a good view of most of the deck. The couples sitting around him looked to be well into retirement, many of the men with bald heads and women with gray or unnaturally dyed dark hair. He was invisible to them, as he drew not even a glance in his direction. He thought of his parents. Had they lived, they would be about the age of the people on the deck, the people laughing, drinking, and eating. Having fun. Enjoying life. *Living.* His parents had been robbed of the chance to see their golden years. After their deaths he was alone in the world, shuttled from foster home to foster home. With no role models, no one to encourage him, to love him, he turned inward and determined his own path in life. If his parents had not died, would he have turned out the way he did? He would never know that answer.

In his loneliness living with strangers he became a voracious reader across many genres, fiction and nonfiction, fascinated by how different writers wove words together to tell their stories or impart their wisdom. He loved cinema, but he didn't just watch movies, he studied them for hours on end, dissecting how lighting, camera angles, mannerisms, and subtle movements told as much or more than the characters' dialogue. Computers … while other kids his age played mindless shoot 'em up games, he wanted to understand how the hardware and software worked. He was removed from one foster home because he took apart the family's computer to get a better look at the components.

During his teen years a switch inside his head turned either on or off. He didn't recall a specific time or event, he just gradually became aware that he was different from everyone around him. He had no empathy or any feeling for other human beings. He had loved his parents—he clearly remembered that—but after they were gone

something drained out of his body, out of his soul. He became fascinated with crime and criminals, especially serial killers. He collected
and read every book he could find about Jeffrey Dahmer, John Wayne
Gacy, The Night Stalker, the Green River Killer, BTK killer Dennis
Rader, and many others. But for Dawdy, one serial killer stood far
above the rest—Ted Bundy. He found a kindred spirit in Bundy, who
was put to death by the State of Florida before Dawdy was born.
Bundy was highly intelligent, charming, good-looking, and seemed
to fit easily into society, but beneath the surface he was a cold, calculating, deceptive killer who took no mercy on his victims. Dawdy
didn't set out to pattern himself after Bundy, it just turned out that way.
Winston Dawdy thought of himself as Ted Bundy 2.0.

The most prized book that Dawdy owned, one that became his
personal bible, was *Practical Homicide Investigation*. The book was
written as a resource tool for homicide detectives, crime scene ana-
lysts, lab technicians, courtroom personnel, and others involved in the
criminal justice system. It was not intended to be a how-to book for
a future serial killer with a great admiration for Ted Bundy, but that
was what it became when Dawdy read it for the first of many times.

Most of humanity would find the pictures in *Practical Homicide
Investigation* to be horrific, but Dawdy was mesmerized by the grisly
portrayal of the aftermath of brutal murder. The photographs, in both
black and white and no-longer-living color, depicted almost every
manner in which one human being could slay another. The book contained more than photographs, however.

Practical Homicide Investigation covered a wide variety of topics
including homicide crime scenes, collection of evidence, identification of victims, autopsy procedures, investigative techniques, and
criminal personality profiling. Twenty-five pages were devoted to
the phenomenon of serial killers, complete with a section about Ted
Bundy.

Dawdy gleaned one important fact from all of the books he read about serial killers—if you knew a serial killer's name, it was because they made a mistake and became known to law enforcement. Dawdy vowed that would never happen to him. He would never slip up. In past *SEE*s, if something went contrary to his plan, he always had a contingency, a Plan B and a Plan C. Adapt and adjust on the fly.

Dawdy declined and settled his tab when his server asked if he wanted another round. He had work to do, as Paul "Dr. Luminol" Winkleman needed to die.

-44-

"I'm sorry to just drop in like this," Marjo said, "but I was afraid that if you knew I was coming you wouldn't be here."

Alita was stunned to silence by her mother's appearance. She seemed to have aged ten years in the three months since she last saw her. Her face was lined, her complexion sallow, and her always perfectly coiffed hair was now short, drab, and a darker shade than she had ever worn before.

"May I come in?"

"Uh, sure." Alita moved aside so Marjo could enter. "I'm just … surprised that you're here."

"I stopped by your shop yesterday hoping we could set up a time to talk. Meg told me you were in Nashville and might be away for a while. I have something I need to tell you and it couldn't wait until you came back home, so I flew up here today. I didn't mean to stop by this late, but I was worn out from the flight and took a longer catnap than I planned."

"So Meg …"

"She told me what you're doing up here. I made her promise not to say anything to you."

Alita felt her brain going into overload with too much to process, including *Meg knew Marjo was coming ... she should have warned me.* But Marjo was here now, standing inside Alita's apartment. *Victoria's apartment.* It was beyond her imagination.

"Can I take your coat?"

"Please."

Alita had another shock when her mother took off her coat and handed it to her. Marjo had dropped significant weight from an already thin frame. She looked almost skeletal.

"Is everything okay?" Alita asked. "You don't look like … you don't look like you're feeling well."

"You don't have to walk on eggshells, Alita. I know I look like crap and I feel like crap, too. Can we sit down?"

Alita's long day now felt like a stroll in the park. "Have a seat on the couch," she said. "Can I get you something to drink?"

"Water would be great."

She fetched a bottle of water from the fridge and poured it into a glass. She didn't know what was going on with Marjo, but she had a good guess.

"Here you go. It's bottled, not from the tap."

"Thank you."

Alita sat in the armchair and saw her mother's hand shaking as she raised the glass to her lips. She often had feelings of dread when around Marjo, but this dread feeling was different.

"I'm sure you're wondering why I'm here," Marjo said.

"It did cross my mind."

The slight smiles they exchanged were the first between them in years.

"I'll get to that. But let's get the elephant out of the room. As I'm sure you can tell, I'm ill. Quite ill."

"What … what is it?"

"Melanoma. Nodular melanoma to be exact. All those years in the Florida sun finally caught up to me."

"Where did they find it?"

"In the middle of my back, where I couldn't see it. For once, having a man in my life would have helped."

"How far along is it?"

"Stage four." Marjo took another sip of water, her hand still shaking. "I had surgery the day after you came by to tell me about Victoria. They cut a big chunk out of my back and took lymph nodes, too. Nodular melanoma is a very aggressive cancer in case you don't know. I won't bore you with the details of everything since then, but it hasn't been a picnic. It's spread to my liver, bones, brain. I start a new treatment on Monday and my doctor thinks it might give me a fighting chance. And I know what you're thinking." Marjo raised her hand and pinched a few strands of hair together, giving a slight tug. "It's still all mine for now, but it's really thin and brittle. I cut it short and colored it because it was turning gray. Lucky me."

No Marjo sightings in New Smyrna Beach now made sense. In addition to the surgery and follow-up treatments, her mother's vanity would have kept her from going out as she normally did.

"You should have told me. I could have taken you to the hospital for your surgery. And to your appointments."

"We didn't leave on the best of terms that day, did we?"

"But this is different, Mother." Alita was stunned by the last word that came out of her mouth. "I would have been there for you. Despite … everything."

"Thank you for saying that, but it's water over the dam now."

"When I get back home, let me know if you need anything."

"No, you have to stay focused on what you're doing here. Meg told me how dedicated you are to finding the person who murdered Victoria. I admire that."

Alita didn't know how to respond to words she never thought she would hear from Marjo. And more than just words, it was her tone: soft, caring, sincere. *Who is this woman?*

"What are you doing about your agency?" Alita asked.

"I've been off since the surgery, but I have good people working for me. And when they sell a house I still make money, so it's all good.

Actually, I've thought about selling the business."

"I think that would be great. You need to focus on you." Alita wanted to take back the words as soon as she spoke them, worried it sounded like Marjo didn't have much time left. *But maybe she doesn't.*

"So … this is where Victoria lived?"

"Yes, for a few months."

"It's a nice place."

"It didn't look like this when she lived here. She was going through a bad time. Meg leased all of this furniture for me."

"That was kind of her. I've always liked Meg."

"She's the best. She's almost like a …" Alita caught herself. "You said your new treatment starts Monday. You're flying back tomorrow?"

"Yes. Quick turnaround. And I'm tired, you're tired, and it's getting late, so let's get to why I came here. It wasn't to tell you I'm sick, but because I'm sick I wanted to tell you this as soon as I could. There are things you need to know. Things I now wish I had told you a long time ago."

"Okay. I'm listening."

Marjo folded her hands together on her lap. Alita saw her shoulders rise and fall.

"First, I want to apologize. Alita, I am so sorry."

"For?"

"Everything. For what I've done, for what I didn't do. For what I'm about to tell you."

Alita sat riveted in the armchair.

Marjo reached for the water glass and took another sip that didn't seem to go down well. A facade was crumbling, and Alita was getting a glimpse of her mother she had never seen.

Marjo set the glass down and looked back at Alita.

"I've spent a lot of time these last three months reflecting on my life. If cancer is good for anything, it's good for that. When the rest of your time on Earth might be measured in months, or perhaps days, you get a different perspective on things."

"Don't talk like that. I'm sure you'll be—"

"Please. I need to get this out. There are things you need to know. You've been angry at me for years. I'm sure you've even hated me, and I can't blame you for that. But you need to hear the whole story."

Alita leaned forward, closer to Marjo. "Tell me. I want to know."

"You weren't around yet, you came along much later, but I pushed Victoria away from the minute she was born. I didn't want a baby, and I couldn't love her. I treated her badly her entire life and I can never forgive myself. Never. I am so sorry now, and I wish I could tell her that. I wasn't even able to … protect her."

"You knew what Daddy was doing. Why couldn't you stop it? Why did you let it keep happening?"

Marjo's small frame seemed to sink deeper into the couch, under a weight much larger than her body mass. "You have no clue what it was like for me, Alita. It's no excuse, but what happened made me who I am. I was threatened with terrible things if I ever talked, if I ever told a soul. Horrible, disgusting things. I was told that no one would believe me, that I would be sent away to an institution and locked up for the rest of my life. When you have those things drummed into your head, it changes you. You feel powerless to do anything. Or say anything. You build walls, and hide behind them."

"What in the world are you talking about? How could Daddy have sent you away? That's crazy."

"Not your father. Your grandfather. My father."

"Your father? I don't understand." Alita saw tears spill from her mother's eyes.

"What happened to Victoria ... what your father did to her ... was the same thing that my father did to me."

Alita felt like all of the air was sucked out of the room. Perhaps she had just heard the single answer to the countless questions she'd had over the years.

"Mother ... I didn't know." Her grandfather died before she was born, and her mother rarely mentioned him. Alita moved from the chair to sit beside Marjo on the couch, taking her mother's hand in hers.

"No one ever knew." Marjo bowed her head. "Except my mother, and she didn't do anything about it. Seems that runs in the family."

"Did Daddy know?"

Marjo shook her head. "Not at first. I was too ashamed. I was afraid he wouldn't love me, that he wouldn't want me anymore." Alita reached for the box of tissues on the end table and handed it to Marjo, as more tears joined the ones already streaking her face.

"But there's more." Marjo dabbed her eyes. She wadded the tissue in her hand and kept it there. "You know that I married your father when I was just seventeen, and that Victoria was born four months later?"

"I was able to do the math."

"I don't think your father really wanted to marry me, but he felt it was the honorable thing to do when he found out I was pregnant. It was different in those days. So we married, and Victoria was born."

Marjo's head lowered. Alita noticed a slight shudder. She waited until Marjo raised her head and was ready to speak again.

"Victoria wasn't your father's child." Marjo's voice was quaking. "She was your grandfather's child."

Alita sagged against the back of the couch. *No, this can't be true.* But it made sense. It was a terrible way to treat your own child, but it did explain the relationship between Marjo and Victoria. And even in the best of times, there was an undercurrent of frostiness between her mother and her father. Family secrets locked away for years rot from the center out, often with devastating results. For everyone.

"I just … I just don't know what to say, Mother. I wish you had told me long before now."

"I know, I know. I should have done so many things differently. I tried to love Victoria, but every time I looked at her I saw my father. It was like she was a constant reminder of what he had done to me. When you came along I finally had something of my own. You were my child, my husband's child. How it's supposed to be. You were a way for me to, if not forget the past, at least push it aside. Can you understand that?"

"Yes." Alita wasn't sure she did.

"When Victoria was older," Marjo continued, "but still before you were born, your Daddy began to suspect that she wasn't his child. He was the jealous type, and he accused me of running around with his best friend before we were married. That never happened, but he would just go into a rage about it. One night he hit me, which made me so angry I just blurted out that Victoria really wasn't his. Just to hurt him back. That was a mistake. He didn't stop until I told him everything, that my father had raped me and was Victoria's father. And that was the worst thing I could have told him. He would have killed your grandfather, but he had died a year before. So, because he couldn't confront my father, he took it out on me. He blamed me for what my father had done. He claimed it was my fault."

"You know it wasn't your fault, Mother. But why would he turn around and do the same thing to Victoria?"

"Because he was sick. All of this was hidden from you. From everyone. He could be a charmer, but he had an evil side, just like my father. I knew what was going on but I couldn't stop it. I was so ashamed, so scared that people would find out. So I just put on this armor shell so nothing could touch me. But in the end, all I really did was fail Victoria."

"She would have forgiven you had she known. I know she would have."

In a moment that Alita could never have expected, she reached for her mother as her mother reached for her, and they held each other in an embrace that couldn't erase the past for either of them.

45

A lita didn't feel like talking. She just wanted to get off the phone. "It's okay, Meg," she said. "I understand."

"But I feel bad not telling you. It's just … she looked so sick that I knew something was really wrong. She didn't want me to say anything, but still, I should have—"

"Hey, I said it's okay. Don't worry about it. It's over anyway, her flight home was at nine this morning."

"So … are you going to tell me why she flew up there?"

"I'll fill you in on everything later. I don't have time now because I'm meeting Luke for lunch and I have some things to do first."

"Tell Luke I said hi. And again … I'm sorry."

Alita had the time to tell Meg all the secrets that Marjo unlocked for her, but that was a conversation meant to be held in person. She also needed space to come to terms with what had happened in her family. Everything she knew about her father, her mother, and Victoria prior to Marjo's visit was traumatizing enough, but the information she now held turned her world upside-down. Victoria was both Alita's half-sister and her aunt; she was also both Marjo's child and half-sister. What then, would that make her grandfather? She didn't want to map out the family tree.

After a shower, she was deciding which outfit to wear when her cell phone rang. She saw the name in Caller ID and answered on the first ring.

"Hello … Crystal?"

"Yeah, it's me."

"It's good to hear from you. How are you?"

"You know, same old shit show. Well, not really. I quit my job and I'm moving to Parkersburg tomorrow."

"West Virginia?"

"Yeah."

"What are you going to do there?" Alita hoped to hear plans of a legitimate job or going back to school.

"I don't know, haven't decided yet."

"Is everything okay, Crystal?"

"Um, yeah. Sure." A short silence. "Say, I saw you on TV yesterday when you got busted. That was cool."

"They ended up letting me go, but it really wasn't so cool."

"Still pretty bad ass. Your interview … I, uh, heard them say there is reward money."

"Yes, there is."

"I was just kind of calling about that."

"Okay." Alita had no idea where this was headed but she was going to let Crystal do the driving.

"I think I deserve the reward."

At last, maybe a good break? Alita's heart felt like it bounced in her chest.

"Crystal, do you know who killed my sister?"

"Nope. I wish I did."

Alita's hopes crashed in a heap. "I don't understand. Then why do you think you deserve a reward?"

"Because I was the one who called the cops."

"I have no clue what you're talking about." Alita wondered if Crystal was high on something.

"Victoria was on her way to meet me downtown when she ran into this guy," Crystal said. "He was going to give her two thousand bucks to hook up in a cemetery at midnight. That sounded crazy even to me, but I couldn't talk her out of it. I tried, I really did, but she said it was too much money to turn down. She also made me swear not to tell Big Red or Lavodis because she was cuttin' Satin Dolls out of it. She was supposed to call me the next morning to tell me how it went, but I never heard from her. When she didn't show up for work, I got worried and called the cops to report she was missing. So I think I deserve a reward for that."

Alita remembered her conversation with Detective Blate on the day they met. *Was Crystal the anonymous caller who wanted to report a missing friend?* Many questions collided in Alita's mind, but one elbowed its way to the front.

"Wait a minute. That night, in the hotel room, you told me you had never heard of my sister, and now you say you knew her? And fairly well, it seems. Is this a scam? Are you lying to me, just trying to get money?"

"No, I'm not lying. I mean, I lied to you that night, but I'm not lying now."

Alita sorted through her thoughts. She was almost certain that Crystal's story was a fabrication, but the key word was *almost.* The police did receive an anonymous call which led to Victoria's identification, and two thousand dollars might have enticed Victoria to go to a cemetery at midnight. What if Crystal *was* telling the truth now?

"Then why?" Alita asked. "Why the mystery, why the lie that night?"

"I didn't trust you. The whole thing with you was freaky at first and I thought I was walking into a trap. When you gave me that extra money and offered to help me I knew you were okay, but I couldn't go back and undo what I already told you about not knowing her."

"All right, I can see that. But when did you call the police?"

"Uh, let me think a minute. She was … she was going to meet that guy on a Saturday. She didn't call me on Sunday, and she didn't show up on Monday night so I had to cover her shift. I think it was the next day. Tuesday. Yeah, Tuesday."

"What did you say to them when you called? Did you tell them about the guy who wanted to meet her in the cemetery?"

"No way. I didn't want them to know what Victoria was doing because that could get back to Lavodis. She would have Big Red beat the crap out of me for not telling them Victoria was freelancing. I just said my friend was missing and I had a bad feeling about it."

"You didn't describe her or anything?"

"Oh, yeah. I did. I told them her name, her height, weight, hair color, that kind of stuff. And her tattoo. I told them about her ankle tattoo. Her butterfly."

"Did you give them your name or your phone number?"

"Nope. I don't trust cops, plus like I said, that could've got back to Lavodis. But I don't give a damn now 'cause I'm not workin' for her anymore."

"Look, Crystal, I really appreciate that you made that call, but the reward money is for information that leads to the arrest of the person who murdered Victoria. None of what you've told me helps in that way."

A long pause. "Well, I might have something else."

"What do you mean?"

"The guy she was going to meet in the cemetery at midnight, the guy who killed her … he gave her two hundred bucks up front that afternoon to show he meant business. When she told me about him she gave me one of the bills. I still have it. Maybe it has his fingerprints on it."

"You're being serious?"

"Yeah, I'm being serious. When I didn't hear from her the next day it was like one of those psychic things, you know? I was sure something bad happened, so I put the hundred-dollar bill in an envelope as insurance. Haven't touched it since."

Alita felt her anger rise—*why didn't she tell the police this?*—but her hope rose again as well. Although this could be nothing more than a spur of the moment scam, she needed to get that hundred-dollar bill if it existed.

"Crystal, if you have time can we meet today? Let me buy you lunch and we'll at least discuss the reward money."

"Sure, I'll take a free meal."

"Tell me where you are and I'll pick you up. And bring that bill with you, okay?"

Crystal was in East Nashville, across the Cumberland River from the downtown area. With light Sunday traffic, Alita was about twenty minutes from the corner where Crystal would be waiting. She called Luke before she pulled out of the Hunting Creek Apartments parking lot.

"Hey, Alita. I was about to call you. Instead of meeting there, why don't I swing by so we can go in one car?"

"I'm sorry, Luke, but I have to cancel our lunch plans. I just talked with Crystal, remember the young girl I told you about who works for Satin Dolls? She just gave me some new info and I have to see her now because she's moving to West Virginia tomorrow. It's my only chance."

"No problem, we can make it another time. But didn't you say she's a little shady?"

"She has issues, but this could be a lead and I just have to check it out."

"Where are you meeting her?"

"I'm picking her up, then taking her to Copper Branch."

"I can still meet you there. It might be a good idea to have somebody with you."

"No, she could get scared and bolt. It has to be just Crystal and me. But Luke, I have to go now."

"All right, but if you need me just call. And please … be careful."

"I'll be fine. Talk later."

***

Crystal was on the corner of Main and N. 8th Street when Alita pulled up to the curb.

"Good to see you again, Crystal." Alita took a close look at the young woman as she climbed in and buckled her seatbelt. Her hair was a deep shade of green. She was dressed in a dirty windbreaker and faded jeans. A small purse rested on her lap.

"Good to see you, too."

Alita detected no hint of sincerity. She pulled from the curb and into traffic.

"I thought we'd try Copper Branch for lunch. Have you eaten there before?"

"Never heard of it. Is it Italian?"

"No, it's uh," Alita stopped before using the *vegan* word. "It's different, but I think you'll like it."

On the short drive to the restaurant Alita avoided any mention of Victoria, the reward, or the hundred-dollar bill she hoped was in Crystal's purse.

"I thought you liked Nashville," Alita said.

"Nah, bunch of losers here. I'm ready to move on."

"What made you decide on Parkersburg?"

"Got a cousin there. She said I could crash for a while."

Alita had read that drug addiction hit West Virginia hard in the last few years. *Out of the frying pan into the fire.*

"I've always wanted to visit West Virginia," Alita said. "I've heard it's a pretty state, especially in the fall when the leaves change colors."

"I don't know, I'm not much of an outdoor person."

Alita wished she knew Crystal's history—who her parents were and what they did; what her childhood was like; where she went to school, and so on. What had gone wrong along the way for Crystal to end up in a stranger's car, working in the sex trade, and about to venture on her own to a place she had never been?

On Sundays it wasn't difficult to find an empty space in the parking garage. As they neared the entrance to the restaurant Crystal stopped and looked at Alita.

"Plant based power food? Is this a health nut place?"

"No, not at all. I mean, it's good food, it's just made out of plants. No animals. Nothing with a face or a mother, as they say."

Crystal shrugged her shoulders. "Okay. You're buyin' so I'll give it a try." She followed Alita inside.

They placed their orders—Tacos Pura Vida for Crystal, a Smoked Maple Tempeh Sandwich for Alita, and Gold Peak Green Tea for both—and it was time to get to the topic at hand. Alita's first question was one that had just popped into her mind. She wondered why she hadn't thought of it before.

"Crystal, the hundred-dollar bill that guy gave to Victoria, the man who might have murdered her ... how did you end up with it?"

"I got it from her. Like, twenty minutes after she got it from that guy."

"But why did she give it to you?"

Crystal's reaction was so subtle and so fleeting that Alita would have missed it had she not been sitting across the table studying her eyes, her face, the slight tilt of her head. She had her answer before Crystal responded.

"Uh, she just gave it to me because ... she knew I was low on cash."

Lie! But stay calm, don't tip your hand. Alita paused just long enough to maintain her composure.

"But yet you didn't spend it?"

"No. Like I told you, I just had this weird feeling that something had happened to her, so I kept it. When I found out she had been murdered, I thought it was a link to the guy who killed her. You know … fingerprints, maybe."

"But thinking that, you still didn't go to the police?"

"No. I already told you why."

Alita accepted those statements as possibly truthful, but she was sure Crystal had lied to the first question. Victoria, kind soul that she was, would have given the last dollar she had to anyone who needed it, but if Crystal was truly short on cash that money would have been spent already. No, Victoria had paid Crystal for drugs, that's how the hundred-dollar bill came to be in her possession.

"Crystal, if that bill leads to the killer and he is arrested, you would qualify for the reward. But first it needs to be tested to see if there are fingerprints or DNA on it. If not, it's worthless to the investigation. I need that bill, to give it to the police. I have a hundred dollars in cash on me, so we can just trade."

Before Crystal could answer, the server came with their food and set the plates in front of them. Crystal looked down at the vegan tacos. When she raised her head, Alita saw a narrowing in her eyes she didn't like.

"If there's no prints or DNA on it I don't get anything, right?" Crystal asked.

"That's right."

"Then I need more than a hundred bucks for it."

"Come on, Crystal. Victoria was your friend. This could be a chance to find the person who killed her."

"I need more, or I'll just keep it and you'll never know."

Alita sighed and opened her purse. She thumbed through the cash in her wallet. "Look, I only have a hundred and fifty-two dollars in cash on me. You're making fifty-two bucks, and if they catch the guy based on that bill you'll get the reward, I promise. Please, Crystal."

"I want five hundred for it."

Alita sat back in her chair long enough for a burst of inspiration. "Okay, fine. But I need to go outside and make a call to get more money. Stay right here."

A few minutes later Alita returned to the table and again sat across from Crystal, who had already devoured her tacos.

"A friend is on his way," Alita said. "It'll be about thirty minutes."

"Fine. For five hundred bucks I can wait."

Alita took two bites of her sandwich before pushing her plate aside. Appetite gone, she sat in the uncomfortable silence at the table as the minutes dragged by. Crystal added to Alita's tab by ordering cheesecake for dessert. As Alita watched her eat, she thought how much easier everything would be if Crystal would get a piece of the crust stuck in her throat and just keel over right there, at the table. *No, fishing through her purse for a hundred-dollar bill while she's turning blue might be a bit cold.*

Crystal's back was to the door. She didn't see it open, nor did she see him until a hand was on her shoulder and she turned and looked up.

"Hello, Crystal," he said.

Big Red plopped his large frame on the chair beside Crystal as Alita savored the mixture of confusion and terror on her face.

"What are you doing here?" Crystal's voice cracked.

"Just helping out a friend. And after what you did to me, you thought you could just disappear? Well ... surprise."

"I'm really sorry, Big Red, but I had to—"

"Save it for later, Crystal. First, you're going to give Alita what she wants."

Alita saw Crystal's hands shaking as she reached into her purse.

She pulled out a white envelope and held it out to her.

"It's inside," Crystal said. "I sealed it to protect it."

Alita took the envelope and held it to the light. She could see the faint image of a bill inside. She put the envelope in her purse and pulled out a hundred fifty-two dollars in cash that she set on the table in front of Crystal.

Big Red put his hand over the money before Crystal could grab it. "You don't have to give her anything, Alita."

"No, it's okay. That's what I offered, she can have it. She can use some of it to catch a cab home."

"Don't worry about that. I'll see that she gets a ride."

"Don't hurt her, Eric."

"I'm not gonna hurt her. We just need to have a little private talk, that's all. And your lunch is on me. My way of apologizing for scaring you that first night."

"Apology accepted."

As Alita rose to leave she took a final look at Crystal. During her phone conversation with Big Red, he confirmed that Crystal had been selling drugs to Victoria for months. He told her other upsetting things as well. Still, she had a measure of pity for the lost little girl who was on a highway to hell, and running out of exit ramps.

46

T he weekend was a roller coaster ride of emotional peaks and
valleys, but when Alita opened her eyes on Monday morning
she was eager to face the coming day.

She was worried about Marjo, though, and with her mother's
sobering diagnosis that was a concern that wouldn't be going away
soon. But love is not a faucet that can simply be turned on at will.
Although she would be there for whatever her mother needed, it would
take time for her feelings to catch up with the pledges she had made.

She found time on Sunday night to watch the Saturday late news
interviews she recorded in her Hulu app. She missed the live broad-
casts because she drove Marjo back to her hotel—her mother turned
down an offer to spend the night in the apartment. She was pleased
with the results from the last forty-eight hours, from finally drawing
attention to Victoria's murder—thanks to a billboard and three local
TV stations—to securing what might be a critical piece of evidence
from Crystal—thanks to Big Red. The upcoming live, in-studio spot
on WKRN's News 2 at 4 p.m. followed by an interview with a reporter
from *The Tennessean*, would only add to the momentum that had
begun. But Alita's first order of business would be a visit with Detective Harold Blate, to give him an envelope that still remained sealed.

She thought about Crystal, and a thin layer of guilt formed despite
all of the girl's lies. Big Red said he wouldn't hurt her but that was no
guarantee, especially after what Crystal had done to him. He didn't
go into much detail during their brief conversation, but a week ago
he had driven Crystal to an appointment with an out-of-towner who'd

had too much to drink and was carrying way too much cash. After the man passed out on the bed, Crystal relieved him of several thousand dollars and slipped out a back exit while Big Red waited in the front parking lot. He searched for her without success in the ensuing days, so when Alita called him from the Copper Branch to ask for help he was more than happy to oblige.

She arrived at the precinct with no appointment and was lucky to find Blate in his office, free to meet with her. He led her to a small, familiar conference room.

"I didn't expect to see you here again," he said. "I thought you were done with me."

"Things change."

"Touché." A slight smile played on his lips. "I understand you had a little encounter with a couple of our boys on Saturday."

Alita tried to discern Blate's mood from his tone but came up empty. At least he didn't seem angry.

"Yes. And they were actually nice to me."

"To protect and to serve, that's what we do."

Was that friendliness or sarcasm? Best stay on guard.

"You know, we've logged a lot of calls since your billboard went up," Blate continued.

"Really? That's great."

"Maybe, maybe not so great. A case like this can bring out the crazies, and your billboard and reward money make it worse. Women wanting to get back at an ex call in to report them as a possible suspect. People call us about a neighbor they think is strange, and we find out the worst thing he's done is chase kids off his lawn. You've created a lot of busy work for us that won't lead anywhere."

Alita bristled. "You're right. You were making so much progress on the case that you didn't need any help."

Blate tilted his head in a half-nod. "Okay, I deserved that. I just wish you had checked with me before you went to the media. At least you didn't say anything you shouldn't have."

"I'll have more chances to say something stupid, point taken, because I'll be on TV again today, and I'm also being interviewed by *The Tennessean*." Alita saw Blate's birthmark darken. "But that's not why I'm here. The billboard and the reward might have already been productive."

"What do you mean?"

Alita opened her purse and took out the envelope. She placed it on the table in front of her.

"This came from a young woman who worked with Victoria at Satin Dolls. I haven't opened it because I didn't want to touch it."

"What's in it?"

"If she told me the truth, it's a hundred-dollar bill that came from Victoria's killer. It might have his fingerprints or DNA."

Blate straightened in his chair. "I'm going to need more of the story."

"Her name is Crystal. I don't know her last name. Lies through her teeth, but this might not be a lie, for what she told me finally makes sense about why Victoria was in the cemetery that night."

"Go on."

"Victoria told Crystal that she was walking down Broadway when a man propositioned her. Two thousand dollars to meet him at midnight in the cemetery. He gave her two hundred dollars in advance, and one of the bills is inside that envelope."

"How did Crystal end up with it?"

"She was selling drugs to Victoria. When Victoria disappeared, Crystal thought she should hang on to it. And your anonymous caller who reported her missing? That was Crystal."

"You're sure about all of this?"

"I can't be sure about anything when Crystal's involved. But isn't it worth looking into? I mean, can fingerprints or DNA show up on currency?"

"Sometimes, yes. But who knows how many people have touched that bill?"

"She said it looks brand new. So maybe just Crystal, Victoria, and her killer."

"And the teller at the bank who gave it to him. Or whoever else passed it along to him."

"Okay, maybe it's a long shot. But can't you at least have it tested? If not, I'll have it done myself."

Blate held up his hands. "Hey, we're on the same side here, remember? I'm just giving you a reality check so you don't get your hopes too high. As smart and as careful as this guy is, he still can't think of everything all the time. Maybe he did slip up with that bill. I mean, he might have thought it would have changed hands many times by now. So of course I will have it tested. But what you said about how Victoria got the bill … she was walking on Broadway?"

"Yes."

"Did Crystal say where on Broadway?"

"No, and I didn't think to ask."

"How do you get in touch with her?"

"I have her number."

"Yeah, I want that. Did she give you a time?"

Alita shook her head. "She just said Victoria met him in the afternoon and was to go to the cemetery that night."

"This is good," Blate said. "Even if the hundred-dollar bill doesn't pan out, we have a day and a street. We'll pull all the security cam footage that's available. It will take time to scrub through it, but if we can spot Victoria we might also get a look at her killer."

47

"Another Monday morning in the City of Broken Dreams," Ed Potter grumbled to himself as he headed down the hallway toward his office. After stubbing his toe on the bed frame and burning his toast, traffic on the 110 had been its usual bumper to bumper crawl. He opened the door to see Sam wildly waving an arm, motioning him toward her.

"Lock it first," she said. "Then come here. You have to see this."

"What the hell's up?"

"Just do it."

Potter bolted the door after closing it. He turned back to Sam.

"Okay, now can you tell me what's going on?"

"It's CNN's website." Sam pointed at her computer screen.

Potter stepped around her desk and leaned down to better see the screen. The small news teaser inches from Sam's finger read: "Florida Woman Vows To Find Sister's Killer, Chains Self To Billboard."

"I locked the door because of that … why?"

"In case someone drops by. Just take a look at this." Sam clicked on the story link and the article opened in a new page, with a photo of a billboard at the top. "That's in Nashville. Check out the name on the billboard."

"What the …"

"Keep reading."

Potter leaned even closer. With each line he read he felt the strength drain from his legs, until he could barely stand.

"Holy fuck," he said.

"I know. I was just catching up on the news and I came across it. We have to call the police."

"No, Sam, we don't. We have to think this through, that's what we have to do. Come on back to my office."

Once they sat down, Sam facing his desk and Potter in his faux leather chair with the broken wheel, he lit a cigarette and opened his bottom right desk drawer for a glass and his bottle of whisky.

"Me, too," Sam said.

Despite her unbridled life outside of work, it would be the first time she joined Potter in a drink at the office. He nodded and poured the amber liquid into two glasses. They each took a gulp.

"Tell me, Ed. And be straight with me."

Another first. Despite years as his secretary and their occasional intimacy, she always called him "Potter" during work hours.

"What?" he asked.

"Did you already know?"

"Know what?"

"This. Dawdy. Did you know?"

"Hell no! Jesus. What's wrong with you, Sam?"

"Okay, I'm sorry. I had to ask. It's just—"

"I know, forget it." Potter looked at her. "Victoria LaRue. He actually used her real name in his book. That takes a set of brass balls you'd have to haul around in a wheelbarrow. What kind of a fool does he take me for?"

"Google her name," Sam said. "See if you can find anything else."

Potter swiveled to his computer and typed "Victoria LaRue" into his browser. He shook his head. "This is crazy. There are videos from TV stations, and a bunch of news outlets have picked up the story." He opened one of the news websites and there again was the photo of the billboard.

"Look at her," he said. "That's Victoria LaRue. Think what he did to her, and then he writes about it in his book."

What snapped into Potter's mind next caused a shudder. The look on Sam's face told him she just had the same thought.

"Mistress Sasha, Sam. What was her real name? It was Pamela something, right?"

"I don't remember."

Potter picked up Dawdy's chapters from the corner of his desk and flipped pages, scanning words and tracing his finger from left to right and back again. "Come on, come on, come on ... here it is. Pamela Dobbins. On Rosewood Drive in Speedway, Indiana."

Potter turned back to his computer and searched "Pamela Dobbins" "Speedway Indiana." He looked at Sam. "There's a Pamela Dobbins on Rosewood Drive. Speedway, Indiana."

"Oh god, she's real, too." Sam's face was ashen. "Is there anything about her murder, about their bodies being found?"

More keystrokes. Potter shook his head. "No."

"Then that means ..."

"Yeah," Potter said. "Dawdy wrote that the dungeon was concealed and airtight. It could be days or months before anyone found them."

"Now we do have to call the police." Sam reached for the phone on Potter's desk, but his hand shot out and grasped her arm.

"And tell them what, Sam? We don't know who Dawdy really is or where he lives. We don't know anything about him. All we have are the chapters he sent, and the cops in Nashville already know what he did to Victoria LaRue. They don't need his chapters for that."

Sam pulled her arm from Potter's grip. "But the other two. They're still there, Ed. In that dungeon, hanging upside-down in that harness."

"And they're not going anywhere. Mistress Sasha didn't have any family and that fat guy's wife is better off not finding out what he was up to, at least for now. So just think about it, Sam. Dawdy doesn't know that we know. We can use that to our advantage."

"Advantage? For what?"

"Dawdy said he was almost done with his book. The next time he calls, I'll tell him we need to seal the deal in person. To sign contracts and everything. We'll pay to fly him here if that's what it takes. That's when we can get the police involved, to set up a trap."

"Dammit, Potter, you're just thinking about his book, aren't you? He could be killing someone right now."

"There's nothing we can do to stop that. Nothing the police can do at this point, either. They don't know who they're looking for, or even where to look. He's a ghost in the wind. We are the key, Sam. This is the only way to draw him out and help the police catch him. And think about this … we have only a few chapters. My guess is he's killed a lot more people and written about it in his book. If we don't get the rest of it, those murders might never be solved. His book will tie him to everyone he's murdered. We'll use the book deal as bait. And once he's caught, you know what we could do with his book, right? A guaranteed best-seller for sure. We'd be able say goodbye to this penny-ante crap forever." Potter took a final puff from his cigarette before crushing it in the ashtray. "So … are you on board?"

Sam threw back her whisky and slid the empty glass across Potter's desk.

"Hit me again and I'll think about it."

48

Every time Alita went online, a few more news sites had picked up the story of the Florida woman who chained herself to a Nashville billboard to help find her sister's killer. None of the websites ran it as a banner story—most buried it as anchor text near the bottom of the homepage where offbeat stories appear. Still, word was spreading and it was exciting. It became more exciting when Meg called.

"It's on CNN's website, Alita!" Meg sounded breathless. "CNN, can you believe it?"

"Wow! Gimme a sec to check." Alita opened her laptop and went to CNN's site. She scrolled down the homepage until she found and clicked the story link. "Got it. Hang on."

The article was five paragraphs long and included two photos, one of just the billboard and the other a close-up of Alita wrapped in chains at its base. She didn't recall having such an angry look on her face, but she was glad that was the moment someone captured.

"This is way more than I could have hoped for," Alita said.

"I know. And you still have that TV interview today, too."

"Don't forget I'm meeting with the newspaper reporter tonight." Alita looked at her watch. "But I better go. I need to take a shower and wash my hair."

"They always say not to wear flashy colors or anything with stripes or busy patterns if you're going to be on TV," Meg said.

Alita had already looked through her suitcase. She hadn't counted on an in-studio interview with one of Nashville's top stations.

"I'm going to wear my pink T-shirt with our Sunriz logo."

"No, Alita!"

"I'm kidding. Talk to you after it's over."

***

Alita cast aside Meg's concern about what to wear for the WKRN interview, but as she sat alone in the green room the seeds of doubt Meg planted were now sprouting. Being interviewed while chained to a billboard did not require any particular clothing choice, but an in-studio, live TV appearance on a major Nashville television station was a different beast, especially if the interview hit the web as well. She went with a solid color, medium blue blouse and dark blue pants. A production assistant helped with her hair and makeup.

Alita's interview was not at the anchor desk but on a nearby set designed for a more relaxed, intimate news segment—two beige stuffed chairs facing a round coffee table. The assistant clipped a lavalier microphone to the front of Alita's blouse and led her to the set where she introduced her to Sydnee Wellington, a statuesque blonde reporter who was a fixture on News 2 at 4 p.m.

"Nervous?" Sydnee asked, once Alita was seated.

"I was more comfortable chained to a billboard."

Sydnee laughed. "Relax. Just tell your story and you'll be fine."

Last-minute bustling by several people on the set added to Alita's anxiety. At the director's cue, the red light on the center camera flashed on.

"I'm Sydnee Wellington, and my guest today is Alita King. Alita's sister, Victoria LaRue, was brutally murdered in Nashville's Mount Olivet Cemetery in the early hours of August third. As Alita will tell you, Victoria's murder remains unsolved and there are no suspects. But first, Alita did something rather unusual on Saturday to draw attention to the case. Take a look."

On a monitor behind the camera, Alita watched a video of her interaction with the first police officer at the base of the billboard. She was relieved when the short clip ended.

"Welcome, Alita. So tell us, why did you do that? Why chain yourself to a billboard?"

"Thank you for having me, Sydnee. As you noted, the investigation was going nowhere with no leads or suspects. I thought if I could get the word out to more people, someone might come forward with information that would help the police. I came up with an idea to rent a billboard that is directly across from the cemetery where my sister was murdered. I asked various media to be there on Saturday for the unveiling—including WKRN—but not a single reporter came. I was a little angry, so I just … did what I did."

"And it seems to have worked, right? You've received some attention?"

"Yes, definitely. The police were there within minutes, but so were reporters from three different TV stations. It made the news on Saturday, and I saw a couple of hours ago that it's spreading on the web."

"I saw that, too. So do you know if all of this has resulted in any new leads?"

Alita wanted to tell Sydnee about the hundred-dollar bill with possible fingerprints and DNA, but she couldn't.

"That's a question for the police to answer," she said.

"Are you in frequent contact with them? Are you happy with their investigation so far?"

So much Alita could say. So much she wanted to say.

"I do talk with them regularly, and I'm satisfied they are doing everything they can. But we need the public's help."

"There is a reward, right?"

"Yes, ten thousand dollars for information that leads to an arrest and conviction. If someone has a tip they need to call Crime Solvers.

They can remain anonymous if they choose."

"I understand you have a website, too?" Sydnee asked.

"Yes, it's who killed Victoria LaRue dot com."

"Okay … wait a second … there it is on your screen, folks. You can go to that website for a lot more information. And please, if you have a tip that could help solve this case, make that call today. But before we close, Alita, if the person who killed Victoria is watching right now, what would you say to him?"

Alita knew that Sydnee was hoping for a dramatic moment, so she would give it to her. She looked directly into the camera.

"I saw my sister's body … what you did to her. You're not human, you're a monster. I hope you *are* watching this, because I want you to know that I will do everything in my power to help hunt you down and put you in a cage where you belong. You can't hide, because we are coming for you."

The set went silent. The red light on a second camera facing Sydnee Wellington blinked on.

"That was Alita King, folks. Thank you, Alita. And now, back to Bruce at the desk."

The camera's red light blinked off.

"That was perfect," Sydnee said.

She stood up and walked away without another word.

***

Nicole Barnes, a reporter with *The Tennessean,* arrived at Victoria's apartment at seven o'clock. Alita wanted the reporter to see her Murder Board and all of the things she was doing to try to help the investigation.

The interview was not what Alita expected. Nicole's initial questions were predictable—*How did you come up with the idea for the billboard? What was it like to be chained to it? How did the police treat you?*—but the reporter was more interested in Victoria's background and the details of her murder. The irony was not lost on Alita. Despite weeks of badgering Detective Harold Blate to release information to the public, she now found herself guarding that same information just as tightly as he had done. She didn't tell Nicole about the fire and the condition of Victoria's body when it was found, or mention the roses, the upside-down cross, or the possibility of a serial killer. She referred her to Blate whenever the questioning landed on an aspect of the case that he didn't want revealed. She did, however, talk about Victoria's hardscrabble life as a sex worker and her struggles with drug addiction. She also circled back several times to restate that, despite her sister's problems and poor choices, her life had meaning and value, and she didn't deserve such a terrible fate.

An hour after the interview began, Nicole Barnes thanked Alita for her time and told her the story would run on Wednesday, both online and in the daily print edition.

Exhausted, Alita went to bed satisfied that soon even more people would be aware of what happened to her sister in Mount Olivet Cemetery.

49

W inston Dawdy shut down his laptop and sat still in the dim light. The pastel-colored walls of his second-floor room in Mount Dora's Lakeside Inn seemed to close in on him. The day's turn of events required a change in plans, which in turn required a walk to clear his mind.

He went down the stairs to the main lobby and didn't give Tremain's Tavern, the inn's cozy bar, a side-glance. Alcohol would only cloud his thought processes.

He crossed the wooden front porch that stretched the width of the inn and went down another set of steps to the sidewalk. It was a pleasant evening with a temperature in the upper sixties, typical for Central Florida in early November. He headed north on Alexander Street and cut through Sunset Park on his way to the public docks on Lake Dora.

The breeze blowing across the lake cooled the air by a degree or two. He passed the Rusty Anchor tour boat, dark and securely moored for the night, and continued along the gangway until he came to the end of the docks where tourists often flock to see the sunset.

Dawdy sat on a bench and listened to the creak of the floating docks as they rose and fell with the lapping waves. He reflected on the events of the last twelve hours. For a day that ended in the toilet, it had started off so well. He had driven from Mount Dora to Lake Sumter Landing in The Villages, to the medical office parking lot where he watched Paul Winkleman arrive via golf cart for his nine o'clock appointment. *Dr. Luminol's going to see a real doctor*, Dawdy thought at the time. He captured several good shots of his next target using the zoom lens on his camera. Once Winkleman entered the building, Dawdy stuck a tracking device to the bottom of the golf cart when he bent over next to it to tie his shoe. From a distance his movements would look normal, and the polymer glove on his hand would not be visible.

When Winkleman left his doctor's office Dawdy followed him for several blocks to test the tracking device.

He returned to Mount Dora and had lunch at The Salted Fry. He planned to spend the afternoon scouting for a proper location outside of town where the Elimination of Paul "Dr. Luminol" Winkleman could be done without risk or detection. But first he went to his room to grab a bottle of water.

He usually waited until the end of the day to review the key-stroke loggers and voice-activated recordings captured from devices he planted in Ed Potter's office. The files automatically uploaded to Dawdy's own encrypted cloud server, and he would download them using a VPN for even more security. However, on some days, such as this one, he would pop in to check a few of the clips and logs just to see what Potter and Sam were up to. It took only a few minutes for him to realize that everything had just changed.

They know about Victoria and Mistress Sasha.

Their multiple early morning shots of whisky and likely stress over what they had found on the web had both of them ready to call it a day and go home well before noon, so within a couple of hours he had listened to all of the audio. He found their plan to set a trap for him—with the details conveniently laid out—impressive. He would come up with his own counterplan, of course, but he had more immediate matters to consider.

It didn't surprise him that Potter and Sam had seen the story about the Nashville billboard and he had not. Although CNN and other websites picked up the story, it was still relegated to the "strange news department" on most of those sites. But now that he was aware of it, he scoured the web for everything he could find about the billboard and Alita King. He had learned of her existence during the Education process for Victoria LaRue. He knew the kid sister lived seven hundred miles from Nashville and owned a small shop in a Florida beachside town, but at the time he had no reason to delve any further into her life.

He had been unable to stream her live interview on WKRN's News 2 at 4 p.m. show, but the station made news programs available in the Video Center section on their website two hours after broadcast. He watched Sydnee Wellington's segment with Alita King, and heard the closing statement that Victoria's sister made.

And then he powered off his computer and went for a walk.

He had the end of the docks to himself as it was well past sunset and no one else found reason to venture that far down the gangway. His next move had to be thought out carefully. The news from Nashville via Ed Potter's office in Los Angeles meant a major reprieve for Dr. Luminol. The pedophile was going to die in a most interesting way, but his Elimination involved many elements that needed to be perfectly timed, and that was not possible now that Dawdy's attention was needed elsewhere. All he could do was hope that any law enforcement agencies that might be on Winkleman's trail would not nab him first.

Dawdy had researched Potter so thoroughly that he could predict his thoughts and actions. Sam, however, was the wild card, the one who concerned him. Potter had talked her out of going to the police for now, but the clock was ticking and Dawdy knew it. If the sample chapters he sent to Potter were turned over to the authorities, his master plan was over. He had to act before Sam changed her mind.

The pieces of a plan finally came together. Dawdy rose from the bench and headed back down the gangway. He cut over to Maggie's Attic and ordered a glass of wine, which he took outside to the courtyard. He rethought each step of his plan multiple times just to be sure it would work. Satisfied, he finished his wine and went back to the Lakeside Inn. In the stillness of his darkened room he opened his laptop, secured his internet connection, and bought an airline ticket to Los Angeles.

50

A lita was awake before dawn on Wednesday morning. She reached for her iPhone on the nightstand. In an hour or two she would go to a nearby convenience store to pick up a few copies of the newspaper, but she wanted to read Nicole Barnes's story online, on *The Tennessean*'s website.

About ten paragraphs into the article she felt nauseous. She forced herself to continue reading until the end before calling Luke.

"Alita … is everything okay?" he asked.

"I know it's really early and I'm sorry if I woke you up, but I wanted to tell you before you heard it anywhere else. I'm sorry, Luke. I'm so sorry."

"About what? What's happened?"

"The paper … *The Tennessean.* I just read the interview online. Their reporter, Nicole Barnes, interviewed me Monday night. I thought the story was just going to be about me and the billboard, but she must have gone to Mount Olivet Cemetery yesterday. She quoted June Wickliff, the woman who works at the cemetery, the one I saw that first day. I hadn't met you yet. I didn't know anything about you, all I knew was your name, and I … I told June you were the one who found Victoria's body. And she told Nicole. It's online now, and it will be in the paper today. I feel so guilty."

Three months of grief, anger, stress, and loneliness boiled to the surface. Alita sobbed so hard she put the phone down on her bed and buried her face in her hands. It was a minute or more before she picked up the phone again.

"Luke? Hello, Luke?"
He wasn't there.

**

Alita soaked a washcloth in cold water and pressed it to her face, holding it there while she thought about the mess she created. Not only had June Wickliff told Nicole Barnes that Luke discovered the body on a training run, she also told her about fire being involved in Victoria's death, something else that Alita brought up that day in the cemetery. And now it was out there for everyone to know.

Luke hates me, and Detective Blate will be pissed.

Alita lowered the washcloth and stared in the mirror. A sad, puffy-eyed woman who looked ten years her elder gazed back at her. She had just fallen off the cloud she had been walking on the last few days and was now plummeting to the ground without a parachute.

Since learning of Victoria's murder she hadn't cared about how she dressed, how much she food she ate, or how much wine she drank. All she thought about was doing whatever she could to help find Victoria's killer. But with the billboard and the publicity and finally getting the word out about the murder to the general public, she felt she had done something positive, that maybe it was time to take a step back to recharge. And in that step back maybe, just maybe, Luke could become more than an ally, more than a friend. But she just blew any chance of ever seeing him again.

She carried her laptop to the couch and forced herself to again read Nicole Barnes's article on the web, hoping that it wouldn't come across the second time as badly as it had the first. That hope faded after a few lines. She closed her laptop and sat in the darkness, arms wrapped around her bent knees, rocking gently back and forth.

First light was breaking when she heard footsteps on the stairs, then a knock at her door. She checked the peephole before opening it.

"Hey, are you okay?" Luke asked gently.

Alita stepped into the hallway and hugged him, not wanting to let go.

"I am now," she said. "I thought you would be really upset with me."

"Of course not. I just jumped in my car and got here as fast as I could."

"I'm so sorry."

"You need to stop saying you're sorry about everything. I don't care that my name's in the paper. Or online. Now, how about we go inside and have a cup of coffee before we wake everyone up?"

They went into the apartment and Alita closed the door behind them.

"Do you mind making the coffee?" she asked. "I need to change and freshen up a bit. I'm sure I'm a sight." In a moment that Alita wished she looked her best, she couldn't recall ever looking worse.

"You look just fine to me. And I can handle a Keurig. Any particular flavor?"

"You pick."

Alita washed her face again and applied enough makeup to be presentable. As she changed from her pajamas she could hear Luke humming in the kitchen.

She thought about their hug in the hallway. It was an impulse, it just happened. She didn't know if Luke had feelings for her. She didn't even know if she had feelings for him. She just knew that the aftermath of Victoria's death had forged a bond between them.

She joined Luke at the dinette table, her steaming coffee mug awaiting her. "I don't know if I look any better, but I feel better," she said.

"There you go again, fishing for compliments." He smiled. "You look great. So what's on tap for the day?"

"I was going to spend it hiding under a rock, but thanks to you I think I'm back on my feet. I don't know what's next, though. I mean, I finally raised awareness with the interviews. And the billboard will be there for as long as I pay to keep it up." Alita pointed to the Murder Board covered with thumbtacked notes. "That thing, though, was a pretty stupid idea. I thought I could play amateur detective and find her killer myself."

"Don't sell yourself short. You might have come up with a critical piece of evidence in that hundred-dollar bill."

"Maybe. But Blate has it now and everything is in his hands. There's really nothing more for me to do. So I'm going back home for a while, to help my mother."

"Marjo?" Luke looked puzzled. "I thought you were estranged."

"There's a lot more to the story now. If you have the time, I have plenty of coffee."

51

E d Potter was stretched back in his chair with his feet on his desk, half-asleep and his work week about to end. Sam rushed into his office.

"He's on the phone, Potter. Winston Dawdy."

Potter sat up, eyes fully open. "What did you say to him?"

"Nothing. I mean, he asked for you, so I said I'd see if you were available. I put him on hold."

"Did he say anything else?"

"No. What should I do?"

"Transfer the call."

"What are you going to say?"

"Jesus, Sam, just put him through before he hangs up."

Sam turned and hurried back to her desk. Mind racing, Potter lit a cigarette to reset his jittery nerves. He took a deep drag and exhaled just as his phone rang.

"Ed Potter."

"Hello, Mr. Potter. Winston Dawdy."

"Winston! Good to hear from you. How's the writing going? Making progress?"

"I'm finished with my book, Mr. Potter. All of it."

"Wonderful. Are you happy with it?"

"You're the one who needs to be happy."

"I'm sure I will be. Look, Winston, I'm confident that I can find a publisher for your book, but I can't shop it until we've taken care of the paperwork. The legal stuff, I'm sure you understand. It's called a

Literary Agent Contract and you need to—"

"I know how it works, Mr. Potter. That's why I'm calling. I would like to sign the paperwork as soon as possible."

"Perfect. We should take care of that here in the office so we can finally meet in person. Book a flight as soon as you can, and I'll reimburse you."

"Not necessary, Mr. Potter. I can stop by your office within the hour."

"You're in L.A. right now?"

"Yes."

Potter paused while he took a drag off his cigarette. With Dawdy already in town, everything he and Sam had planned needed to be rethought. Immediately.

"And you have the book with you, Winston?" he asked. "All of it?"

"Yes. I can be at your office in thirty minutes."

Potter was not comfortable with how fast things were moving, but he had no choice. "I'll be here. Do you need directions?"

"I know where you are. See you soon."

Potter was so focused on his call with Dawdy that he didn't notice Sam in front of his desk until he looked up.

"He'll be here in half an hour," he said.

"Potter, I don't like it. We don't have enough time to set up a trap. We have to call the police."

"No. Not yet. Let me think, let me think." Potter took a couple of deep drags from his cigarette before crushing it in the ashtray. He couldn't tell Sam, but the only thing more important than catching Winston Dawdy was to make sure the police were not aware of his book when they cuffed him and hauled him away. Potter had to get the rest of the book and have Dawdy sign the paperwork. Once that was done, Potter would have all of *Stay Downwind* and the legal right to represent it, but if the police seized the book first it would never be returned to him.

"Okay, I've got it," Potter said. "Here's the plan. You're going to go home and—"

"I'm not going home."

"I don't have time to argue with you, Sam. This will work, trust me. Go home, and be ready to call the cops. Not 911, you'll need to call the station on North Wilcox. As soon as Dawdy signs the paperwork and I have the book, I'll text you. I'll tell him you're as excited about having him as a new client as I am, and that we want to take him out for dinner and drinks to celebrate. I'll make up a restaurant, he won't know. When you get the text, that will be your cue to call the cops. Again, make sure you have the number of the one on Wilcox. Tell them I'm on my way to their station with a known serial killer. Tell them he killed Victoria LaRue in Nashville. That billboard story is on the web, they can verify that in a few seconds. I'll be going up Vine, taking a left on De Longpre, and then go south on Wilcox. That way Dawdy won't know where we are until we're in front of the station. The cops need to be out there with guns drawn. Describe my car, and make sure you tell them I'm driving, he's the passenger."

"What if they don't believe me?"

"Then I'll crash the damn car into their building. Jesus, Sam, just convince them."

"Okay, okay. How long will it take you to get there?"

"It's only a couple of miles away, but I'll take my time locking up and everything. Make it fifteen minutes after my text. That should give you and them enough time. After you call them, text me back and say 'on my way.' If there's any hitch or delay, text me and say 'running late.' I'll stall until you text me that you're on your way, code for they're ready. Got it?"

"I think so."

"It can't be I think so, Sam. Do you have it or not?"

"Yes, I've got it, dammit."

"Then go."

Sam turned and took a few steps. She stopped and turned back to him. He saw the worried look on her face.

"Ed … be careful."

Potter smoked two cigarettes while waiting on Dawdy to arrive. He thought about making a deal with God to quit smoking if he survived the night, but he didn't believe in God and he knew he'd never quit.

He checked his watch. *Five-thirty.* At that time on a Friday night he'd be the only one still working in any of the small offices on the second floor of the building, but the nail salon and the vintage record store on the ground floor both stayed open until seven. *If needed, help is only one floor away.*

Sam's house was twenty-five minutes from the office, maybe fifteen minutes more with early Friday evening traffic. Potter ran the timeline through his mind. With Dawdy due any minute, he would have to buy enough time to make sure Sam was home and waiting by her phone for his text. If he stalled Dawdy while completing the paperwork, the plan should work. *As long as Sam doesn't screw things up.*

Potter was about to light another cigarette when he heard three knocks on the office door. It swung open, and a man toting a backpack came through the doorway.

"Hello, Mr. Potter."

"Winston! I'm so glad to finally meet you."

"Same here, sir."

Potter had no idea what the evil monster who took such delight in killing people would look like. Dawdy was white, maybe early thirties, dressed in jeans, a black T-shirt, and a Dodgers ball cap. Even though he was good-looking, something about his face just seemed off. The coloring, the contours, Potter couldn't pinpoint what it was, and he didn't want his gaze to linger.

They shook hands. Potter hoped his sweaty palm wasn't noticed. "Come on back to my office and we'll get the paperwork out of the way," he said. "Do you have anywhere you need to be tonight?"

"No."

Potter led Dawdy past Sam's desk on the way to his office, thinking a knife was about to be thrust into his back. *Stop it, that doesn't help! He doesn't know you know. Be cool, act natural, and this will all be over soon.*

"Have a seat."

Dawdy sat in the chair facing Potter's desk. Potter patted him on the shoulder as he passed by to sit in his chair. "This is a big day for you, Winston."

"I know that, sir."

"You brought the rest of your book with you, right?"

"Yes, of course."

Dawdy pulled a stack of pages bound by a large rubber band from his backpack. He removed the rubber band and handed the pages to Potter.

"Stay Downwind, by Winston Dawdy." Potter looked up from the title page. "Sounds like a bestseller to me, don't you think?"

"With you, anything is possible, sir."

"I hope you're right. Let's see, you're under eighty-five thousand words. Good." Potter thumbed through a few pages at the beginning, middle, and end, but didn't see what he was looking for. "The chapters that you already sent to me, the ones about the hooker and the dominatrix … are they here, too?"

"Yes."

"Do you have a digital copy you can give me?"

"Yes." Dawdy unzipped a pocket in his backpack and brought out a flash drive. He set it on the desk. "It's in Word."

"Fine." Potter put the flash drive in his middle drawer. "Winston, what you'll be signing is a standard Literary Agent Contract. You're giving me the exclusive right to represent and market your book. For my services I will receive a fifteen-percent commission on all sources of income, including hardcover, paperback, ebooks, audiobooks, film rights, etc., etc. All royalties are sent directly to me. I take my commission and send you the balance. Again, all standard stuff. And, of course, you retain ownership of the copyright to your book. Do you have any questions about any of that?"

"No, Mr. Potter. I've done my research."

"I'm sure you have. But one more thing. I drew up this agreement between Potter Literary Associates and Winston Dawdy. That is your real, legal name?"

"I told you it was when we first talked, Mr. Potter."

"You did, but I just had to confirm. And since you didn't give it to me before, you'll need to write in your address, phone number, and e-mail. Also, your social security number, for tax purposes."

Potter rotated the contract and pushed it across his desk along with a pen. "Take your time, look it over."

"I trust you, Mr. Potter."

Potter watched as Dawdy filled in the blanks on the contract. It was upside-down, so he couldn't read the writing. Dawdy finished and put down the pen.

"Congratulations, Winston. I'm going to make you famous." Potter reached over the desk and again shook Dawdy's hand.

"I have no doubt about that, sir."

Potter glanced at his watch. *Sam should be home now, but give her a little more time, just in case.*

"How long will you be in town, Winston?"

"I'm leaving tomorrow morning."

"You came here just to drop off your book and sign the contract?"

"Yes."

"Well, if you don't have any plans, Sam—my secretary, you've talked with her—we'd like to take you out and have a celebratory drink. And dinner if you're hungry. It's not every day an author signs his first agent agreement."

"That's nice of you, sir. To be honest, I could use a drink right about now."

Ah, another way to buy more time. "Well, I just happen to have a little Johnnie Walker Black right here," Potter said. "If that suits your fancy."

"That would be great."

Potter opened his bottom drawer and took out the bottle of whisky and two glasses. He screwed the cap off the bottle and poured a generous amount into each glass. He handed one of them to Dawdy.

"Here's to your book, Winston. I wish you great success."

"Thank you, sir."

Potter took a sip and savored the smoky flavor and warm, throaty burn of his favorite whisky. Dawdy took a taste, too.

"Good brand, sir. But before I forget, would you mind making me a copy of our agreement? I think I should have one."

Potter slapped his forehead with the palm of his hand. "Of course. Sam usually handles those things, but I should have thought of it. Just give me a second."

Potter picked up the agreement and headed to the copy machine in the outer office, near Sam's desk, to make two copies of the original. With the privacy partition blocking the view between them, Potter took a peek at the last page of the agreement to learn Dawdy's address—a town in Idaho he'd never heard of.

"Here we are," Potter said upon return. He handed one of the copies to Dawdy.

"Thank you." Dawdy folded the agreement and put it in his back-pack.

Potter took another sip of whisky. "Winston, I've represented many authors and many books over the years, but you're the most intriguing writer I've ever met."

"I've always been a little different from everyone else, sir."

"Use that to your advantage, my friend," Potter said. "I hope you have plans for another book."

"I do. I'll be writing the first chapter in a few days."

"Ah, good. The same genre? Another serial killer book?"

"Yes. As they say, write what you know."

Potter thought his heart skipped a beat. *Did he just admit to being a serial killer?*

"I majored in criminology," Dawdy continued. "I've always been fascinated by serial killers, so writing about them comes easily to me."

Potter took no comfort from Dawdy's answer. His fear level inched higher. He took more than a sip from his whisky glass this time. He stubbed out the butt of the cigarette he had neglected and pulled another one from the pack.

"Do you mind if I smoke?" he asked.

"Of course not. It's your office."

Potter tried to hide the tremor in his hand as he flicked his lighter and held the cigarette to the flame.

"I need to quit these damn things before they kill me."

"Cancer is a slow, painful death, Mr. Potter. But there are worse ways to die."

God, he's a weird son-of-a-bitch. Potter took another swallow of whisky, but it had done nothing to tamp down his nerves.

"Your new book," Potter said. "So you've already started your research?"

"Yes. And I'm going to Florida from here. I have a couple of places I need to visit. New Smyrna Beach and The Villages."

"I'm sure you'll be thorough. You write such vivid scenes, Winston. They seem so real." *That was stupid, you idiot! Time to get the show on the road before you say too much.*

"I feel I owe that to the reader, sir."

"That's what makes a g-good ... uh, a ... good ... writer."

Potter reached to pick up his cigarette from the ashtray but his fingers weren't working in tandem with his brain. A strange dizziness swept over him. His arms were heavy lead pipes and his feet were numb against the floor.

"What's ... what's happening to m-me?" Potter's tongue felt too thick for his mouth. "I think I'm ha-having a ... stroke."

"I'm not a doctor, Mr. Potter, but it's definitely not a stroke. I think you must have ingested something. Maybe bad whisky."

"You ... you did this. Put s-s-something in ... my glass. When I was ... was at ... copier ..."

"I've waited a long time for this, Mr. Potter. Almost a lifetime, really."

"What ... you ... talk ... ab-"

52

P otter's eyes opened and closed as he drifted back into awareness. Drool trickled from the corner of his mouth. He tried
but couldn't raise his hand to wipe it away. He looked down at the
ropes that secured him to his chair. Winston Dawdy stood in front of
his desk.

"Welcome back, Mr. Potter. But take this as a warning. If you yell
for help, no one will hear you. And you won't wake up the next time."

"Why are you doing this to me?" Potter couldn't move because of
the ropes, but he was alert and able to speak again.

"Because you and Sam know the truth about my book, thanks to
Victoria's sister and her billboard."

"We just came across it online," Potter said. "But we weren't going
to the cops, I swear. Smell the money, Winston. I can still sell your
book while you stay in the wind. We'll set up a Swiss bank account
or something to get your royalties to you. I'll figure that out. And if
you keep doing what you do, there could be more books … movies
… the sky's the limit. No one has ever done anything like this before,
Winston. A book by a real serial killer who's still out there killing."

"You haven't changed a bit, have you, Mr. Potter?"

"What do you mean?"

"*SEE*. Selection, Education, Elimination. You know my process,
right?"

"Yes."

"I can multitask, Mr. Potter. I selected my first victim many years
ago, and Education has been ongoing since then. So long, in fact, that

I know more about him than he knows about himself. Care to take a guess who he is?"

Potter struggled against the ropes. "You can't get away with this," he muttered. "I was supposed to text Sam. She didn't hear from me, so the cops are on their way right now."

"Oh, I know all about your little plan to deliver me to the doorstep of the police station. I've taken care of that, Mr. Potter. I used your cell phone to text her. She thinks I didn't give you my book yet, so you're taking me out for dinner and drinks by yourself. You told her not to worry, you'll call her later tonight once you have it."

"She won't believe that."

"Of course she will. She knows you want my book more than you want me arrested."

"Winston … please …"

"Mr. Potter, my name really isn't Winston Dawdy. That's just an anagram of the title of my book. Winston Dawdy—*Stay Downwind.* Get it?"

"Then who are you?"

"I've had many names. But my birth name? Artemus Logan, Jr."

"My god … you can't be."

"Yes, Mr. Potter. My dad was Artemus Logan. I think you read his book, *The Devil's Finest Hour.* In fact, I know you read it. Because you stole it from him."

"But that was a long time ago, and I paid a heavy price for it. And your family … your mother received seven figures from the lawsuit, and millions more from book sales."

"And she invested most of it in Apple stock before she died, and that became mine when I turned twenty-one. This isn't about money, Mr. Potter. It's about making things right. An eye for an eye, as they say."

"How does this make anything right?"

"Because I hold you responsible for my father's death."

"Your dad died in a car accident. Before I even called your mom. How am I responsible for that?"

"My father was a teacher, but his dream was to be a writer. And of all the literary agents out there, he picked you, Mr. Potter. He put his faith in you. After he sent you his manuscript, he went to the post office every day to look for your response. For weeks he did that. He was driving home from the post office the day his car slid on black ice. He was hit head-on by a snowplow and died instantly. You were the reason he was on the road that day, Mr. Potter. That's why I selected you first."

"Winston ... Artemus ... I'm sorry. But without me, you'll have no chance of getting your book published. And that's what you want, right? To be a published author like your dad?"

"No, Mr. Potter. I know my book can never be published because it's the only thing that links all of my victims. I sent you those chapters to see what you would do. When you found out my book was about real murders, Sam wanted to call the cops but you talked her out of it. You didn't care if I kept on killing as long as you got your greedy little hands on my book. I was going to send you a few more chapters before paying you a visit, but the meddling by Victoria's sister changed everything."

"How did you know we found out about Victoria? And ... our plan tonight?"

"Mr. Potter, you so underestimate me. There are six office suites on this floor and rarely are all rented. The office down the hall on the left that's vacant now? Remember about a year ago when it was rented for a few months by a psychologist? A psychologist you never saw, who never seemed to have any patients? That gave me a key to the main doors, and at night when everyone was gone it was easy to get into your office. I hid tiny spy cams so I could see and hear everything.

Your computer is hacked, Sam's is hacked. I could go on and on. Oh, I also knew about the bottle of Johnnie Walker Black you always keep in your bottom drawer. When I said I could use a drink, I knew you'd pull it out. You're so predictable."

"But Sam knows what you did. You can still walk away now, and we won't say anything."

"Unfortunately for Sam, I'll be paying her a visit soon, too. Hope you don't mind if I borrow the house key she gave you. But now it's time for you to go silent while I tidy up." Dawdy reached into his backpack and pulled out a roll of duct tape. He came around the desk and stood next to Potter.

"Please, Winston. Don't do this."

Dawdy tore off a strip of tape and held it close to Potter's mouth. "You might want to take a deep breath, Mr. Potter. Sorry I can't offer you one last cigarette."

Potter saw movement behind Dawdy, who must have sensed something because he started to turn around. If Dawdy saw the gun in Sam's hand or heard any of the shots, no one would never know.

A warm, red spray hit Potter's face as Dawdy slumped to the floor.

"Dammit, Sam! You shot me, too."

53

A lita slept in and was about to fix breakfast when she heard the custom ringtone on her phone.

"Hello, Mother. How are you feeling today?"

"Like a steamroller ran over me. The treatment's worse than the cancer."

Alita could hear the discomfort in her mother's voice.

"Do you need me to fly home?" she asked.

"No need to do that. If you were here I'd still be just as sick. But that's not why I called. Am I interrupting anything?"

"Not at all."

Alita once went long stretches without any interaction with Marjo, and now they were talking on a daily basis, and not just about her treatments. They were in uncharted waters, but a renewed mother-daughter relationship—once thought impossible—now seemed within reach.

Marjo coughed roughly several times, and the sound was painful for Alita to hear.

"I want tell you something," Marjo said, her voice raspy. More coughing. "And also ask you to make a promise to me."

"Of course."

"When I flew up to Nashville to see you, and we had the talk about … well, the family and everything. I would have told you then, but we were both worn out and I had given you enough for one night. But it's important to me that you know this, too. In case something happens to me sooner rather than later."

"What is it, Mother?"

"I was there that day," Marjo said. "For Victoria's funeral. Not in the cemetery, but I drove by out front. Several times, before and during the service."

"Why didn't you stop?"

"I just couldn't. And I regret it so much now, like I regret so many other things. But I wanted you to know I was there. At least driving by. That's what I wanted to tell you."

"I don't know what to say, Mother. I know now how difficult that had to be for you. Just that you tried means a lot to me, and I'm sure Victoria knew you were there."

"I hope so. But there's more, and it involves Victoria. I want you to promise me you'll do this." More coughing.

Alita had no idea what was coming, but she already knew she would do whatever her mother asked.

"I'm hoping I'll get better, that the treatment is going to work. But if it doesn't turn out that way, I want you to promise you'll do one last thing for me. Promise?"

"I promise, Mother. What do you want me to do?"

***

It was after eleven-thirty in the morning and it had been a chore for Alita just to move from the kitchen to the couch in the living room. She was still processing her mother's phone call.

She realized that she never really knew her mother. She could say the same about her father, her grandfather, and her grandmother who turned the same blind eye to incest that her mother did. Strangers all. The only family member she had ever known, *really known*, was Victoria, and at one time Marjo had done her best to destroy that relationship, too.

But Marjo was changing. Or had she always been there, just covered in layers of guilt and denial and pain that were finally dissolving? Alita could not fathom what her mother's childhood had been like, but now that she knew the truth, how could she judge her any longer? She couldn't.

Alita finally made it off the couch and returned to the kitchen to think about making lunch when her cell phone rang again. She didn't recognize the number but she answered it anyway.

54

66 I 'm glad I was able to reach you, Miss King. Thanks for coming in so quickly." Detective Blate's face was blank. "Have a seat."

This was a conference room Alita had not been in before. Blate closed the door behind them.

Is this about the article in The Tennessean? Or is he still upset about the billboard and all the false leads it might have caused?

Alita took the chair on the opposite side of the table.

"I have news for you about Victoria's case," he said.

Alita studied his face but there were no tells, and the birthmark on his forehead retained its usual color. His expression remained blank, but there were no traces of anger. A small relief.

"I hope it's good news," she said.

A sparkle seemed to come into Blate's eyes as his face softened.

"Alita, they got the son-of-a-bitch."

"Got him … like he's actually in custody, or you just know who he is?"

"He's not in custody. He's dead."

"Who? How?" Monosyllables were all she could produce.

"It went down in Los Angeles. In his literary agent's office."

"His *literary* agent?"

"Yeah. It gets complicated and it's going to take time to sort it all out. I got a heads up yesterday from a detective out there, but I wanted to wait until they were sure of what they had before I told you. They called me again this morning, and I called you right away."

"Was he really a serial killer?"

"Definitely. Victoria was one of possibly many victims."

"What's his name? I need to know his name."

"Artemus Logan, Jr. He was writing a book about his victims using the name Winston Dawdy. Do either of those names mean anything to you? Did Victoria ever mention them?"

"No. But a book … about what he did? To Victoria?"

"And others. The L.A. cops don't have much to go on at this point, just what they're getting from the literary agent that Logan wanted to represent him. That guy's name is Ed Potter. He's still pretty shook up because Logan was going to kill him, too. I don't know the details yet, but Potter's secretary showed up at the office just in time. Emptied her gun into Logan, but accidentally winged her boss in the shoulder, too. He'll be all right. They're both extremely lucky, though. Potter said Logan was going to go to the secretary's house and kill her later that night."

"This is just such a shock … I mean, not only that he's dead, but he was writing a book? If the literary agent knew he was a serial killer, why didn't he call the police?"

"He didn't know at first. He didn't have the entire book, just a few chapters, and he thought it was fiction. Potter found out because of you. He saw the story on the web about you chaining yourself to the billboard. Logan actually used Victoria's name in the chapters Potter had, so he put it all together. I might have called it the 'stupid billboard idea' at one time, and if I did, I'm sorry. Without you, Logan would still be out there."

"You said the book wasn't just about Victoria. How many others?"

"No idea yet. Potter told the detectives about two possible murder victims in Indiana, and they in turn notified cops there. They found two bodies in some sort of hidden dungeon. I don't know any more about that. But they have the entire book now, so there's a lot of things that need to be sorted out. The investigations will take time because there are multiple jurisdictions involved—here, L.A., Indiana, and who knows where else. But Alita ... thanks to you, it's over."

She wanted to rush around the table and give Blate the biggest hug he'd ever had, and even kiss that beautiful birthmark on his forehead that was shaped like the state of New Jersey. Instead, she sat just there, totally and completely drained.

It truly was over.

-Epilogue-

Luke was in Austin meeting with a hot new country band when Alita called to tell him the serial killer who murdered Victoria was dead. Luke was elated for Alita, but sad that he was so far away and unable to be with her.

Alita remained in Nashville for a few days to close out Victoria's apartment. Jamila had been kind to her from the beginning, so Alita gave her the bulletin board, office supplies, and the Brother copier/printer/scanner. She also surprised her with generous gift certificates to her favorite hair and nail salons, and also to the best barbecue restaurant in the city.

Alita boxed and shipped to Florida the few items of Victoria's that she wanted to keep. The last thing she took off the wall was her father's photograph. She tossed it in the trash bag. Everything else—sheets, towels, silverware, cups, plates, etc.—went to the laundry room for any resident to take.

When the leasing company removed the last piece of furniture the apartment was empty. She walked through each room one last time before pausing at the door to look back at the living room and the small balcony on the other side of the sliding glass doors. She had always felt Victoria's presence in the apartment, but that feeling was gone now. She hoped that Victoria's spirit was finally at rest.

Alita returned to work with Meg at the shop, and to a daily routine of leaving her footprints on the beach and watching the sunrise.

She was thrilled when her mother invited her to Thanksgiving dinner. Marjo had responded to the new treatment regimen and was feeling a little stronger, although she was exhausted by the end of most days. Still, she insisted on preparing the holiday meal, including a small turkey for herself and Meg, and a plant-based roast for Alita. She even set an honorary place at the table for Victoria.

Detective Blate contacted Alita to report that testing of the hundred-dollar bill that Crystal claimed Victoria gave to her did not contain Artemus Logan's DNA or fingerprints. Alita decided it was just another one of Crystal's many lies. It didn't matter anymore.

Ed Potter applied for the reward money that Alita offered through the Crime Solvers program. Two days later, Sam Brocklesby applied, too, claiming that she should be the sole recipient because she was the one who actually shot and killed Logan. A decision was made by the Crime Solvers board to split the reward equally between Potter and Brocklesby, a solution that didn't satisfy either of them. The dispute apparently didn't affect their working relationship, as Sam Brocklesby was still employed by Potter Literary Associates.

Alita learned from Detective Blate that there were a number of discrepancies in the stories told by Potter and Brocklesby, and L.A. investigators felt they were withholding information. Potter had turned over Logan's book to authorities, but there were rumors that he had a digital copy and was discreetly shopping it to New York publishing houses. Alita shuddered at the thought that she might one day see *Stay Downwind* in her local bookstore.

Marjo continued to improve and was returning to most of her normal activities. She was delighted to meet Luke when he flew down to spend a few days with Alita over Christmas. She went with them to The Garlic for dinner, and the next day she joined them for drinks at The Breakers. Alita marveled at the kind, warm, engaging woman her mother had become once she finally unburdened herself of the guilt she carried for decades.

Luke talked Alita into flying back to Nashville with him to celebrate New Year's Eve, and they rang in the new year with two hundred thousand other people at Nashville's Big Bash. During Alita's five days in Music City she enjoyed a private tour of the Ryman Auditorium and a beer at Tootsie's Orchid Lounge. They sat in on a recording session, and Luke introduced her to country music stars, A-list pickers, record company executives, and anyone they encountered who was connected to the music business. He was so unassuming for someone so important in the industry, one of many traits she found attractive about him. She didn't know if a long-term relationship was possible because his work tied him to Nashville, and she couldn't bear to leave her shop or New Smyrna Beach. For now, they decided to enjoy each moment together and not worry about the future.

Marjo relapsed in February and testing showed that her cancer had spread throughout her body. Her doctors could do nothing more for her. Alita moved in with her mother, and Meg was there as often as possible to help out. Hospice care began in mid-March, and Marjo passed peacefully in her sleep on the third day of April. She had wanted to be cremated and not have any public memorial service, requests that Alita honored.

A few weeks later, Alita also kept the promise she made to her mother on the phone months earlier. On the second Sunday in May, with Meg at her side and Phil Krynak standing solemnly in the background, Marjo King's ashes were placed for eternity with her late daughter, Victoria LaRue.

Thank you

This book rose from the ashes of the first draft of a novel I wrote decades ago. I kept about ten percent of that original writing, and along the way I changed the plot, characters, settings, and even the title. All my love to my patient wife, Linda. She never lost faith that I would one day finish *Stay Downwind*, and her input was invaluable. (Don't tell her I just started writing a new book ...)

I want to thank my editors: first my *Family Reunion* coauthor and best friend Mark Davis. He ran out of red pens many times during the editing process. When I finally thought my book was ready, I made the mistake of sending it to him for a "final look"—and of course he tore it apart yet again. But he was right. Thank you, Bro, for helping me make it the best it could be. Thanks to Lesley Kellas Payne, who edited that first draft years ago and told me it was great for nine chapters, then I went off the rails. She was right. Thanks and love to my editor daughter, Brandy Foster, who made sure I kept Alita authentic. A special thanks to my good friend and nemesis Lisa Rast Fish, for giving so freely of her editing skills.

I am truly humbled and deeply honored that Lauren Graham Cunningham let me use one of her amazing oil paintings, "Athena," as my front cover art.

Thanks to Lisa Rast Fish (yes, her again), for being the face of Victoria in promotional materials, and thanks to TJ Fish for the photograph.

Thanks to Wendy A. Lavezzi, M.D., for sharing her expertise in forensic pathology. I hope I got it right. If not, that's on me, not Dr. Lavezzi.

Thanks to Porsche guy Mason Gilchrist for tips on how to start a 2014 Carrera 4 GTS Cabriolet.

Thanks to Crissy Stile, Barrel of Books and Games, Mount Dora, for your friendship, inspiration, and for keeping my book in stock!

Thank you

A big thank you to my 2024 – 2025 beta readers
Lee Baker, Cathy Baker, Fran Bast, Ken Bell, Neta Bell,
Amy Braun, Cassandra Clark, Don Cooper, Linda Cooper,
Mark Davis, Jan Davis, Katie Eriksen, Raquel Fagan, Jeff Forte,
Kathy Forte, Brandy Foster, Lauren Graham Cunningham,
Jeanann Hand, Mary Johnson, Ellen MacDonald, Cindy Matyi,
Ana Moulder, Karen Price, Lisa Rast Fish, John Schwab,
Crissy Stile, Tony Taylor, and Dave Tisdale

Thank you across the years

Special thanks to Cory Cooper for the Mac technical support;
Christopher Cooper and Patricia Jeffrey for Nashville updates; Don
Cooper, Joy Cooper, and Carol Cooper for your encouragement; my
daughters Brandy Foster and Mandy Cotterman, who were there at
the beginning of that first draft; my parents, the late Don and Marge
Cooper, for their love and support; and to Queenie, Kuja, Chloe,
Tybee, Zoe, and Miley Cypress, my beloved dogs over the decades
who were often at my feet as I worked late into the night.

Thanks to every member of every writers group I've ever been a
part of. I always submitted Chapter 1 for feedback, thus it has to be
one of the most critiqued chapters ever.

From the first draft of that novel whose bones led to this book:
I no longer remember the names, but thanks to the Chief Forensic
Investigator in Nashville who gave me a behind the scenes tour of
the facility (and I saw everything); the kind and helpful woman with
Mount Olivet Cemetery who gave me a pamphlet about the Confed-
erate Circle, and was thrilled the first chapter was set there (note:
June Wickliff is not based on her); and two names I do recall, Sgt.
Brooks Harris and Officer Bill Sneed of the Metro Police Depart-
ment, who showed me around their headquarters.

And my deepest gratitude to the late Robert A. Liebert, who helped
make that first draft possible so long ago. *Thanks, Bob.*

ABOUT THE AUTHOR

Rick Cooper lives in Central Florida with his wife, Linda, and two poodles, Zoe and Miley Cypress. He finds peace and paradise kayaking the nearby Dora Canal, taking close-up photos of gators and snakes.

He grew up in Ohio, and it was through the guidance of Marion Hemphill, his Composition teacher at Indian Lake High School, that he developed his lifelong love of writing. His first suspense novel, *Family Reunion* (coauthored with Mark Davis under the pseudonym Nicholas Sarazen), was published in 1990 by Pinnacle. In addition to novels and nonfiction books, he has written award-winning poems and short stories. He is a songwriter with songs released on fifteen different albums by various artists. McGuffey Lane, John Schwab, Bobby Ross, J.D. Blackfoot, Mel Besher, Sirens, The Dollyrots, Jeff Allen, Sol Varon, and The Bruise Brothers have recorded his songs.

He is a graduate of The Ohio State University, with a major in criminology. An avid runner, he completed thirty-two marathons across the country, including the Boston Marathon two times. He has been a vegan since 2011—for the animals.

Thank you for reading *Stay Downwind*. If you enjoyed it, tell your friends. I welcome your comments: rick@rickcooper.com

For more information about the author:
rickcooper.com

ABOUT THE COVER ARTIST

Lauren Graham Cunningham's work explores the complexity of representation—from the transcendent to the mundane. Her compositions are imbued with two-dimensional atmosphere, emotion, and impression, and capture the sardonic, energetic, and deceptively domestic qualities of human experience.

For more information about the artist:
laurengrahamcunningham.com